Ludwig Uhland, Walter W. (Walter William) Skeat

The Songs and Ballads of Uhland

Ludwig Uhland, Walter W. (Walter William) Skeat

The Songs and Ballads of Uhland

ISBN/EAN: 9783744797894

Printed in Europe, USA, Canada, Australia, Japan

Cover: Foto ©Andreas Hilbeck / pixelio.de

More available books at **www.hansebooks.com**

THE SONGS AND BALLADS OF UHLAND.

TRANSLATED FROM THE GERMAN

BY

THE REV. W. W. SKEAT. M. A.
LATE FELLOW OF CHRIST'S COLLEGE, CAMBRIDGE.

WILLIAMS AND NORGATE,
14, HENRIETTA STREET, COVENT GARDEN, LONDON;
AND
20, SOUTH FREDERICK STREET, EDINBURGH.
1864.

LEIPZIG: PRINTED BY B. G. TEUBNER.

THE POET'S PREFACE

TO THE FIRST EDITION, PUBLISHED IN 1815.

Songs are we, our father sends us
  Through the world afar to roam;
Where the critic's spleen attends us,
  On the stage he bid us come.
Deem us not too overweening,
  Lend us a propitious ear
Whilst — your kind indulgence praying —
We our prologue brief are saying;
Once did frogs with croak unmeaning
  On the Grecian stage appear!*

Some may choose to call us mournful,
  Weeping, grieving ceaselessly;
Some — that we of *life* are scornful,
  Making men and mice to *die*.

* Alluding to the "Frogs" of Aristophanes.

A *

Yet should each on youth who ponders,
  Youth, with fullest life that glows,
Know—the vine doth weep, tho' teeming;*
Yea, the vine whose juice, dark-gleaming,
'Mid the gifts that Autumn squanders,
  Kindling strength and gladness, flows.

Yet, although to boast were folly,
  Some of us are here to-day
Whence hot summer suns have wholly
  Dried the dew of tears away:
As, of yore, the Jester sprightly
  Hand in hand with Death would pace,
Some are cheerful, some distressing,
Some — 'tis hoped — some wit possessing;
Truthful lays may oft run lightly,
  Free from idle sorrow's trace.

Ballads are we — mere romances,
  Framed with touches light and few;
Every soul that sings or dances,
  Pipes or harps, may run them through.
Yet the thoughtful man, essaying
  Gentle hints with care to find,

---

* Alluding to a transparent exudation from the branch of the vine.

Here and there may soon discover
Deeper thoughts veiled lightly over:
Every part to him betraying
  One sole source — our Author's mind.

Should too many seem but trifles,
  Think, they mark this age of strife,
Which — like snow deep-drifted — stifles
  Every sign of struggling life.
When we groaned 'neath Thraldom's rigour,
  Song declined beneath its blight;
Now that, long extinct in ashes,
German Freedom brightly flashes,
Soon shall Song win life and vigour,
  Soaring in unclouded light.

May we then but herald others,
  Other more exalted rimes,
Larger-statured, stronger brothers,
  Rising up in after times.
Lest we should but promise vainly,
  This we leave to Heaven above.
Ye perchance, more skilled in seeing
Future things by those in being,
By these opening buds may plainly
  Guess at what the fruit will prove!

PREFACE.

Ludwig Uhland was born on the 26th of April, 1787, at Tübingen, in Würtemburg; and died at Stuttgardt, November the 14th, 1862, at the advanced age of 75 years, after a long, laborious, and useful life. He himself alludes to the month of his birth in the fragmentary poem called "Fortunatus", where he says of Fortune,

"In changeful April has she fixed the morn,
In changeful April was her poet born."

He early applied himself to the study of the law, although — like Metastasio when engaged, in the same pursuit — he felt himself far more easily attracted by the reading and cultivation of poetry. Accordingly we find him saying,

"When to law I gave my studies,
'Gainst the impulse of my heart,
And from Poetry's allurements
Half had torn myself apart,
To the God who wears the fillet
Oft I gave some idle song,
None to thee, O blindfold Goddess,
Sternly severing Right from Wrong."

He matriculated at the university of his native town in 1805 — took the degree of Doctor of Laws in 1810; and in 1812 began to practise as advocate in the town of Stuttgardt.

His life was alternately one of political excitement and of retirement and literary employment. He was especially active in the political world at three periods.

The first of these — to which most of his political poems may be referred — began with the national movement against the French in 1813, in which year occurred the memorable battle of Leipsic, to which he so often refers. Two years later, king Frederick of Würtemburg proposed to frame a new constitution for that country, and though he died in the ensuing year before any reforms were completed, his successor, William I. (the lately deceased king) persevered in the liberal course which had been thus commenced, and to him the country was ultimately indebted for its present excellent constitution.

Uhland was at all times among the foremost advocates of freedom and of liberal ideas, and was elected as member of the representative assembly in 1819. His spirited "Patriotic Poems," (among which must be reckoned the last twelve of the "Songs"), commanded indeed no little influence, and are especially interesting to the historical student, as precisely indicating the national feeling at that time. Three of them were written on the second, third, and fourth anniversaries respectively of the last day of the struggle at Leipzig (October 18, 1813).

It should be added that the constitution which was at first offered by William I. to his subjects in 1817 was condemned as inadequate to their wants, and further concessions were demanded. This supplies the key to "Patriotic Poems," 9 to 12.

The second of the periods in which the poet appeared as a politician was in 1838, when he was chosen as a deputy to the Diet; and the third and last period was ten years later, when he was again elected as a persevering advocate of liberal opinions.

Many of his poems were written before his entrance upon these stirring scenes. Among his first productions were his contributions to a publication entitled the "Deutscher Dichterwald" (the German Minstrel-forest) to which he refers in Song 41.

A visit to Paris in 1810, immediately after taking his degree, gave him a great opportunity for making literary researches, of which he availed himself largely. The influence of French and Spanish mediæval literature is clearly traced in the "Poems from the Old French" — in the Ballads of the time of Charlemagne (Ballads 69—71) — in "Taillefer" (Ballad No. 72) — and in the imitations of the Spanish *romanceros* in Ballads 34—38. Again, the 42nd Ballad introduces us to imitations of the Provençal Minnesang, whilst Norse literature is represented by "the Dying Heroes," and "the Blind King." At the same time, many of the most spirited of all his poems remind us that he was by no means neglectful of the old Suabian legends, but preferred them indeed to all others, as became so true a patriot; the district called

Suabia being partly included in the modern Würtemburg. The celebrated Nibelungen Lied was with him an especial favourite, and he often adopts the name of the hero Siegfried or Sifrid. See Sonnet 5 (II).

His fondness for mediæval literature led to his publication of several works upon that subject, such as "Walther von der Vogelweide", "On the myth of the Northern legend of Thor", and a very valuable collection of "ancient High and Low German popular songs;" and his reputation for philology was so great that in 1830 he was appointed professor extraordinary of the German language and literature.

In his dramatic efforts he was less successful. He wrote a drama called "Louis the Bavarian," and a tragedy entitled "Ernst, duke of Suabia," the prologue to which will be found below. (*Pat. Poems.* No. 14.) Included in his poems are also four dramatic fragments, one only of which appeared to me of sufficient interest to be here inserted, viz. the one entitled "A Norman Custom". Of the one called "Schildeis" the best passage is perhaps the following:

My best belovèd ones, the life of man
Is a short blossom and a long decay.

And, interwoven with this gradual course,
The seasons' swift and many-coloured changes
Occasion unto man, who witnesseth
But cannot follow them, unnumbered woes.
When Autumn strips the fields of flowers and leaves,
The joyous mind of youth grows sad to think
That thus he tastes old age before the time.
More mournful still — when Spring the earth revives,
Then 'gins the graybeard's cheek to glow afresh,
And the o'erwearied heart half hopes for youth.
Short-lived deception! for the withered stem
Puts forth a weakly leaf, but bears no bloom."

It includes also the following songs: —

"Enter two wanderers; the first sings.

O Fir-tree! thy rejoicing spray
Through all the year is green;
Like thee, my love for many a day
Hath fresh and hopeful been;
O Fir-tree! blossoms bright and gay
On thee are never seen;
Like thee, my love doth wear for aye
A garb of gloomy green.

The second sings.

O Birch, that 'mongst the firs around
The wanderer gleaming sees,
That art with leafy verdure crowned
Before all other trees,
My early hopes — my youthful dreams —
Like thee, O Birch, are they?
Thy verdure soon and brightly gleams,
Yet fades and falls away!"

Another fragment, "the Serenade", contains merely a serio-comic dialogue between a music-master and a refractory pupil. The fourth and last one is entitled "Conradin", and refers to the ill-starred expedition to Italy of Conradin, the youthful duke of Suabia, in the autumn of 1267. The passages in which Italy is contrasted with Germany are too characteristic to be passed over.

"Son of our princes, this Italian land
That with false glitter blinds thy dazzled eyes,
What is it — but a whited sepulchre?
Lay thee among these flowers fair, and straight
The viper venomous shall sting thy heel!
Or slumber to the sound of amorous lutes,
On some warm night, and from the walls creeps forth

The scorpion — the malignant Tarantella!
The sun's broad flood of light breeds poisonous plagues,
And smites the frame with leprosy and sores;
The very soil on which thou setst thy foot
Is treacherous; beneath it yawns a hell.
The crater bursts asunder, spitting flames,
Then quakes th' unstable earth, and o'er thy head
Rends the o'erarching roof, and whelms the tower.
In every nook assassination lurks:
The women's burning eyes consume and waste
The pith of heroes; e'en the friendly cup
Is poisoned, yea! the Host itself is death!"

And now look upon this picture;

"O think upon that mount, that high and steep
Arises, fairer than all Suabian hills,
And on its kingly narrow-pointed peak
The Hohenstaufen's olden castle bears!
Lo! far around, beneath the sun's soft ray,
A green and fertile land, far-winding vales
Gleaming with torrents, pastures rich in herds,
Woods stocked with game above, and far below
The neighbouring chapel's vesper-bell's soft chime!

And far and wide, in every town and fort
A race most blest of God, true-hearted men,
And women fair, yet modest and reserved,
Yea! (as our Walter sang), like very angels!"

Uhland's poems also contain a fragment called "Fortunatus", a rambling poem in the metre of Tasso. Though I have translated it for my own satisfaction, I think it is so far inferior to his other poems as to possess but little interest, on which account it is omitted. For some of my facts I am indebted to an article on "Uhland" in the English Cyclopædia. It contains so very just an estimate of Uhland's poems, and expresses their character with such accuracy, that I shall best assist the reader by quoting the passage unaltered.

"His songs, ballads, and romances form the most valuable portion of Uhland's literary works. His songs are distinguished by their spirit and energy, their truth and depth of feeling, their lively and picturesque representations of nature, and their varied subjects; his patriotic songs in particular contain some most heart-stirring appeals to all the better national feelings that were likely to arouse his countrymen, and in them is a mixture of earnestness and jocularity, with a fervent love of country, and aspiration after the great and good inspired by the recollections of their ancestors. His ballads and romances are remarkable for their apparent symplicity, the result of a most carefully exercised art, shewn by the extreme skill and felicity in the choice of words, and the masterly way in which characters are sketched perfectly but briefly."

A translation of nearly all Uhland's poems by Alexander Platt was published at Leipzig in 1848, but is not very easily accessible in this country. My own translation is an independent one; indeed, I was not able to obtain a copy of the above till my own was already in the press. I have endeavoured to make it especially suitable to the English reader, whether acquainted with the original or not; and have also aimed at rendering it as far as possible self-explanatory—to the avoidance of many footnotes—and at divesting it as far as is consistent with fidelity to the original of that listless formality which translations are but too wont to assume. Thus, whilst the metres of the original have been nearly always adhered to, the rimes are less frequent, and double-rimes in particular have been avoided in many instances; for it is in general wrong to represent double-rimes in German otherwise than by single-rimes in English. On this point see Marsh's Lectures on the English Language, First Series, pp. 536, 537. English hexameters are in most cases but poor, or as Tennyson calls them, "barbarous," but they may serve to translate German ones, in moderation, and have therefore been employed. Several of the Ballads are in "Asonante" verse, in imitation of the Spanish. Two have been rendered into this verse by way of example. Its peculiarity is that the rime is confined to the *vowel* only; or speaking more correctly, to the *vowel-sound.* It requires that the same vowel-sound shall recur in the last syllable but one of the second, fourth, sixth, &c. lines of a trochaic measure in which each line contains four trochees, or else three trochees and a half. See Ballads 34 and 38. In this manner, such words as *famous, sailor, neighbour, favour*, &c., may be used as *assonant;* but we should not admit among these such a word as *father*, (as is often wrongly done), because in this case the vowel *sound* is really altogether different.

In conclusion, it is fair to suppose that the poet would have wished the attention of the critic to be especially directed to his 39th Ballad.

CAMBRIDGE, 1864.

INDEX.

The occurrence of a *name* after any of the following titles of Songs or Ballads indicates that such piece has been *also* translated by the person mentioned.

Songs.

Patriotic Poems.

Epigrams.

Sonnets.

Poems in Ottava Rima.

Bouts Rimés.

A Norman Custom; a dramatic Poem.

Ballads and Romances.

Ballads from the Old French.

CORRECTIONS AND ADDITIONAL NOTES.

P. 13, line 4 from the bottom; for "gra" read "gray".

P. 42, stanza 3. More correctly thus: --

Thy mother died full early;
This mournful loss expressed
Thou shouldst derive no solace
From any earthly breast.

Note to pp. 103, 151. I have here alluded to William I, of Würtemburg, as being still alive. His decease took place after these expressions were written, in June, 1864.

P. 174, line 6 from the bottom. There should be no inverted commas at the beginning of the line.

P. 176, line 1. A comma is required at the end of the line.

P. 199, last stanza. This stanza should have been thus translated: —

"Why, why was he so daring?
Him wherefore didst thou slay?
His care the flowerets tended
That now must droop for aye!" —
"He dared to say, the fairest flower
That grew within his garden
Should be his true love's dower."

P. 242, stanza III. The first two lines may be more correctly rendered thus: —

Ne'er might the champion's death be wrought
by beauty's tender glance;
Ne'er might his noble breast be pierced
by thrust of sword or lance.

P. 245, line 6 from the bottom; for "t e" read "the".

P. 259. The ninth stanza of this ballad has been accidentally omitted. After

Rising from her funeral bier!

insert

From the death-like trance awaking,
Healthful bloom her cheeks hath dyed;
Light her step, as though the cerements
Were but robes that clothe a bride.

Note to p. 318, line 4:

Where stands the fort, hight "Woman's Truth;"

The story goes that Frederic, duke of Suabia, being besieged in the castle of Weinsberg by Conrad III, was obliged to surrender at discretion. "The emperor granted the duke and his chief officers permission to retire unmolested; but the duchess, suspecting Conrad, begged that she and the other women in the castle might be allowed to come out with as much as each of them could carry, to be conducted to a place of safety. The request was granted, and to the surprise of the emperor and his army, the duchess and her fair companions staggered forth each carrying her husband. A. D. 1140." *Epitome of Russell's Modern Europe.* In allusion to this story, Mr. Platt translates the first stanza on page 88 thus:

Are not thy dames a glory —
Domestic, kind, and true?
And *Weinsberg's* noble story
In memory ever new?

Whether his version or mine is here more correct, I hardly know.

Note to p. 331, last line of ballad 65. The German word *Schwabenstreich* means either *a Suabian blow* or *a Suabian trick.* The latter phrase was used proverbially as a synonym for a piece of stupidity or clumsiness.

SONGS.

---

1. The Poet's Evening Walk.

When wandering in the evening light —
(The time when poet's dreams are won) —
Oft turn thee to direct thy sight
Where brightly glows the setting sun.
Then high thy ransomed spirit soars,
Within the Temple peers thy glance;
Thy soul all holy things explores,
And heavenly forms each sense entrance.

But when, to hide this Holy Place,
Roll down the sombre clouds of night,
Then all is done — thy steps retrace,
Made joyful by the wondrous sight.
In mute emotion homeward fare:
Within thee dwells a blissful lay;
The light that thou beheldest there
Shines round thee on thy darksome way.

---

2. To Death.

Thou, who oft at twilight hours
  Through earth's garden wand'rest free,
Gathering golden fruits, bright flowers,
  Planted there by God for thee,
Spare, O Death, the smiling prize,
  Clinging to the quickening breast,
  Lulled by soothing songs to rest,
Gazing at its mother's eyes!

Spare the earth's strong sons, Oh spare
  Those in fervid strains who sing
Till throughout the forests bare
  Joyously loud echoes ring.
Spare the sage's fires to slake,
  Round whose holy sunlike glance
  Hovering close in steady dance,
Youthful moons their circuits take.*

Buoyed on clouds all silver-white
  Seek, when Eve's bright star appears,
Him who, gray with age, each night
  Consecrates his hearth with tears.

---

* By "moons" the sage's pupils are meant.

Name his loved ones gone from hence,
  Place him in thy garland's rim,
  Where no parting tears bedim
Eyes that beam with joys intense.

Seek the youth whose ardent breast
  Love hath filled with fierce alarms,
Who, impelled by wild unrest,
  Stretching out his open arms
Tow'rds the flow'r-strewn floor on high
  Bright with stars, looks up love-warm;
  Friendly take him arm in arm,
Bear him to yon far blue sky!

There, 'mid bridal pomp and mirth,
  (Breathing love), may round him flow
All that stirred his heart on earth,
  Greeting him with greetings low.
There his soul her holyday
  Fresh with newer life, may keep,
  Filled with inspiration deep,
Filled with songs that last for aye.

---

3. Harper's Song at a Marriage-feast.

Sounds of mirth and festal clang
  Through the lofty halls have sped
Till the answering echoes rang
  From the vaults that hold the dead.
'Mid the joys to-night hath brought
Of your ancestors ye thought,
Singing glorious deeds of might
Rescued from the past's dim night.

Oft with scenes of festal cheer
  Hath this ample chamber shone;
As the tree, when May draws near,
  Puts its radiant blossoms on.
They that here, a joyous crew,
True love's ties more closely drew,
Now, alas! together prest,
In their sleeping-chamber rest.

Thither man with tempest-speed
  Flies, and leaves life's rapid race;
In the hearts of friends, indeed,
  Lingers he a little space.
Down the hall, in bronze and stone,
Stand long lines of heroes gone,
Powerless their eyes to move,
Speaking not sweet words of love.

No bright deed, for ever green,
  Keeps thee from the vault's dim night;
None the thunder's path hath seen,
  None the wings of Zephyrs light.
How to God you raised your look,
How your friend's dear hand you took,
How you gave love's kiss of fire,
All doth with your life expire.

Both the child who laughingly
  Nestled 'neath his mother's arm,
And the grandsire who with glee
  Clasped his grandson close and warm,
And the bride, with love possessed,
Hanging on the loved one's breast,
All a well-spent life have sealed;
Praise to all my song shall yield.

---

4. The King on the Watch-tower.

There slumber they all, those dark gray hills,
  And the darkling vales sleep gently there;
Now slumber reigns, and no sadness fills
  With its wail the ambient air.

'Mid strifes and struggles my realms I won,
  'Mid cares have I drunk of the sparkling bowl;
Heav'n gleams with stars and the night's begun:
  I seek to rejoice my soul.

O writing of gold in the stars revealed,
  To you I lovingly gaze aloft!
Thou wondrous music from man concealed,
  How I list for thy murmurs soft!*

My hair is hoary and dim my sight,
  In the hall are hung both shield and spear;
In word and deed have I fostered right,
  Ah! when shall my rest draw near?

Ah! how for that blest repose I yearn,
  Ah! beauteous Night, why slacks thy speed?
Thou Night, when the stars shall yet brighter burn,
  And their music be heard indeed!

---

* Alluding to the fabled "music of the spheres".

5. A May-dirge.

Flingeth still the sun of spring-tide
  Far o'er mead and mere its light?
Still do verdant boughs, o'er-arching,
  Form sweet bowers of calm delight?
Ah! the maid my heart remembers
  Gives no more her May's bright gleam,*
Wanders not through groves full-blossomed,
  Rests not by the bubbling stream.

Yes! there once were days more happy,
  When, in files with garlands crowned,
Through the grove young lads and lasses
  Wandered, as o'er sacred ground;
When the maid, her pitcher bearing,
  Oft to fountains cool would rove,
Whilst the wanderer, smit with longing,
  Craved at once a draught and love!

Ah! the din of ruthless tempests
  Hence that golden spring did tear;
Castles rose aloft, and turrets —
  Sadly sat the maiden there,

---

* If the poet here compares his loved one to the sun, let it be remembered that "sun" is *feminine* in German.

Nightly, for a dear voice listened,
  Saw the battle rage beneath;
Saw, amidst the press of weapons,
  How her warrior sank in death.

Then an age, all sad and gloomy,
  Brooded darkly o'er the earth,
Like a dream dissolving wholly
  Youth's bright love and buoyant mirth.
They who hoped, close yoked for ever,
  Souls to mingle, heart to heart,
Now with saddened glances greeting
  Pass with hurried steps, and part.

Fade, ye trees and lovely blossoms,
  Deepen not true love's sad smart;
Wither, wither, springing branches,
  Pine and die, thou swelling heart!
Sink, ye youths, in lonely darkness,
  Rest within the silent tomb;
Alders in the breezes rustle,
  O'er your graves sweet roses bloom.

---

6. A Poor Man's Hymn.

The poorest of the poor am I,
  And lonely linger here;
I would my heart might yet once more
  Be filled with joyous cheer.

Once in my dearest parents' house,
  A happy child, I played;
Sharp poverty's my portion now,
  Since they in graves were laid.

I see the rich man's garden bloom,
  I see the golden corn;
But mine is that unfruitful path
  By care and sorrow worn.

Yet gladly here, all grief suppressed,
  Amid men's joyous swarm
I linger, wishing each "good day"
  With grateful heart and warm.

Thou hast not wholly, gracious Lord,
  Abandoned me to wo:
Sweet comforts for the whole wide world
  From heav'n unceasing flow.

For still Thy holy house is seen
  In every village here;
The organ's tone and anthem sweet
  Thrill through the gladdened ear.

Still shine the sun, the moon, the stars,
  With kindly love on me;
And when is tolled the vesper-bell,
  I commune, Lord, with Thee.

Thou soon shalt ope Thy banquet-room
  For righteous men made fit;
In marriage-garb I then may come
  And at Thy table sit.

---

7. The Song of Young Men.

Youth is sacred! youth-endued,
  Enter we the Temple-halls,
Where in dusky solitude,
  Echoing loud, the footstep falls.
Noblest resolutions should
  Bright in youthful bosoms burn;
Each in sober thoughtful mood
  All his sacred strength should learn.

Go we forth o'er fields to roam
  Proudly spread beneath the skies,
Which, in an o'er-arching dome,
  O'er the gifts of spring-time rise.
Buds and blossoms soon shall bring
  Fruitage in abundant store;
Sacred is the time of spring,
  Youth should con its lessons o'er.

Seize the cup while Pleasure reigns,
  See how gleams the purple wine,
Blood from lavish Nature's veins!
  Drain we then the draught divine!
Let the sacred strength of wine
  With the strength of manhood blend;
Sacred is the cheering vine,
  Youthful fancy's genial friend.

See yon maiden hither come!
  She in sport unfolds her power;
Soft desires within her bloom,
  Sweet and tender feelings flower.
She who grows in sunny gleam
  Gives us strength when tempests blow;
Sacred should the maiden seem,
  'Tis for her we riper grow.

Enter then youth's fane divine,
  Feed on thoughts of high emprise;
Gather strength from spring, from wine,
  Sun yourselves in beauty's eyes.
Youth, and Spring, and festive bowls,
  Maiden in her beauty's pride
To our earnest, youthful souls
  All alike be sanctified!

---

8. To a Child.

From out the keen distress that circled me,
Have I, sweet child, preserved myself for thee;
That I mine eyes and heart may feed and bless
  With thine angelic happiness,
With this sweet innocence, this morning-gleam,
This yet untroubled, heav'n-descended stream.

---

9. The Chapel.

There aloft the chapel standeth,
  Peering down the valley still;
There beneath, by fount and meadow,
  Rings the shepherd's carol shrill.

Sadly booms the bell's slow knelling,
Solemn sounds the last lament;
Hushed are all the boy's loud carols,
Still he stands, with ears attent.*

There aloft are borne to burial
They who filled the vale with glee;
There aloft, O youthful shepherd,
Men shall chant the dirge for thee!

---

10. Genial Days — Early in Spring and late in Autumn.

I hold so dear the genial days
When in the Spring-tide's earliest birth,
The sky its blue expanse displays
And sheds its cheering warmth on earth.
The valleys still with ice are gra,
The hill shines bright beneath the sun,
In open air the maidens stray,
And children's sports are fresh begun.

---

* A word occurring in 2 Chron. VI. 40.

I stand on yonder mountain's height
  And gaze around with heartfelt peace;
My breast receives an impulse light
  That doth not to a wish increase.
I feel a child, and mark intent
  Boon Nature's pranks, with joy possessed;
And by the calm she thus hath sent
  My soul is lulled to tranquil rest.

Those genial days are likewise sweet,
  When to the soft and sunny plains
Old men their sad farewells repeat
  And Nature's Sabbath-season reigns;
No more she bud or fruit supplies,
  Each active power awhile expires;
In self-collected calm she lies,
  And to her inmost depths retires.

My soul, late soaring high, returns
  To earth, and ends her daring flight;
A resignation sweet she learns,
  Remembrance now contents her quite.
A silence deep my soul doth bind
  That Nature o'er me softly throws;
I seem descending slow, to find
  The stillness of the grave's repose.

11. In Autumn.

Hail! as though sweet spring were nigh,
Golden sun and azure sky!
Hark! from yonder bowers above
Strains I hear of mirth and love.

Think'st thou, soul, again to hear
Spring's sweet carols, soft and clear?
Lo! how sere the forests seem;
Ah! thou didst but fondly dream.

---

12. A Wonder.

A child was she but yesterday,
  To-day a child no longer — no!
The bud its flower doth now display,
  And now—half closed—scarce seems to blow.
What means this wonder, who can say?
  Or am I mocked by outward show?

Such childish thoughts her words express,
  So artless seem her glances bold,
Yet fuller meanings oft I guess
  And depths without an end behold;
Such wonders Love's first dawn confess,
  For Love hath wonders manifold!

---

13. My own Song.

Think ye that joys I never knew,
  That ever thus my lay was sad?
Not so — my days once brightly flew,
  With lays of love my life was glad.
The presence sweet of her I loved
  Made flow'rs to bloom throughout the year;
What morning's dreams had promised, proved
  Reality when eve drew near.

To joys of mine might witness bear
  The sky's bright blue, the streamlet's sheen,
The grove with sprouting branches fair,
  The garden gay and meadow green.
For these have oft beheld me glad,
  For these full oft have heard my lays;
But ah! they now seem alway sad,
  No charms fair nature now displays.

But witness thou, my love, mine own,
  That art so far and yet so near,
Thou mind'st my childlike happy tone,
  Thou mind'st my looks of blissful cheer.
Each knew so well the other's thought,
  Our eyes alone our meaning told;
For us life's stream dashed onward, fraught
  With music gushing uncontrolled.

Thou partedst hence, the world to me
  Was void, I shrank within my breast;
The soothing plaints of minstrelsy
  Were all my comfort, all my rest.
What can I, save in mournful strain
  Recount the past so dear to me,
And still expect, with longing pain,
  The golden love-time yet to be?

---

14. The Monk and the Shepherd.

Monk.

Why stand'st thou here in silent wo?
  O shepherd, tell me true;
A wounded heart I too can shew,
  That draws me, friend, to you.

Shepherd.

What need to ask? cast round thine eyes
  On this mine own dear vale;
This meadow broad no blade supplies,
  And every tree doth fail.

Monk.

Yet murmur not! How light thy wo!
  'Tis but a vision drear;
Soon from the soil new grass shall grow,
  And buds on trees appear.

This cross that oft I kneel before
  Within this orchard fair,
Nor blooms, nor buds, but evermore
  A Dying Form doth bear.

---

15. The Shepherd's Song on the Lord's Day.

  The Lord's own day is here!
Alone I kneel on this broad plain;
A matin-bell just sounds: again
  'Tis silence, far and near.

  Here kneel I on the sod;
O deep amazement, strangely felt!
As though, unseen, vast numbers knelt
  And prayed with me to God.

  Yon heav'n, afar and near —
So bright, so glorious seems its cope
As though e'en now its gates would ope —
  The Lord's own day is here!

---

16. A Nun's Song.

Lift up your heads to heav'n above,
  Ye sisters, with devotion meet;
  Let rosy clouds sustain your feet;
  There o'er us gleams the Spotless Sun,
  There, blithe as when sweet spring's begun,
Of Thee we sing, Immortal Love!

Tho' every tender bloom should wane
  From earthly love's impassioned force,
  To Thee, of fadeless youth the source,
  We turn, who fill'st our souls for aye,
  Undying Flame! whose steady ray
Our hearts and altars both retain.

To earth Thou cam'st, eternal Light,
  To lie, a smiling heav'n-born child
  In Mary's arms, the Virgin mild.
  On Thy clear eyes she fixed her view,
  And thence celestial lustre drew
Till o'er her glowed a "glory" bright.

With love divine, past human speech,
  Thou on the cross didst stretch Thine arms.
  Lo! earth doth quake, the storm alarms;
  Hither from farthest regions wend,
  Ye dead! the grave's strong portals rend!
With open arms He claspeth each.

What wondrous love, what joys are mine!
This life a sleep to me doth seem,
Of Thee, and only Thee, I dream:
The hour of waking soon shall be;
Oh joy! to be absorbed in Thee,
A sunbeam of the Sun Divine!

---

17. The Boy's Mountain-song.

The mountain shepherd-boy am I,
Yon castles all beneath me lie;
Here first the rising sun doth shine,
His last departing rays are mine;
A mountain-child am I!

Here springs the torrent's parent-rill,
From this, its source, I drink my fill;
It leaps adown its craggy way,
My hands receive its dripping spray;
A mountain-child am I!

This mountain-peak is all mine own,
The tempests gather round its cone;
From North and South they rave along,
Yet o'er them all rings out my song;
A mountain-child am I!

Lightning and thunder 'neath me rave,
Around me spreads the blue concave;
I know them well, and loudly cry,
"My father's hut in peace pass by!"
  A mountain-child am I!

And when th' alarum thrills the air,
And beacons on the mountains flare,
Then down I wend to join th' array,
And swing my sword and sing my lay:
  A mountain-child am I!

---

18. Bridal Song.

My blessing and praise with the house abide,
That hath lately been graced by a beauteous bride,
  Like a Garden it seems to bloom.

From the bridal chamber the Sun* doth gleam,
  Like a Nightingale's voice is the flute's soft strain;
  Each table is bright as a flower-deck'd Plain,
And the red wine runs in a sparkling Stream.

* I. e. the Bride, "sun" being feminine.

Like Lilies and Roses the maidens bloom,
And like Breezes that stray
Amid Flowerets gay,
Caressing and kissing are heard through the room.

---

19. A Resolution.

Today she seeks this quiet vale,
With courage firm I'll dare to speak;
What need before a girl to quail
Who no one's hurt or harm would seek?

All they that meet her, greet her too;
I dare not speak, but pass her by;
I lift not up my face to view
The brightest star in all the sky.

The flowers, that down towards her bow,
The song-birds full of lusty cheer,
All utter many a tender vow,
What need have I alone to fear?

To heav'n I oft the live-long night
Full bitterly my vows repeat;
To her I dare not speak outright
The simple phrase — "I love thee, sweet!"

She past this tree doth daily walk,
  And 'neath its shade myself I'll lay,
And feign that in my dreams I talk
  Of her, my life's most cherished stay.

Yea! I'll — but ah! what terror! hush!
  I see her come — she'll see me here;
I'll slip behind this sheltering bush,
  And thence behold her passing near.

---

20. The Course of Events.

Along the path across the lea
    At eve I often stray,
From out her arbour peepeth she —
    It stands beside the way:
'Tis not that we appointments make,
'Tis but the course events *will* take.

    Howe'er it chanced I cannot guess,
      I've learnt to kiss her, long;
    I ask her not — she saith not "yes",
      Yet never saith — "'tis wrong":
When lip on lip doth softly rest,
We leave them so, we seem so blest!

The Zephyr with the rose doth play,
  Yet asks not — "Think'st me dear?"
The bud that loves the dew's cool spray
  Needs not to say — "Come near."
I love her well — so loves she me,
Yet neither saith — "I pine for thee."

---

21. A Song of the Woods.

I seek the woods with courage brave,
  I fear no robber's snares;
A loving heart is all I have,
  For that no robber cares.

Who breaks, who rustles through the bush,
  A murderer threatening death?
My lover forward springs, and — hush!
  With hugs nigh chokes my breath!

---

22. A happy Death.

I perished, slain
   By love's fierce bliss;
Buried I lay
   Her arms within;
I lived again
   By her sweet kiss,
And in her eyes
   A heaven did win!

---

23. Inconstancy.

Thou long hast held unbounded sway
Both o'er my heart and o'er my lay,
   And yet to-night — O dream unkind!
Henceforth, my heavy heart, be free!
There seated 'neath our trysting-tree
   A stranger's form, close-veiled, I find.

How strong thine influence o'er me still!
I hasten on with anxious thrill;
   The stranger lifts the muffler light,
And then — O joy! I recognize
Thy deep, thy blue, thy truthful eyes,
   And all the strangeness fades outright.

---

24. Retirement.

At length have I my darling gained
'Mid bustling crowds so lately thrown;
Thou in mine arms art closely chained,
Now art thou mine — yea, mine alone.
At this still hour all nature sleeps,
We wake, but all is hushed beside,
As in the ocean's silent deeps
The sea-god clasps his goddess-bride.

The day's loud roar no longer moans,
That of thy words bereaved mine ear;
The murmur of thy tender tones
Is now the sole sweet sound I hear.
The earth close-veiled in darkness lies,
No light shines out o'er dyke or plain;
This lamp alone with light supplies
The tiny realm where Love doth reign.

---

25. Contentment.

Beneath a linden shady
With me my little lady
Sat resting, hand in hand:
No breeze the leaves stirred wildly,
The sun shone out so mildly
Far o'er the peaceful land.

We sat in silent leisure,
With deep unuttered pleasure
  Our hearts beat soft and low;
What more could we be saying,
What questions more be weighing?
  No more we sought to know.

No source of rapture failed us,
No vain regrets assailed us,
  No transport could we miss;
With glances glances greeting,
And lip with lip oft meeting,
  We rendered bliss for bliss.

---

26. Love Sublime.

In loving arms enraptured rest,
  Ye whom the joys of life enthral;
A single glance my lot hath blest,
  Yet makes me rich beyond you all!

The joys of earth I hold but light,
  And, like the martyr, upward gaze;
For o'er me in the distance bright
  Its open portals heav'n displays.

---

27. Nearness.

I wander through thy garden,
  Where art thou, dearest, where?
The butterflies flit lonely
  Along the gay parterre.

Yet with what dædal fulness
  Thy beds their blossoms shew!
With what sweet perfumes laden
  The Zephyrs round me blow!

I feel thy gladdening presence
  Fill all these solitudes,
As o'er all worlds created
  The Great Unseen One broods.

---

28. The Evening Before.

Who past me in the twilight goes?
  Is't not the maid I prize?
Doth not the fragrance of the rose
  From out her basket rise?

To-morrow come the sports of May,
To-morrow's sun how blest!
For then she'll shine in garments gay,
A rosebud on her breast.

---

29. The Gossamer.

As through the fields we walk, a thread
Of gossamer flits o'er the lea,
An airy phantom, fairy-bred,
And knits a band from thee to me.
I take it for a warning sign,
A sign how love too oft doth fare.
O hopes in Hope's wide realms that shine,
From vapour spun, dispersed by air!

---

30. By Night.

To yon still house I raise mine eyes,
Against a tree reclined;
For there in soft repose she lies,
To sweetest dreams resigned.

And oft to heav'n I glance from thence,
  Dark clouds obscure its blue;
But lo! tho' seem the clouds so dense,
  The moonbeam glimmers through.

---

31. A bad Neighbourhood.

I seldom from my chamber stray,
  Yet work will ne'er proceed;
Wide open lie my books all day,
  But never a page I read.

The flute so well one neighbour plays,
  I pause to hear the air;
Then pause again, to slily gaze
  At yonder neighbour fair.

---

32. Precepts for Peasants.

In Summer with thy sweetheart walk
  Through field and garden oft,
For then the days are long for talk,
  The nights are mild and soft.

In Winter let the tender band
  Be fastened firm and strong,
Lest 'neath the chilly moon ye stand
  'Mid frozen snows too long.

---

33. Hans and Grete.

Grete.

I find thine eyes oft peeping round
  As though they sought to meet me;
Take care! thou scarce wilt keep them sound
  If so o'ertasked to greet me!

Hans.

Unless thou round wert peeping too,
  How couldst thou ascertain it?
Thy neck, my love, is fair to view,
  Take heed, then, lest thou strain it!

---

34. The Smith.

'Tis my darling I hear!
    His hammer he's swinging,
    His strokes are out-ringing,
    Their music is stealing
    (Like bells that are pealing)
Through streets far and near.

In the dark forge at night
Oft rests he to ponder;
Then past it I wander,
The bellows 'gin roaring,
The flames begin soaring
And clothe him with light.

---

35. Hunting-song.

To me no pastime sweeter seems
Than through the woods to go,
Where throstle sings and falcon screams,
Where leap the hart and roe.

O would my love a throstle were
And sang on yonder spray;
Or, like a roe, came bounding fair —
I'd hunt her all the day!

---

36. The Shepherd's Winter-song.

O Winter, biting Winter!
The world is then so small;
Thou mak'st us seek the valleys,
In huts thou shut'st us all.

And when I seek the cottage
  Where dwells my treasure dear,
Scarce through the little window
  Her little head can peer.

And when with heart love-brimming
  I softly close the latch,
She sits 'twixt father and mother,
  And scarce a glimpse I catch.

O Summer, glorious Summer!
  The world is then so wide,
The higher I climb the mountain,
  The broader grows its side.

If on the heights thou standest,
  I shout thy name so dear;
The echoes roll it onward,
  Yet none, but thou, canst hear.

If in mine arms I hold thee
  On the open mountain-plain;
We see vast tracts around us,
  But are not seen again!

---

37. Song of a Prisoner.

How sweet the refrain,
O Lark, of thy strain,
How it floats from the height thou hast won!
I rejoice, I am free,
I am singing with thee,
We ascend through the clouds to the sun.

O Lark, thou descendest,
Thy carol thou endest,
Thou sink'st to yon meadow so fair;
Then in silence I'm bound,
I descend to the ground,
And Oh! to what gloom and despair!

---

38. The Churchyard in Spring.

Silent garden, bloom apace,
Deck thyself with verdure young:
Be the red earth's latest trace
Hid with roses, thickly sprung.

Haste to close yon darksome grave,
Thus to view it grieves my heart,
Though, in sooth, it doth not crave
Aught wherein my love hath part.

Stay, this grave myself will share,
  Now shall earth receive her due;
Nay, not yet — in upper air
  Many a task I've yet to do.

---

39. Songs of Springtime.

1. Spring's Approach.

O breeze so soft, so dear!
    Soon, soon thou wilt bring
    Sweet songs of the spring,
And the violet-buds will peer.

2. Faith strengthened by Spring.

Awakened are the breezes light,
They blow and rustle day and night,
  Fresh life and strength they give;
O perfume fresh, O voices glad!
No more, poor heart, be dull and sad;
  Now all shall change, and live!

The world grows lovelier day by day,
We know not what 'twill next display,
  New buds each hour doth give;
Now blooms the gloomiest, deepest dale,
Be calm, poor heart, forget thy bale,
  Now all shall change, and live!

3. *Spring-repose.*

Lay me not in the grave's deep gloom,
Let not the turf my corse entomb;
For buried soon I hope to lie
'Mid waving grasses, close and high.

'Mid grass and flowers well-pleased I lie
And list some flute's low-warbling sigh,
And watch above me, changing fast,
The radiant clouds of spring fly past.

4. *Spring's Holyday.*

Genial, golden, vernal day,
Waking thoughts delicious,
If I e'er could weave a lay,
Sure, to-day's propitious.

Wherefore, though, when nature's gay,
Need a task molest me?
Spring's a gladsome holyday,
Let me pray and rest me.

5. *The Praise of Spring.*

Cornfield's greenness, violet's sweetness,
Skylark's carol, ousel's lay,
Rains in sunshine, Zephyr's fleetness —
Whilst of these I gladly sing,
Lacks there yet some greater thing
Thee to praise, thou vernal day?

6. Spring's Consolation.

Why fear'st thou, heart, in days so fair,
When e'en the briers roses bear?

7. A future Spring.

Serene and gentle bloometh
The spring-time, year by year;
Have faith and wait: there cometh
A Spring more bright and clear.

For thee doth God ordain it,
When life's short journey's done;
On earth thou long'st to gain it,
In heav'n 'twill be begun.

8. Springtime: By a Critic.

'*Tis* the Spring, there's no denying:
'Twill be nice — 'tis scarce worth doubting —
Now at last to venture out in
Weather not too keen and trying.

Storks and swallows fast are coming,
None too early, none too early,
Bloom, my tree! and be not surly,
'Tis on my account you're blooming.

Spring, I hail thee somewhat gladly,
Yea! the skylark seems improving,
Philomel is almost moving,
E'en the sun shines none so badly!

May none guess my joy, to mock it,
  Nor to see me strolling ponder:
  Forth awhile I'll deign to wander,
"Thomson's Seasons"* in my pocket.

---

40. To one I name not.

On some tall mountain's summit
  Might I with thee but stand,
And o'er ravine and forest
  A prospect wide command,
There might I shew around me
  The world, when spring doth shine,
I'd say — Were this mine only,
  I'd make it mine and thine!

Within my soul's recesses
  Oh! would thou couldst but see
Where all the songs are sleeping
  That God hath given to me!

---

* The original has "Kleist's Spring". Christian Ewald von Kleist wrote, among other things, a descriptive poem on Spring, which soon became popular, though it was only one of many imitations of Thomson's Seasons. Kleist was born in 1715, died in 1759.

There shouldst thou soon discover
  My heart's sincerest aim;
What passion 'tis thou wakest
  That dares not breathe thy name!

---

41. Free Art.

In "The German Minstrel-forest"*
  Whoso can, should sing his lay;
Joy and life are shewn whenever
  Sounds a voice from every spray.

Minstrel-art is not restricted
  To a small and glorious band;
Scattered are its seeds prolific
  Over all the German land.

All thy heart's most mighty passions
  Boldly tell in manly tone!
Be thy love revealed in whispers,
  Be thy wrath in thunders shewn!

---

* "The German Minstrel-forest" (Der Deutsche Dichterwald) is the title of a publication to which Uhland contributed.

Though not all thy life thou singest,
  Sing when youth is fierce and strong;
Only in the month of blossoms
  Nightingales outpour their song.

Canst thou not collect in volumes
  What the hours, in passing, teach;
Toss the leaves for winds to scatter,
  Trust that youth will snatch at each.

Fare ye well, ye arts mysterious,
  Necromancy, Alchemy;
Formal rules are weak to bind us,
  Now our art is Poesy.

Sacred still we deem the spirits,
  Though their names like vapours flee;
Worthy still we deem the master,
  Though the art to all is free.

Not in chilly marble-statues,
  Not in ruined fanes abides,
But in dewy groves, the Spirit
  Who o'er German art presides.

---

42. A Request.

Kind singers, have compassion!
  Too lofty themes ye sing;
Not thus in saintly fashion
  Your dulcet tones should ring.
Whoe'er would prove how truly
  He fights in God's own name,
Should stoop to combat duly
  This world of sin and shame.

---

43. To a Dancer.

When thou the sprightly dance dost lead,
When on the ground thou scarce dost tread,
  In youthful beauty hovering light;
I read in every gazer's feature
The thought, thou art no earthly creature,
  But wholly Soul, ethereal quite.

Yet this I fear: if, hence upborne,
Thou wert from earth for ever torn,
  How wouldst thou, Soul, preparèd be? —
Yet in the dazzling butterfly*
O'er blossoms hovering, some could spy
  A type of immortality!

---

* The Greeks considered a *butterfly* an emblem of the *soul*, and expressed both by the same word, "psyche."

44. On a Poet, starved to death.

This was thine earthly portion,
  To live by grief subdued;
Thyself hast thou expended
  As every poet should.

The Muses, at thy cradle,
  Thy destiny implied,
And kept thy mouth devoted
  To songs — and naught beside.

Thy mother died full early;
  This mournful loss expressed
Thou shouldst derive thy vigour
  From no mere mortal breast.

The world with all the treasures
  Its wealth could e'er produce,
Was thine — for thee to gaze on,
  But kept for others' use.

The spring thy life might quicken,
  Its buds thy dream might be;
Another pressed the vintage,
  Another stripped the tree.

Thou hast on days unnumbered
  Upturned thy water-cruse,
While round the festive table
  Thy strains would mirth infuse.

E'en here thou wert in glory,
  And scarcely more than soul;
Now liv'st thou 'mongst immortals
  Where nectar crowns the bowl.

Be to the churchyard carried
  What seems thy corse to be;
Thou'lt press the earth but lightly,
  May earth lie light on thee!

---

45. The Valley.

How wilt thou open on my gaze,
  Beloved valley? Ah, how strange!
Yet, since so oft in childhood's days
  I saw thee, thou hast known no change.
The setting sun hath vanished now,
  But brightens still yon torrent's spray;
No breezes come to cool my brow,
  Yet through yon wood they softly stray.

Again doth olden love inspire,
  Again old hopes their joys impart,
I feel the old poetic fire
  Revive this cold and withered heart.
Sweet scenes! I need such hours as this,
  Such soothing, such love-breathing hours,
To make this heart regain its bliss
  And strengthen all its drooping powers.

When next the world shall make me grieve,
  Again I'll seek thee, tranquil vale;
Thy minstrel faint with woes receive,
  And soothe, as now, his heavy bale!
And if I sink, worn out by pain,
  With fracture light thy soil divide,
Receive me, close the cleft again,
  And let fresh grass its traces hide.

---

46. The Vale of Rest.

When, while evening gilds the west,
  Golden cloud-built hills arise
    And Alp on Alp appears,
    I ask myself with tears,
Where, amid yon summits, lies
  My longed for vale of rest?

---

47. Evening Clouds.

Clouds I see at evening's hour
  Tinged with sunset's loveliest glow,
  Clouds as bright as gleaming snow
That but now were dark and grim;
Yes! my heart's prophetic power
  Tells me that — tho' late its light —
  Comes the sunset, rendering bright
Mists that now my soul bedim.

---

48. May-Song.

Little hath the glorious spring
  Hitherto on me bestowed,
All its loveliness can bring
  Naught to ease my spirit's load.
How can any heart be gay,
  Torn, like mine, by ceaseless pain?
Now I first perceive 'tis May,
  Now these flowers are crushed by rain.

---

49. A Lament.

Should one be buried living,
His lot hath evil proved;
Yet fate may bring an evil
Not far from that removed;
'Tis this — in passion's springtime,
In youth's most hopeful prime,
To be by grief and anguish
Made old before the time.

---

50. A Vindication.

Full many a splendid vision
The hopes of youth embrace,
With vehemence and weeping
It storms the starry space.
Heav'n hears its supplication,
In mercy answers, no!
And puts aside the craving
With all its load of wo.

But when from baseless visions
  The heart, grown wiser, turns
And but for truth, for pureness
  For men's affection yearns,
And yet with all its striving
  Can never reach the bourn,
Then may we freely pardon
  The man, howe'er he mourn.

---

51. On a Cheerful Morning.

Blue sky succeeding days of cloud,
How canst thou calm my wailings loud?
But he, whose woes are caused by rain,
Finds warmth and sunshine heal his pain.

Blue sky succeeding days of cloud,
Thou yet canst calm my wailings loud;
This healing hope thou bidst me borrow —
Eternal joys shall end my sorrow!

---

52. The Greeting of Souls.

She. Are the bonds of earth dissevered,
Are at length my pinions free?
May I, in th' eternal haven,
Dearest, soon be one with thee?
Yea! thy spirit, hovering o'er me,
Oft to heaven my glances drew;
Now in light, in life I find thee,
Never lost from memory's view.

He. Say, what hear I? Dost thou draw me
Downward, or dost upward steer?
Smiles again my earthly springtime,
Or a fairer, blooming here?
Yes! in these celestial mansions
Thee I missed, and only thee;
Come! I feel thy presence, waking
(E'en in heav'n) fresh life in me!

---

53. The Ferry-Boat.

Lo! the stream that once before
I in youth was ferried o'er;
Here — the fort in evening's glow,
There — the mill-dam roars below.

In this fragile vessel tossed,
With me two companions crossed,
One a father's aspect had,
Young the other, hopeful, glad.

One his life in quiet spent,
Quietly from hence he went;
Whilst in storm and battle-strife
Ceased the other's restless life.

Thus whene'er on bye-gone days,
Happier far, I fix my gaze,
Oft I miss my comrades dear
Torn from me by fate severe.

Friendship most the man controls
When the soul meets kindred souls;
Spiritual those hours I found,
Hence am I to spirits bound.

Boatman, come, thy fare receive,
Thrice thy fare I gladly give,
For, unknown, unseen by thee,
Spirits twain have crossed with me.

---

54. The Larks.

How ye scurry! how ye veer!
Cloud of larks, you're welcome here!
This one skims the meadow's rim,
Rustles that thro' thickets dim.

Numbers, soaring tow'rd the skies,
Wing their way with piercing cries,
One whose joyous song excels,
Fluttering, in my bosom dwells!

---

55. The Poet's Blessing.

As I went the fields along,
Listening to the skylark's song,
Was I of a man aware,
Labouring hard, with grizzled hair.

"Blest — said I — shall be the field
Which such faithful toil hath tilled.
Blessings on thy withered hand
Strewing still with seeds the land."

Answer made his look severe;
"Poet's blessings speed not here;
Cruel as the heav'ns in scorn
Flowers he gives in lieu of corn."

"Friend! my poor poetic powers
Ne'er will plant too many flowers,
Scarce enough the corn to trick,
Which thy grandson soon may pick."

---

56. May-dew.

On the forest, on the meadow,
  When the morning first is gray,
Drips, from Paradise out-welling,
  Soft and cool, the dew of May.
All that fills May's sacred temple
  With each fresh and fair delight,
Leaf's enamel, blossom's beauty,
  Scent and fragrance prove its might.

When such dew the oyster drinketh,
  Soon is formed a pearly drop;
When in oaken trunks it sinketh,
  Honey-bees soon swarm atop;
If the bird, while onward flying,
  Dip therein his tiny bill,
Soon he learns the happy carols
  Which through solemn woodlands thrill.

With the dew from May-buds shaken
  Oft the damsel wets her face,
Oft she bathes her golden ringlets;
  Shines she then with heavenly grace.
Many an eye that's red with weeping
  Finds how fresh the dewdrops are;
Soon beholds how friendly shineth,
  Dim with mists, the morning star.

Pour on ME thy kindly healing,
  Gentle balm for every smart!
On mine eyelids softly trickle,
  Give to drink my thirsty heart.
Give me youth and love of singing,
  Give me heavenly forms to view;
Aid mine eyes to bear the sunlight,
  Soft, refreshful morning-dew!

---

57. Wine and Bread.

Odours such as these revive me,
  Far dispersing thoughts of pain;
On the mountain blooms the vineyard,
  In the vale the golden grain.

Soon the threshing-floors will thunder,
  Soon the whirring mills will go;
And when these at last are weary,
  From the press the wine will flow.

Hostess good, with topers round thee,
  Fain would I be briskly sped;
Come, with wine fill up the beaker —
  On the table lies the bread.

---

58. The Summer Solstice.

Now the sun at length must finish
  This his longest, grand career,
How he lingers ere he turns him
  Tow'rd the sea serene and clear!
Nature now with sad forebodings
  Feels her youthful God's decline;
Far around, the evening landscape
  Seems in mournful calm to pine.

But the quail, who always early
  By her chiding wakes the day,
To the sunbeam faint and fading
  Sings a final 'larum-lay;

And the skylark soars in singing
  Far above the misty vale,
For a moment more to hover
  In the beam that 'gins to pale.

59. The Poppy.

Behold how rocked by Zephyrs
  The poppy's blossom gleams:
The flower that best adorneth
  The slumberoüs God of dreams.
Here, scarlet like the cloudbanks
  Which sunset renders bright,
There, pale and white and ghostly
  As 'neath the moonbeam's light.

I've heard men say in warning,
  Should one 'mid poppies sleep,
His senses soon are buried
  In heavy dreams and deep;
Awaking, he retaineth
  This fancy strange and dim,
That all things true or lovely
  But shadows are to him.

In lifetime's early morning
  I too once rested there,
By flow'rets hidden wholly
  In a valley bright and fair.
So drowsy seemed their odour
  That, ere I felt aware,
My life became a picture,
  Its truths but dreams and air.

Since then the power hath lasted
  All things as then to view;
The world but seems a picture
  And only dreams are true.
The shadows round me flitting
  Distinct as stars I trace;
O Poppy! flower of poets,
  My head for ever grace.

---

60. The Mallow.

Hast thou come again, pale mallow,
  Hast thou put thy blossoms on?
Yea! a mournful sight hath met me,
  All the spring at once is gone.
Thou art still the rose of Autumn,
  Born when lower wheels the sun;
Thou art staring, thou art scentless,
  And thy blossoms are as none.

I would gladly greet thee, mallow,
  Wert thou not so rosy red,
Hadst thou not my loved one's blushes,
  Hers, who blossomed — and is dead.
Cease to feign that Spring continues,
  For thou need'st not glow so bright,
Thou canst blend a dusky sadness
  With a radiance soft and white.

---

61. Travel.

Must I, friends, set out on travel,
  Must I breathe a foreign air?
Would ye have me wish to wander
  From the tracks of daily care?
Yet amid these scenes so homely
  I have deeper learnt to sink,
Yea! I feel (by these surrounded)
  Freër, happier, than ye think!

Ne'er can I exhaust my rambles,
  Ne'er this vale can fathom quite;
E'en the old familiar footpaths
  Yield me ever fresh delight.
Oft whene'er the thought arises
  That the path is lone and drear,
Close beside me, e'en in daylight,
  Flit the forms of comrades dear.

When the sun from hence departeth,
  Still my heart no quiet knows,
With him from the mountain-summits
  Tow'rds romantic isles it goes;
Then the stars start out above me,
  Challenging my earnest view
Till to heights for aye receding
  I a heavenward track pursue.

Dreams of youth, both new and olden,
  Past and Future equally,
Limitless celestial spaces
  All are present here to me.
Therefore, friends, *far hence* I'll travel,
  Mark my road, appoint a goal;
In my home's familiar circles
  Roves *too much* my vagrant soul!

---

62. Songs of the Traveller.

1. Farewell.

Farewell, farewell, my dearest love,
  To-day must see us sever;
A kiss, a kiss at parting give,
  I leave thee, love, for ever.

A blossom, blossom, break for me
  From the tree i' the garden blowing;
No fruit, no fruit, dear love, for me,
  I may not wait its growing.

2. *Parting and Starting.*

From thee must I be starting
  Who mad'st my life so blest!
Thou kissest me at parting,
  I press thee to my breast.

Say, dearest, is it *starting*
  While fondly you caress me?
Say, dearest, is it *parting*
  While closely thus you press me?

3. *Far away.*

Beneath the trees I'll rest me here,
  And list the songbirds sweet;
Why seek ye thus my heart to cheer,
How know ye of our love so dear
  In this remote retreat?

I'll rest beside this torrent clear
  'Mid flow'rets sweet and gay;
Who, floweret sweet, hath sent thee here,
Art thou affection's token dear
  From her that's far away?

4. *Morning-song.*

As yet the sun's first rays are pale,
The matin-bell down yon dim vale
  Not yet its peal is flinging;
How still the spacious woodlands seem!
The birds but twitter in a dream,
  As yet no lays are ringing;
Long time I've paced the fields along,
And thus betimes have framed the song,
  Which loudly now I'm singing.

5. *Travelling by Night.*

Across a darksome land I ride,
Both moon and stars their radiance hide,
  The chilly winds are hissing;
I oft have passed the selfsame way
When laughed the sunshine's golden ray
  And wanton winds were kissing.

Across a garden dark I go,
Through faded trees chill breezes blow,
  Leaves drop from branches dreary;
Here was I wont, when roses bloomed
And all things Love's soft looks assumed,
  To wander with my dearie. —

'Tis quenched, 'tis gone, that gladsome sun,
The rosebuds withered every one,
  The grave my love is holding;
Across a darksome land I ride,
'Mid winter's storms, no light to guide,
  My mantle round me folding.

6. *Winter Travelling.*

So cold the wind is blowing,
  The roads are void and bare;
The waters still are standing,
  I only onward fare.

The sun shines out but dimly,
  And soon must pass from sight;
Love's fires are all extinguished,
  All joys have vanished quite.

At last the wood is traversed,
  The thorpe I gladly gain;
Here may I warm my fingers,
  Tho' cold my heart remain.

7. *Going Away.*

Thus now at length I leave the place
  Where late I've dwelt for many a day;
I quit the streets with sturdy pace,
  With none to cheer my lonesome way.

At parting none my coat have rent,
'Twere pity, sure, such cloth to tear;
Nor on my cheek I find the dent
Of teeth pressed close in strong despair.

None found last night their slumbers gone
That I so soon from hence must go;
They all in peace could slumber on,
Yet one dear face to lose — is wo!

8. *The Inn.*

A kind and gentle host was he
With whom I stayed but now;
His sign a golden apple was
That dangled from a bough.

Yea! 'twas a goodly apple-tree
With whom I late did rest;
With pleasant food and juices fresh
My parching mouth he blest.

There entered in his house so green
Full many a light-winged guest;
They gaily frisked and feasted well
And blithely sang their best.

I found a couch for sweet repose
Of yielding verdure made;
The host himself, he o'er me spread
His cool and grateful shade.

Then asked I what I had to pay,
Whereat his head he shook;
O blest be he for evermore
From root to topmost nook!

9. The Journey Home.

O break not, bridge that tremblest so!
O fall not, rock that threat'nest wo!
Earth, sink not down; thou heav'n, abide
Until I reach my loved one's side!

---

63. Dedication of a House.

Right well is the new-built house begun,
The roof's not on, nor the walls quite done;
Still from above the rain may fall,
And the sunlight wander at will o'er all.
Then pray we to the world's great king
That He from heaven's high vault will bring
His priceless treasures forth, and o'er
The open house His blessings pour.
And first may He, all-bounteous, deign
The barn to fill with ripened grain;
With honest thrift the parlour bless,
The kitchen with order and cleanliness;
The stalls make healthy for horse and kine,
And the cellar stock with generous wine;

The wickets and windows consecrate,
That evil may ne'er pass in thereat;
And grant that from out this new-made door
Gay laughing children may often pour.
Now, builder, finish the walls and roof,
God's blessing hath made it evil-proof.

---

64. A Tardy Nuptial Lay.

The Muse not seldom fails me
  When most her aid I need;
She sweeps to worlds far distant
  And will not slack her speed.
She, wrapped in trances, dreameth
  Full oft the hours away;
Nay more, she e'en neglecteth
  A happy bridal day.

So now, to greet your bridal,
  She cometh all too late;
She prays you treat her kindly
  Nor count her fault as great;
For, trust me, fortune poureth
  On you her brightest ray,
If friends both late and early
  May sing your bridal lay.

---

65. A Song of Tea.

With gentle finger touch the string,
  Awake its murmurs soft and low
To celebrate the daintiest thing,
  The daintiest that the earth can shew.

Where reigns eternal spring, O Tea!
  O'er India's* far, mysterious clime
Dost thou, thyself a mystery,
  Consume thy days of blooming prime.

Wee lips of bees alone may dare
  Sip honey from thy calix sweet;
Bright birds alone of plumage rare
  Their songs of eulogy repeat.

When lovers haste to tell their love
  Beneath thy shade in happy hours,
Thou gently dost thy branches move
  And o'er them strewest fragrant flowers.

Thus on thy strange domestic strand
  Thou growest, fed by sunshine fair;
Till here, in this far-distant land,
  We learn at last thy nature rare.

---

* We generally suppose China, not India, to be the home of the tea-plant. Neither does the fourth stanza agree with our usual ideas of the plant's size.

For ladies fair and none beside,
  Like mothers, keep thee safe from ill;
We watch them o'er the cups preside
  Like nymphs that guard a sacred rill.

It scarce can e'er to men pertain
  To know thy hidden powers aright;
Soft female lips alone may gain
  Acquaintance with thy magic might.

Myself, thy poet, call thee rare,
  Yet scarce thy wondrous powers perceive;
But *all* that female lips declare
  With trust devout I aye believe!

Then gently touched, O sounding string,
  In murmurs whisper, soft and low;
A woman's voice alone should sing
  The daintiest thing that earth can shew.

---

66. A Song of Pork.

To-day, as oft in former years,
  A porker have we slain,
Weak Jews are they and over-nice
  Who meat like this disdain.

Hurrah for swine, both small and great,
In tame, or else in savage state,
The white ones and the brown!

Then tarry not, my trusty friends,
The sausages to eat;
And let the flagon fast go round
To crown the savoury treat.
They rime so neatly — *Wine* and *Swine* —
They fit so closely — *Wurst** and *Thirst* —
We needs must drink with *Wurst*.

Then there's our noble *Sauer-kraut*,
(To pass it by's unmeet),
Invented by some German brain
For German mouths to eat.
When meat so soft, so white as this
Lies in the *Kraut*, a picture 'tis
Of Venus rose-embowered!

And when by fair white hands therein
The fair white meat is placed,
'Tis this that makes a German's heart
Of happiness to taste.
Young Love draws near and laughs, y-wis,
And thinks, whoe'er would snatch a kiss,
Hath but to wipe his mouth!

---

* *Wurst* means a sausage; *Sauerkraut* is a preparation of pickled *red* cabbage, which occasions the introduction of the simile of "Venus among the *roses*".

Let none reproach me now, good friends,
  That I of porkers sing;
For oft some mighty thought depends
  On some most trivial thing.
Right well that saying old ye know,
That here or there, as luck may shew,
  "A pig may find a pearl."*

---

67. Drinking Song.

A year so thirsty ne'er was known,
My throat's as parched as any bone,
  My liver dried away;
I seem a fish on driest sand,
I seem a tract of sunburnt land;
  A draught of wine, I pray!

How dry is every passing gale!
Nor rain, nor mist, nor dews avail,
  All drinks my anguish mock;
Deep draughts I drink, and drink again,
Yet down my throat they're poured in vain
  As 'twere a heated rock.

---

* A common German proverb. It requires a slight acquaintance with German customs in order to appreciate this poem.

What star now reigns, so hot, so fierce?
Its heat doth e'en my marrow pierce
And pains me to the core.
My friends must think I pine with love,
And sooth, who gives me drink shall prove
Beloved for evermore!

All ye that suffer thus with me,
Pray oft that wine may plenteous be,
All ye whom drinking stays;
Saint Urban*, justify our trust,
Grant us this year much precious must,
That we may hymn thy praise!

---

68. Drinking-Song.

One glass — 'tis not the first — we'll drink;
Of this and that we'll freely think,
Of grand and stirring scenes.

We'll think of forests dark and drear
Where raves the roaring blast,
The hunter's ringing horn we hear
As horse and hound go past.

---

* Urban I. was consecrated Bishop of Rome in A. D. 223. St. Urban's day is May 25.

The stag doth through the torrent go
  While floods around him brawl,
We hear the huntsman's wild hallo
  And shots, fast pattering, fall.

One glass — 'tis not the first — we'll drink;
Of this and that we'll freely think,
  Of grand and stirring scenes.

Next think we of the sea's wild dash,
  We hear the boisterous waves;
O'erhead the rolling thunders crash,
  The whirlwind howls and raves.
Mark! how the vessel groans and reels,
  How masts and timbers break!
The minute-gun full sadly peals,
  And sailors curse and quake.

One glass — 'tis not the first — we'll drink;
Of this and that we'll freely think,
  Of grand and stirring scenes.

Next think we of the battle-field,
  Where Germans join the fray;
The broad swords clash, the lances yield,
  The mettled chargers neigh.
To roll of drum and trumpet's blare
  The storming hosts rush on,
The deafening cannon rends the air,
  And wall and tower are gone!

One glass — 'tis not the first — we'll drink;
Of this and that we'll freely think,
  Of grand and stirring scenes.

Next think we of the Judgment-day,
  We hear the trumpet's call,
With thunderous sound the graves obey,
  Stars shoot from heav'n and fall.
There roars the pit of hell and night
  With seas of surging fire;
And there aloft in golden light
  Is heard the heavenly choir.

One glass — 'tis not the first — we'll drink;
Of this and that we'll freely think,
  Of grand and stirring scenes.

And when we've thought of chase and wood,
  Of storms and tossing spray,
Of German warriors stout and good,
  And of the Judgment-day;
Then think we of ourselves awhile
  How boisterously we sing
And how we jest, and cheer, and smile,
  And how the glasses ring!

---

69. Song of a German Poet.

I sang in days of leisure
  Full many a joyful lay,
Of old and homely sayings,
  Of love and wine and May.
Of these my songs are ended —
  Mere toys, at leisure planned —
The shield of war is ringing
  We shout for "Fatherland".

'Tis told us of the Catti: —
  A ring each warrior wore
Which, till he slew a foeman,
  As badge of shame he bore.*
So must I chain my spirit,
  Fix on my lips a lock
Till well I've served my country
  Amid the battle's shock.

And though I was not nourished
  For lofty hero-hood,
And though my song be suited
  To please a thoughtless mood;

---

* "Fortissimus quisque ferreum insuper annulum, ignominiosum id genti, velut vinculum gestat, donec se cæde hostis absolvat." *Tacitus*: *De Germaniâ*.

Yet in this holy warfare
  My proudest boast would be
The noble right, to herald
  My country's Victory!

---

70. To a Poet's Daughter.

Thou'rt welcome, poet's daughter sweet,
  For thee life's golden portals ope;
I bring for thee a present meet,
  Prophetic words and songs of hope.

In troublous times thou blossomest,
  In days that stir the anxious soul,
When, breaking through thy baby-rest,
  A holy warfare's thunders roll.

Yet slumber on in guileless ease,
  And dream as poet's daughter should
Of stars and flowers and budding trees,
  Of heav'ns bright sheen and waving wood.

Then as the tempest dies away
  And warfare's pangs and horrors wane,
Shalt thou thy maiden bloom display
  And far extend Love's gentle reign.

The soft desires and dreams of love
  That fired thy father's minstrelsy
Shall then descend from realms above
  To wake to perfect life in thee.

---

71. Forwards.

Forwards! on! whate'er betide;
Russia shouts the word of pride;
      Forwards!
Prussia hears the word of pride,
Hears it gladly, spreads it wide,
      Forwards!
Up, thou mighty Austrian crew,
Forwards, do what others do;
      Forwards!
Up, thou ancient Saxon-land,
Onward ever, hand in hand;
      Forwards!
Bavarians, Hessians, strike! combine!
Suabians, Franks, defend your Rhine;
      Forwards!
Forwards, Dutch and Belgian lands,
Swing your swords in freemen's hands;
      Forwards!

Swiss, may God your league sustain;
Burgundy, Alsace, Lorraine,
Forwards!
Forwards, Spanish, English lands,
Give to brothers helping hands;
Forwards!
Forwards, ever onward steer,
Fair the wind, the port is near;
Forwards!
"Forwards" is a marshal's name*,
Forwards, soldiers known to fame,
Forwards!

---

72. The Tidings of Victory.

The hours were heavy, dull, and dead,
Around us crept a rumour dread
That croaked as 'twere an evil bird,
Of swarthy hue, at twilight heard.

The evil rumour swiftly spread,
With vile reports of phantoms dread;
It hinted feuds and traitorous deeds
And perishing of precious seeds.

* Marshal Blucher was nicknamed Marshal Forwards.

The friends of evil lose their fear,
With spite they grin, aloud they sneer;
The good stand resolute and dumb,
Waiting to learn what end will come.

Then o'er the Rhine a something flies
And breaks the mists that veil the skies;
Is 't sunny flight of eagles proud,
Or tuneful swans with voices loud?

From golden clouds this song doth break —
"The Lord His own will ne'er forsake;
He guards from scorn all righteous powers,
God fights for us, the Victory's ours!"

---

73. To my Fatherland.

I fain would consecrate to thee
  These songs, dear German Fatherland;
For thou, to life restored and free,
  Dost all my hopes and prayers command.

Yet heroes' blood for thee hath flowed,
  For thee hath died youth's choicest flower;
When gifts like these have been bestowed,
  These songs must seem a worthless dower.

---

74. The German Philological Association. 1817.

Some learned German men
Who the German language ken
  Their labours now combine
Its powers and use to sound,
Its varied rules to bound
  And fixedly define.

While these to fix and trace
Each word's true form and grace
  Their useful toil pursue,
Your silent aid afford,
Your active help accord,
  Ye German folk, thereto!

Yea! give them language chaste,
Pure phrases culled with taste
  From purest hearts that flow;
Speak fiery words and free,
Let all the nations see
  How German minds can glow!

Then from your speech expel
All words where lies may dwell,
  Be truth on all conferred;
Implant in every youth
The love of honest truth
  With every German word.

Let not your words of might
In amorous ditties light
  Be tamely made to move,
But honour's code express,
Or maid's pure flame confess,
  Or sing true strains of love.

Ne'er let them, as at court,
Like girls or jugglers sport,
  Nor idly lisp — for shame;
But consecrated be —
Unweakened — to the free
  Who speak in Freedom's name.

When thus your noble speech
To greater force shall reach,
  And every grace combine;
Of Germans men will say,
That — greet where'er they may —
  There speaks the Voice Divine!

---

75. Seriousness of the Age.

When first were garlands twined from flowers,
  Or balls tost up with dexterous aim?
When first did dancing speed the hours,
  When first was learnt some "forfeit-game?"

Ah! sure in some forgotten age!
  These times with no such sports are rife,
For bitter war the nations wage,
  And traitors brew internal strife.

---

76. The New Fairy-tale.

Fain would I once more inherit
  Thoughts from golden Fairyland,
But an all-commanding Spirit,
  Whilst I play, controls my hand;
Freedom's now my chosen Fairy,
  Right my knight, my champion good;
Up then, knight, be keen and wary,
  Slay the dragon's hateful brood!

---

77. Looking forward.

Must my songs be sung for ever
  In this high and earnest strain?
Must the field of grace and beauty
  Hence for aye untilled remain?

When the axe has cleared the forest,
When the swamps are drained away,
Then the eye with tranquil pleasure
Views the sun's unclouded ray.

---

78. To Mothers.

Mothers, who fresh vigour win
Gazing on each infant face,
Who with prescient pleasure trace
All their future fate therein,

Once again with earnest love
Gaze on us, and thence declare,
Will the wounds the fathers bear
Fruitful to the children prove?

---

79. To Maidens.

Hapless maids, my pitying heart
Most for you feels sorrow's smart,
Since ye to an age belong
Seldom cheered by dance or song.

Beauteous maids in youthful prime
Blossom but a little time.
Must ye then put forth your bloom
Whilst the days are wrapt in gloom?

Yes! methinks your prime is left
Wholly of delights bereft,
That your after lives may prove
Blest by true devoted love!

---

80. The New Muse.

When to Law I gave my studies
  'Gainst the impulse of my heart,
And from Song's delicious music
  Half had torn myself apart,
To the God* who wears the fillet
  Oft I gave an idle song,
None to thee, O blindfold Goddess†,
  Sternly severing right from wrong.

---

* Cupid.

† Themis, or Justice, also (like Cupid) represented as being blindfolded.

Times are changed, and changed the Muses;
  Now in this all-earnest age
Naught so fiercely stirs my bosom,
  Naught so wakes my minstrel-rage,
As when thou with sword and balance,
  Awful Themis, throned in might,
Bid'st the nations cry for vengeance,
  Warnest kings to render right.

PATRIOTIC POEMS.

1. On the 18th October, 1815.

To Burgomaster Klüpfel, State Deputy of the town of Stuttgart.

The fierce momentous fight was o'er,*
From German soil withdrew the foe;
But still the ransomed country bore
Full many a trace of former wo.
And as in cities long o'erthrown
The forms sublime of Gods are found,
So many a right may prove our own,
Long hid beneath some rubbish-mound.

'Tis now the time to save, to build,
Yet progress must imperfect prove,
If king and people be not filled
With concord, mutual trust, and love.
To regal power a due respect
At all times hath the German paid;
Yet loves he still to walk erect
And free, as by his Maker made.

---

* The battle of Leipsic, Oct. 18, 1813.

In steadfast league, ye guardians bold
  Of freedom's cause, united be;
Ye build upon foundations old
  The welfare of posterity.
Unmindful of reward on earth
  Still prove industrious, firm, and true,
And to the People's honest worth,
  As to the King's, give reverence due.

Then while this festal day we keep,
  On which a thousand fires we light,
(Which, where from hills they flare not, deep
  In patriot hearts, are glowing bright),
What can adorn or grace so well
  The banquet that unites us here,
As that man's praises forth to tell
  Who aye has proved a friend sincere;

Who, in this township born and bred,
  Hath alway sought its truest weal,
To whom our hearts by love are led,
  Who guards our rights with watchful zeal;
Who, when terrific clouds did lower,
  Unmoved endured the tempest's strife,
And now, collecting all his power,
  To wise reforms devotes his life.

Ye, Fathers of the people, know,
  No words for warmest thoughts are found;

No language can, ye senate, shew
  How closely ye to us are bound.
When lately in the lofty hall
  The people thronged your words to hear,
The silence that pervaded all
  Spake more than could the loudest cheer.

Then may such silence please thee well
  When at the feast thou meet'st us all;
And if sad musings with thee dwell,
  Think on some future festival:
When blessings, from that battle's storm
  Resulting, shall be clearly shewn,
And seeds shall take their proper form,
  By you, in this the Seed-Month,* sown.

---

2. The Good Old Right.

Whene'er the man of Würtemburg
  On good old wine doth light,
The foremost of the toasts he gives
  Shall be — "The Good Old Right!"

---

* October is sometimes called Sämond, *Seed-month.*

The Right, that like a pillar strong
  The prince's house upholds;
And safe against intruding steps
  The peasant's cot enfolds.

The Right, that gives us honest laws,
  That render despots weak;
Such laws as love an open court
  And truthful verdicts seek.

The Right, that moderate taxes asks
  And keeps accounts with care,
That on the cash-box watchful sits
  And poor men's toil doth spare;

That o'er church property keeps guard,
  A patron just and wise;
That science and creative thought
  With aid and fire supplies.

The Right, that weapons dares to place
  In every freeman's hand,
Wherewith he for his king may fight
  And for his native land.

The Right, that leaves us wholly free
  To other climes to rove;
And binds us to our native soil
  By none but chains of love.

The Right, whose well-deservèd fame
  Long centuries approve;
Which all men, like God's Holy Word,
  Revere at heart and love.

The Right, to which an evil age
  A living burial gave;
Which now with energy renewed
  Hath risen from the grave.

Yes! may it strong and stronger grow
  When we are gone from hence,
And prove to children yet unborn
  Their welfare's best defence.

And when the man of Würtemburg
  On good old wine shall light,
The foremost of the toasts he gives
  Shall be — "The Good Old Right!"

---

3. Würtemburg.

What is it that thou lackest,
  Mine own dear Fatherland?
The rumours of thy riches
  Are heard on every hand.

They say thou art a garden
  Where Eden's wealth is found;
What hast thou yet to wish for,
  When all thy praises sound?

We read, an ancient worthy
  Hath written thus of thee:
"Though men should seek thy ruin,
  Thou couldst not ruined be."

Do not thy fruitful cornfields
  Like some vast sea extend?
While from a thousand hill-tops
  Red streams of must descend?

And swarm not shoals of fishes
  In every dyke and stream?
Do not thy forest-copses
  With game exhaustless teem?

Roams not o'er every mountain
  The shepherd's fleecy care?
And hast thou not strong horses
  And heifers everywhere?

Is not "Black Forest" timber
  In every land extolled?
Hast thou not salt and iron,
  And even grains of gold?

And are not all thy women
  Domestic, pure, and true?
Blooms not in every province
  A vineyard* always new?

And are not all thy yeomen
  Industrious, honest, blunt?
In arts of peace accomplished,
  And brave in battle's brunt?

Thou land of corn and vineyards,
  Whereon such blessings 'light,
What lack'st thou? *One*, yea, *all things* —
  Where's now the Good Old Right?

---

4. A Dialogue.

What? always praise the olden right?
  Still fondly o'er it brood? —
I am antiquity's true knight
  Because 'tis just and good.

The Better shouldst thou rather praise,
  And not the Good alone: —
Of Good I see some certain trace,
  But of the Better — none.

---

* By "vineyard" is meant a family of young children. "Thy wife shall be as the fruitful *vine:* upon the walls of thy house." Psalm CXXVIII.

But should I point it out indeed,
  Be guided then by me: —
I pin my faith on no man's creed,
  Man's rights I claim like thee.

Think'st thou wise counsel brings no gain?
  Whence kindlest thou thy light? —
That homely sense I still retain
  Dear to the homely wight.

Quick zeal and projects vast, I see,
  Thou canst not comprehend: —
I rather praise such industry
  As slowly gains its end.

True genius dares aloft to soar
  And all men with it raise: —
The plant is rotten at the core
  That never bud displays.

Thou canst not as a whole discern
  Mankind's most bitter smart: —
Thou mean'st it well, but canst not learn
  How beats a Patriot's *heart.*

---

5. To the Representatives of the People.

With your noble work proceed,
Be ye firm, let wisdom lead,
Let not praise your thoughts disturb,
Let not blame your efforts curb.

Blame the overwise, (who wind
Round their special sun), will find;
Closer hold the righteous cause,
Keep the time-tried, simple laws.

Scoffs are from the hard and cold,
Those who zeal for folly hold;
Let your noble ardour's fire
Flame but brighter, clearer, higher.

Slanders are from those who fear
All men's plans are insincere;
Therefore but the clearer prove
How ye truth and justice love.

For the truths by you restored
We our grateful thanks accord;
And for what ye hope to do
We can wait, with trust in you.

6. On the 18th of October, 1816.

(The Third Anniversary of the Battle of Leipsic.)

Should now some spirit here alight,
At once a bard and warrior brave,
Such as in Freedom's glorious fight
His life to serve his country gave,
He soon to German ears would bring
A stirring, sabre-edgèd song,
Not such as I alas! shall sing,
But thunder-loud, divinely strong: —

"Men speak of triumphs loud and gay,
Of bonfires bright in years gone by,
But who is found to tell to-day
What such rejoicings signify?
'Twould seem that spirits must descend,
Lured from the dead by holy zeal,
To shew you where their wounds extend,
Wounds that your hands may plainly feel.

And first, ye dukes and princes, tell
Have ye forgot that battle-hour
When on your knees ye humbly fell
And magnified a Higher Power?
If for your fame the people fought,
If ye have ever found them true,
'Tis yours, to vow no more for naught,
But what ye praised in them, *to do!*

Ye people, who have much endured,
  Have ye that day of toil forgot?
That day, that matchless fame procured —
  How comes it that it profits not?
The *foreign* hordes ye taught to flee,
  There shines *at home* no guiding light;
Ye art not free, ye are not free,
  Ye have not aye held fast the right.

Ye sages, must I hint to you
  In learned works so deeply read,
How well th' unlettered simple crew
  In Freedom's cause their life-blood shed?
Think ye that in the flames of strife
  The age was, phœnix-like, re-made
Only to bring the eggs to life
  That ye so busily have laid?

Ye councillors and courtiers all,
  With tarnished stars on breasts of stone,
Who of the fight by Leipsic's wall
  Till now, perchance, have never known,
Know that upon this festal day
  God holds a solemn court on high —
But ah! ye hear not what I say,
  Or deem a spirit's voice can lie!

The lay I yearned to sing is o'er,
  I seek the skies from whence I came;

What here has come mine eyes before
I to the heavenly host proclaim.
I censure not, nor glorify,
Small hope on every side is found;
Yet saw I many a kindling eye
And many a heart I heard to bound!"

---

7. Tares among the Wheat.

Say, who this year such refuse
Amongst the corn hath shed,
Rank weeds and wheat that's blighted
That stupefies the head,
Vile darnel, and that greatest bane,
Strong tares that choke the growing grain?

The shooting-match but lately
These hurtful weeds betrayed;
Half blinded seemed the marksmen,
Not one a "bull's eye" made.
The new-made beer was most in fault,
Vile tares were mingled with the malt.

We needs must bolt and winnow
What seems so marred by blight,
The sieve must cleanse it throughly
From chaff and refuse light.
Remove at least that greatest bane,
The tares that choke the growing grain.

So ye, by us appointed
  The seeds of truth to sow,
Sift out the trashy refuse
  That wrought such harm and wo:
Weeds, darnel, and that greatest bane,
The tares that choke the growing grain.

8. Traditional Domestic Customs.

Come in across the threshold,
  Thou'rt freely welcome here;
Take off thy cloak, and yonder
  Thy staff beside it rear.

Sit highest at the table,
  Such place befits the guest;
Thy day's long journey ended,
  Refresh thyself and rest.

If harsh unrighteous vengeance
  Hath driv'n thee from thy home,
Beneath my roof content thee
  A welcome friend to come;

But *one* thing I beseech thee —
  Despise not, nor dispraise
My fathers' simple customs,
  Our household's ancient ways.

---

9. A Patriotic Heart.

Upon our fathers' labours
  With reverence to build,
To sow the seeds they left us
  Within the fields they tilled,
By thoughts of them assisted
  To plan the nation's weal,
To glory in our honour
  And shame for wrong to feel,
To sink all selfish passions
  In public joy or smart —
All this implies most clearly
  A patriotic heart.

Whate'er our fathers builded,
  Devoid of shame, to waste,
To rear our fancy's structures
  On airy nothings based,
To blame, devoid of feeling,
  The men ourselves did choose,
Because they have not honoured
  Our new-adopted views;
When naming names once famous
  To act the scorner's part,
All this implies as clearly
  No patriotic heart.

Now that bright hope is quickened
  To newer, purer light,
And History's Muse — expectant —
  Her pencil grasps to write,
O Prince! for whose forefathers
  Zeal set our hearts a-flame,
'Neath whose victorious standard
  Our youth have fought for fame,
With none to stand between us,
  Thyself behold our smart;
And shew, above all others,
  A patriotic heart.

---

10. A New Year's Wish. 1817.

Who truly to his country clings
  Should wish it now a fruitful year;
From frost, sharp hail, and blighting things
  May all good angels keep us clear;
Together with the welcome corn
  And with the wine we need so sore,
Soon may It, from Its plenteous horn,
  Dispense our ancient rights once more!

Men's wishes oft are much amiss,
  They wish too much, both bad and good;
But *we* wish nothing strange, y-wis,
  We but desire the things we should;

If man would keep his frame alive,
  His daily bread he surely needs;
And would he wish his mind to thrive,
  Such growth true freedom only breeds.

---

11. To the Representatives of the People.

On St. Christopher's Day, 1817; the fourth anniversary of the battle of Leipsic.

Again stern Fate her balance sways,
  The olden battle lives again;
This day began the righteous days
  That sundered first from chaff the grain;
Then first at length the false and true
  Men learnt with opened eyes to scan;
The dauntless and the timorous crew,
  Th' imperfect and the perfect man.

Now men shall him "Illustrious" name,
  Whose mind its light from justice takes;
And him shall men a "Knight" proclaim,
  Who ne'er his knightly promise breaks;
Him men shall deem a true "Divine",
  In whom a godly spirit glows;
And he as "Citizen" shall shine,
  Who how to guard his city hnows.

Now let your worth, Ye Men, be shewn,
  Still onward with decision move,
Lest ye a burden to *your own*,
  A jest to *other* countries prove.
Of schemes ye have a plenteous host,
  Long speeches have been duly heard;
Enough is written and engrossed* —
  Then speak your *last* decisive word!

And if, alas! it prospers not,
  Back to the people's ranks return;
Be it your proud, your glorious lot
  No precious rights to lose or spurn.
With patience in this hope abide —
  "The dawn hath come of Freedom's day,
A God its sun doth wisely guide,
  And naught its onward course can stay!"

---

12. Prayer of a Würtemburger.

Thou who from Thine eternal throne
  Dost guard the nations, small and great;
  Thine eye surveys our little state;
Thou seest how we, derided, groan.

---

* The original has "gesandelt", *sanded*; sand being used instead of blotting paper in Germany; I have substituted the word "engrossed" as being more easily understood.

To our good king Thy servant, Lord!
  The people's voice still fails to reach;
  Had he but heard our pleading speech,
We long had had our rights restored.

To Thee is every passage clear,
  No barrier can Thy path control;
  Thy word is heav'n's loud thunder-roll,
Speak *Thou* within our sovereign's ear!

---

13. The Charter.

No prince is so supremely first,
  No king so high a stand can take,
That if the land for freedom thirst,
  Unaided he that thirst can slake.
He cannot in his single hand
  Of Justice such a store possess,
As to distribute to the land
  Just what shall please him — more or less.

Though from the throne sweet Mercy flows,
  Yet Justice is a common good,
In every son of earth it glows,
  It runs in every vein like blood.
And when for freedom heroes strive
  And faithfully join hand in hand,
Then justice proves itself alive —
  A Charter makes it surely stand.

A Charter! hence, to bless the land,
  Proceeds the frame of righteous laws,
Uniting by its holy band
  The prince's with the people's cause.
Though in a palace one be born
  And rest in gilded cradle find,
Not unto him is fealty sworn
  Till lies The Charter sealed and signed.

For this we strove, and still contend,
  Yet is not all as yet attained;
The wreath that crowns a prosp'rous end
  Ye have not yet, ye warriors, gained.
No! as an ensign, wounded sore,
  His standard keeps 'mid hottest fight,
So, worn with toil yet daring more,
  Ye view your well-defended Right.

No herald will your triumph shew
  With roll of drum and trumpet's blare,
Yet will this hope take root and grow
  In German acres everywhere: —
"That wisdom ne'er shall bury Right,
  Nor wealth set honest claims aside,
But every honest Suabian wight
  Shall find his Charter ratified."

---

14. Prologue to the Tragedy of "Ernest, Duke of Suabia".

To celebrate the new Constitution of Würtemburg, on the 18th October, 1819, the above tragedy was played at the Royal and National Theatre at Stuttgart. The whole play, as well as the prologue, was written by Uhland.

A tragic show will pass before you soon;
The curtain rises on a former age
That long hath sunk beneath the stream of time;
And battles, long decided, will once more
Before your eyes be stormily renewed.

Two men, both noble, honest, pious, brave,
Two friends, still firm and faithful e'en to death,
Chief names of Germany's heroic times —
These will ye soon behold in exile roam,
And, desperately fighting, sink in death.

'Tis aye the curse of that unhappy land
In which pure freedom and just laws lie low,
That still the noblest and the foremost men
Consume themselves in most unfruitful toil:
That they whose patriot feelings warmest glow
Are branded as betrayers of their land;

And they — their country's saviours lately called —
Must to a foreign hearth for refuge flee.
And whilst the best men's strength is brought to naught,
There flourish — growing by the power of hell —
Pride, violence, base meanness, coward acts.

How different, when from a stormy time
Pure laws and order, freedom and just rights
Have struggled forth and, firmly fixed, struck root!

Then they, who grudgingly would stand aloof,
Now gladly join once more the burgher's ranks;
Then every hand and every spirit works
Fore-reaching, active, for the general weal;
Then gleams the throne, then thrives the town, then teem
The fruitful crops, then men look proud and free;
The prince's and the people's rights are twined
Together, as the vine entwines the elm,
And for the sanctuary's secure defence
Each gladly ventures both his lands and life.

Men gladly turn themselves from troublous scenes
To revel in the happy realms of art,
And for the sicknesses of painful truths
Men turn for healing to the poet's dreams.
To-day, however, should the stage's shows
Wound any, let him think (to comfort him)
What feast we celebrate in sober truth!*
Then may he know for what true heroes die.

Still Deities descend to visit earth;
Still do those noble thoughts awake to life
Which men in every age have loftiest deemed.
Yes! in the middle of a 'wildered age
Arises, moved spontaneously, a Prince,
Who nobly to his people gives his hand
In willing pledge of order and just laws.†
This have ye seen, ye all can witness this;
Let history on her tablets grave it deep!
Hail to this monarch, to this people hail!

---

* Battle of Leipsic, Oct. 18, 1813.

† Alluding to King William I. of Würtemburg, to whom that country is indebted for its excellent constitution. He began to reign in 1816, and is still living (1864).

15. Wandering.

I took my staff to wander,
  I ranged the German land;
The German mind and manners
  Were praised on every hand.
I went not near the country
  Where orange-blossoms glow,
But fain would that examine
  Wherein potatoes grow.

I sought the princes' palace
  Where German art is crowned,
Where statues godlike, graceful,
  On every side abound.
A tree, that ne'er was nourished
  In German soil, was there;
Or rather, one that flourished
  With roots upturned in air!*

I sought a famous college,
  Pure light I hoped to gain
Where from the chair prophetic
  I heard true freedom's strain;

---

* The meaning is, I suppose, that the poet likens „German art" to a tree growing in a tub, or even upside down. This poem is *ironical* throughout.

There daily the professor
  Supplies our mental needs,
The while he none so badly
  His earthly body feeds.

I sought the "minstrel-forest"
  Where freshening breezes play,
There sat a worthy poet,
  Who plucked a laurel-spray;
No time had *he* to ponder
  Upon a nation's smart;
He only could consider
  His own poor blighted heart.

A temple next I entered,
  There heard I Christian words;
Within — were all men brothers,
  Without — were slaves and lords;
The subject of the sermon
  Was — "Bow thyself, be still!" *
As though despotic statutes
  All Holy Writ did fill.

---

* I cannot find any such text in the Bible; the nearest seems to be — "Take heed, and be quiet." Isaiah VII. 4; where Luther's translation has "Hüte dich, und sei stille".

A burgher's house I entered,
  I muse thereon with joy,
There bloom content and virtue,
  Nor party-strifes annoy.
Live on in homely comfort!
  Ere long we hope to see
One house — from Rhine to Jutland –
  One lodging house, may be!

The hospital I entered,
  There all was clean and fair;
Good store of groats and cabbage,
  And snowy beds were there;
There too deserted children
  A pitying care engage.
Who careth for the needy
  Deserted *in their age*?

Next in the council-chamber
  I sat, and slept, and thought
The hospital still held me
  Which lately I had sought,
While one that in a fever,
  An ague-fever, lay,
Exclaimed — "Say naught, my brother,
  About that Diet-day!"

I mingled with the people
  That 'gan the square to throng,

Where through the flying dust-clouds
  Lean horses whisked along.
There learnt I that the riders
  Hold over-haste in fear,
And that the time is shortened
  By sausages and beer.

(With wings displayed) an Eagle
  Our scutcheon bore of late;
I saw him still in being
  At Nürnberg, o'er the gate.
"God grant it" 's now the motto;
  None care on wings to sail;
Twin Crabs are the supporters,
  The scutcheon bears a Snail.

When this I apprehended,
  My staff I homeward bore;
When Freedom comes in earnest,
  I'll wander forth once more.
I may not live to see it,
  Yet, guided by the hand
Of Zeal, my ghost shall visit
  Mine own free fatherland!

———

Distiches.

To Apollo, the Butterfly.

God-like child of the Alps! unto these my songs be propitious!
Thou o'er the deep dark cleft flutterest, sporting in light.

Achilles (1).

Thou through the turmoil of battle didst pass on, alway in safety,
Oft from Scamander's stream didst thou in safety emerge;
'Twas when receiving the hand of thy bride in the temple of Concord
Thou, O hero divine, fell'st by the arrow of death.*

Achilles (2).

Far hence reigneth Achilles, a God, i' the land of the Blessed;
Waters embrace it, and thou, goddess of waters! a son!†

---

* One account says that Achilles loved Polyxena, a daughter of Priam, and going to receive her (without his armour) into the temple of Concord, was there slain by Paris.

† Thetis, a sea-goddess, mother of Achilles.

Narcissus and Echo.

Strangely, O Love, thou sportest with men — Narcissus an echo
Loveth, the whilst with love pineth an echo for *him*.

This might comfort her still — the words of her timorous lover
Back to re-echo, but *he*, changed to a flower, is dumb.

Mournfully thought Narcissus — "O were I again but a stripling!"
E'en so Echo — "alas! were I a maiden again!"

This is thy sport, O Love! now calling to amorous Echo,
Now Narcissus, all gold, twirling in infantine hand!

The Gods of Antiquity.

Perishing Gods of old Greece, flow'rs bloomed wherever ye wandered,
Scarcely may *ye yourselves* blossom in poesy now!

*Tell's Platte.**

Here is the rock-formed slab, where Tell
leapt out from the vessel;
Lo! an eternal sign here of the hero is
seen.
Not yon chapel I mean, where yearly they
sing for him masses,
No! 'tis the hero's self. See'st thou how
noble he stands!
Now with the one firm foot on the soil —
thence sacred — he treadeth,
Whilst with the other away thrusts he the
tottering ship.
'Tis not of stone, this figure — nor brass,
nor the labour of craftsmen,
Yet to the free man's mind riseth it, vivid
and clear.
Yea, and the wilder the storm, the louder
the roar of the breakers,
Then doth the hero's form grander than
ever appear.

---

* The name given to the slab of rock (on which a diminutive chapel now stands) where Tell leapt ashore in the storm.

The Ruins.

Wanderer! thee it behoveth to sleep in the city of ruins,
So may'st thou in thy dreams grandly upbuild it again.

Burial.

Scarce in the churchyard's soil had the just man's coffin been hidden,
Ere kind heaven thereon sprinkled its silvery snow.

Mother and Child.

"Look toward heaven, my child! there happily dwelleth thy brother,
Ne'er did he vex me, and now angels have borne him away!"
"May no angel approach, nor bear me away from thy bosom,
Mother, O tell me, I pray — how may I vex thee the most?"

A Night in March.

Hear! how roareth the storm and the rain-swoln stream in the darkness!
Feeling both awful and sweet! Beautiful Spring, thou art near!

May.

Blossoms and buds how bright! leaves circle the trees like a "glory";
Heav'n, o'erclouded remain! Earth hath a gleam of her own.

Exchange.

Keenly the swift breeze blew, and the flow'rs were scattered in fragments,
But on the low-bent stalk rested a butterfly still!

Love's Arrow.

Love! thine arrow of might my heart hath mortally stricken;
Now in Elysian realms wake I, already in bliss!

Interpretation of Dreams.

Yesterday I in a dream saw her whom I love at the window;
What saw I when awake? only the flowers she gave.
But in my dreaming to-day, bright flow'rs I saw by the window;
Surely to-day will ere long shew me the darling herself!

Roses.

Oft in the olden days she gave me sweet-
smelling roses;
One hath but lately bloomed o'er the
belovéd one's grave.

The Answer.

The rosebud which thou gav'st to me,
(This morning plucked, dear love, by thee),
Could scarce survive till eventide,
But pined for home, and early died;
And nów its spirit hence doth flee
And wafts this simple lay to thee!

The Slumberer.

When downward droops thine eye's soft lid,
Thine inner eye, from gazers hid,
Begins its vivid dreaming;
Thy glance is inwards beaming!

To Her.

Thine eyes have not the blue of heaven,
Thy mouth no redness of the rose,
No lily seems thy breast or arm.
Ah! what a wondrous spring were here,
If in the vales and on the heights
Such lilies and such roses bloomed!
And if a heaven surrounded all
As clear, as blue as are thine eyes!

Words of an Old Man. (1).

Never say more "good morning", or "good day",
But ever say "good evening" and "good night";
For evening now surrounds me, and the night
Draws on apace — ah! would it now were here!

Words of an Old Man. (2).

Come here, my child! O thou my dear, dear *life!*
Nay come, my child, O thou my dearer *death!*
For all that's bitter should be callèd *life*,
But all that's sweet, should bear the name of *death*.

On the death of a Village Priest.

If with departed souls the power doth dwell
Again to visit scenes once loved so well,
Thou wilt not come when moonlight floods the skies,
When only sadness wakes, and longing sighs.
No! when the summer's morning softly breaks,
When the blue sky is free from cloudy flakes,
When wave the corn-fields high of golden hue,
Enwoven bright with flowerets red and blue,
Then through the fields thou'lt wander as erewhile
Greeting each reaper with a friendly smile.

Elegiacs.

I.

Thou, mother, saw'st mine eyes' first glance
Drink in the light of earthly day;
On thine expiring countenance
I saw descend a heavenly ray.

II.

For thee, O mother dear, a grave is made,
And in a quiet spot, to thee well-known;
Above it broods a home-recalling shade,
And even flowers are at its threshold strewn.
E'en as thou diedst, there thou liest hidden,
Unchanged, with every trace of joy or smart;
To live again thou art not e'en forbidden —
For this thy grave is dug within my heart.

III.

The tolling of the funeral bell
May fade, and sink, and die;
But, in my breast, a mournful knell
Shall ever softly sigh.

IV.

Thou scarce with earth wast covered, ere
A friend with pensive pace

Drew near, and decked with roses fair
    Thy silent resting-place;
Two at thy head that softly glow,
  Two dark ones at thy feet;
Two white ones that for aye shall blow
  Above thine heart smell sweet.

V.

A leaf is falling at my feet,
Weary alike of rain and heat;
Ah! when this leaf was green and new,
I still had parents fond and true.

How soon a leaf doth pass away,
The child of spring, the autumn's prey!
And yet this leaf that downward dives
So much that was so dear survives!

On a Tombstone.

Engraven on this burial-stone
  Two hands together clasped you view,
A sign of earthly union
  That ended soon, tho' deep and true.
They hint to us that parting hour
  When hand clasps hand in bitter pain,
How souls are knit with bonds of power,
  And how they greet in heaven again!

In an Album.

Time, in his ceaseless flight, not only strips
The field of flowers, the forest of its leaves,
Youth of its brightness and elastic force,
But ruthlessly despoils th' ideal world.
All that was beauteous, noble, godlike, rich,
And worthy every sacrifice and toil,
Becomes so colourless, so false and small,
So humble that ourselves are humbled too.
And well for us if still the embers keep
One trembling spark, and if the cheated heart
Becomes not all too faint to glow afresh.
Reality is but a quivering spark;
Imagination soars beyond the fact,
Pretence has more existence than the truth.
He who sees truth alone, hath ended life.
Life is a play; and when the hollow show
Begins at length to fade, the curtain falls.

On William Hauff's early death.

To that young life, so fresh, so brightly hued,
To that rich spring which autumn ne'er ensued,
To him as funeral offering let us bring
A spray plucked newly off, still blossoming.

But lately with this springtime's gladsome light
Our country glowed. Upon a rocky height
Where stood a ruined fort*, there rose in air
A cloud-capt tower, a structure wondrous fair;
Whilst in the cavern where the gnomes of
earth
With silent toil give shapes mysterious birth,
By Fancy's flickering flambeau-light betrayed,
We saw majestic hero-forms displayed;
And every sound in cleft or rift that stirred
Became instinct with life, a pregnant word.
With painted garlands and with warrior-
troops,
With shapes of Satyrs and with festive groups
The ancients the sarcophagus adorned
That hid the burnt remains of him they
mourned;
E'en so hath he for whom our tears are shed
With lively images his tomb o'erspread.

His ashes rest — his soaring spirit flies
To life, whose fulness we can scarce surmise,
Where even Art its heavenly goal may gain,
And mortal types beside th' Immortal wane.

---

* Alluding to "Lichtenstein", an historical novel, by Hauff. Lichtenstein is the name of a ruined fortress.

Fate.

Yes! Fate, I understand thee now;
Not to this world belongs my bliss,
But only blooms in poet's dreams.
Thou sendest me a many griefs,
But send'st with every load — a lay.*

At Sea.

At midnight, on the trackless sea's expanse,
When all the lights on board have long been quenched,
When e'en in heav'n above there gleams no star,
Still glimmers on the deck a little lamp,
A wick protected from all gusty winds,
That shews the needle to the steerer's gaze,
Revealing most unerringly his course.
So — would we heed it — burns within our breasts
A steady light, to guide thro' every gloom.

---

* There is here a play upon the words "Leid" and "Lied".

SONNETS.

I. A Legacy.

A bard — in days when knights had honour meet —
Who fought right nobly in the Holy Land,
Pierced through with arrows, stretched upon the sand,
His faithful followers 'gan thus intreat:
"Enclose my heart, when it hath ceased to beat,
Within the urn that from my native strand
I brought, (with many a pledge of love's sweet band),
And therein bear it to my lady sweet!"
Thus I, belovéd, who thy praise have sung,
Now bleed to death, far off, thro' love's sharp pain;
My cheeks are deathly pale thro' fond regret;
And when death's veil is o'er thy minstrel flung,
This truest of all hearts receive again,
Within this sonnet's golden casket set.

II. To Petrarch.

If thou of Laura hast but *truly* sung,
Her look sublime, her port of heavenly grace,
Not that I question thou didst truly trace
The love for her, thine inmost soul that wrung;
Was she indeed a Bough, from Eden sprung —
An Angel, clothed in fleshly garments base —
A tender Pilgrim o'er this earth's rough face
Who homeward turned while yet her life was young;
I needs must fear that 'mid the twinkling lights
Which thou, now glorified, hast reached at last,
Thou canst not yet thy soul's desire receive;
For she, meanwhile, hath reached remoter heights,
To spheres more holy still her soul hath passed,
And thou in plaintive strains once more must grieve!

III. In Varnhagen's Album.

When turrets, walls, and bars — by Phœbus'
aid —
Decked Nisa's kingly town* with strong
array,
Upon a coping-stone that near him lay
His gold-strung harp, still vibrating, he laid.
The battlement was ne'er so far decayed
But that the stone, e'en to the latest day,
A soft melodious strain would gently play
When gliding fingers lightly o'er it strayed.
So also on this Album-leaf I place,
(This leaf thou'lt stir — in turning o'er —
full oft),
Some tones that from my lowly harp have
rung;
Yet much I doubt if ever thou wilt trace —
When coming to this page — a murmur
soft;
I am not Phœbus, nor from Phœbus sprung.

---

* Nisa was the old name of Megara. Alcathöus "restored the walls of Megara, in which work he was assisted by Apollo. The stone upon which the God used to place his lyre while he was at work, was believed, even in late times, to give forth a sound, when struck, similar to that of a lyre."

Smith's Classical Dictionary: Alcathöus.

IV. To Kerner.

'Twas in the sorrowful November days
I wandered to a silent fir-thronged wood;
Against the tallest fir I leaning stood,
And in my hand wide open held thy lays.*
Absorbed in thought, I conned each pensive phrase;
With awe "St. Alban's stone" my mind imbued,
Next "Regiswind in rosy light" I viewed.
Then "Heliccna's Minster" caught my gaze.
What pleasing wonders wrought thy soothing strain!
The heights were touched with May's fair golden trail,
The voice of spring breathed through the trees o'erhead;
But soon the magic spring dissolved again;
It might not settle in that dreary vale,
But lightly touched earth's highest tops, and fled.

---

* Some of Kerner's poems are mentioned in this sonnet. He is not to be confounded with the more celebrated Körner.

V. On Karl Gangloff's death.

In this sad age when noble deaths abound,
When heroes fall while youthful hopes are high,
'Twas not thy fate on victory's field to die
To be by honour's oaken garland crowned.
Insidious fever did thy powers confound,
And whilst thy parents stood lamenting by,
Thou from thy home wast carried forth, to lie
Where only flowers, not bloodshed, paint the ground.
But no! thou yet wast whelmed 'neath glory's tide;
A battle-picture thou wouldst fain pourtray,
Memorial of thy country's warriors tried.
Thou, dying, seem'dst to hear the battle-cry;
Around thee men, steeds, weapons joined the fray,
And thus 'twas thine 'mid battle-scenes to die.

Author's Note. Karl Gangloff died May 16, 1814, at Merklingen in Würtemburg of a nervous disease. This and the two succeeding sonnets refer to the last paintings and sketches of this ingenious young artist.

Thou wouldst but high and worthy things pourtray,
Despising both the trivial and untrue;
And thus thy pencil's skill would fain renew
The Nibelungen Lied — that wondrous lay.*
Now Hagen's greatness would thy spirit sway,
Now fierce Kriemhildé stood before thy view;
But most that gentleness thy liking drew
Which Sifrid brave and Giselher display.
With justice didst thou Giselher bemoan
Who fell, in youth's fair prime, in hottest fight;
Like his, an early death hath proved thine own.
Was then thy spirit so completely won
By that strange lay, where fate's mysterious might
Calls each *to die*, that *death* thou couldst not shun?

---

* Of the Nibelungen Lied, a most famous mediæval poem, the principal characters are those mentioned in this sonnet. For an explanation of it see Chambers's *German Literature*, p. 19. Sifrid or Siegfried, the dragon-slayer, was Kriemhilde's first husband, and was slain by Hagen. Giselher was Kriemhilde's youngest brother.

How well that solemn, tranquil picture throws
A meaning o'er thine artist-life's glad end,
Where Abraham and all that with him wend
Survey the land which God on them bestows!
There o'er their pilgrim-staves they forward bend,
While cliff and wood their figures half enclose;
And underneath them, stretched in fair repose,
Broad acres, filled with corn and vines, extend.
So likewise, O departed soul, hast thou
This earthly life's rough wilderness passed o'er
And reached the happy goal where pilgrims rest:
Yea, through the hollow sepulchre's dark door
Upon the happy fields thou gazest now,
The heavenly Promised Land, by saints possessed.

——

VI. To the Invisible One.

Thou, whom we seek by many a darksome way,
But whom our groping thoughts can never feel,
Thou once didst leave Thy throne, which clouds conceal,
Amidst Thy people visibly to stay.
How happy those who could Thy face survey,
And hear Thy words, so full of sweet appeal;
Who round Thy table sat and shared Thy meal;
Most happy he who on Thy bosom lay!
We scarce can deem the burning zeal o'erwrought
Of countless pilgrims who from home set out,
And armies who on coasts far-distant fought
That they beside Thy grave but once might pray,
And once might kiss with fervour most devout
The holy soil o'er which Thy feet did stray.

VII. Presentiment of Death.

Who knows whence thoughts of death the mind assail?
In wondrous wise they've haunted me to-night;
My limbs already owned the conqueror's might,
I felt my heart's retarded beatings fail;
Unwonted tremors made my spirit quail,
My spirit which so seldom knows affright;
Yet now 'twas quenched, and now restored to light,
Like some dim torch that feels a passing gale.
Did dreams molest my sleep, with terrors rife?
The skylark sings, the ruddy morning glows,
New longings bid me wake to bustling life.
Or hath the dread Death-angel near me sped?
Yon flowers that freshly bloomed at evening's close
Droop from their stem, dry, withered, scentless, dead!

VIII. Extinguished Love.

We were as if new-born — so brightly-dyed
On us the light of love's soft morning beamed.
How, Laura! glowed thy lips! thy features gleamed!
How flashed thine eyes! how swelled thy heart's full tide!
Me, too, what founts of love revivified!
With higher thoughts my restless bosom teemed,
So that my wonted sleep I needless deemed;
A briefer waking dream its place supplied.
Yes, love is higher life in common things;
Such were the tokens of its living fires
Which now I seek, in thee or me, in vain;
Laura! for thee and me my sorrow springs,
We both are proofs how faded love expires;
The death of loveless life our love hath slain.

IX. Ghostly Life.

Severed from thee, like one entombed I lie;
No sounds of vernal winds my senses greet;
No skylark's song, no balm of odours sweet
Nor beam of morning sun can life supply.
When living men in slumbers seem to die,
When rise the dead from out the tomb's retreat,
O'er gulfs, o'er heights careers my spirit fleet
Which, whilst I wake, approach to thee deny.
Then to forbidden Paradise I come,
Thro' gates I pass whose bars did erst repel,
Yea! e'en to beauty's silent sanctuary!
Doth ghostly breath affright thee, tender bloom?
'Tis love's soft sigh that breathes on thee — farewell!
The cock crows shrill — to seek my grave I fly.

X. A Desolate Spring.

To youthful dreams my fancy often veers,
Albeit it fails again those joys to bring
When, in the first sweet days of genial spring,
The teeming buds my bosom freed from fears;
Then fancy bore me hence to distant spheres,
As birds essayed their earliest lays to sing;
Then Hope would seek the light, forth venturing
As from the budding trees fresh green appears.
But o'er me now, who late such bliss have known,
Just severed from the closest bonds of love,
Thrust forth from Paradise to wander lone,
O'er me what joy can sprouting germs diffuse,
Or lonely ousel's lay from yon dead grove,
Or violet meek, tho' ne'er so sweet with dews?

XI. The dear Spot.

The spot where I, upon my winding way,
That maiden met, in beauty's mould designed,
Who, passing swiftly as the hasty wind,
Gave me such bliss as beauteous looks convey;
Gladly to that loved spot I fain would stray,
There carve love-emblems on the tree's fair rind,
With fairest wreathèd flowers my temples bind,
And in cool shade — to dream — my body lay.
But so her glances bright confused my mind,
So was I blinded by her beauteous face,
That long I tottered like a drunken man;
And now, tho' strive my thoughts the best they can,
Howe'er across the field my steps I trace,
That spot so dear I cannot hope to find!

XII. The two Maidens.

I saw two maidens on a grassy mound,
Both fair alike in face and gentle mien;
They sat and gazed upon the evening scene,
In sisterlike embrace together wound.
The one her right arm raised and moved it round,
Pointing to mountain, stream, or pastures green;
The other held her left — her eyes to screen —
Against the sun, and watched with gaze profound.
What wonder that the sight sweet yearnings raised,
And that the tender thought within me burned,
"Oh! that I might but sit in either's place!"
But when I longer at the darlings gazed,
My pitying heart this soft reply returned,
"Not so! to part them were a sin most base!"

XIII. The Wood. — A Dream.

Whate'er of verdure fresh or shade serene
With tranquil calm could heart or senses slake,
Methought encircled me, and seemed to make
A still retreat, a pleasant forest-scene.
Whate'er of springing buds or blossom's sheen
Hath round me glowed — in dreams, or whilst awake —
Shaped like a huntress fair, all lightly brake —
(Herself the forest-flower) — thro' bushes green.
She fled; I followed fast with many a prayer,
And now mine arms were almost round her thrown,
When lo! my morning-dream dissolved in air!
O fate! thou bringst my every hope to naught!
Not only hath the lovely vision flown,
But e'en the wood wherein she might be sought!

XIV. The Nosegay of Flowers.

Since flowers — in nosegays — tender meanings veil,
Since *love* is hinted by the blushing *rose*,
"Forget-me-nots" by name their drift disclose,
The laurel *fame* implies, the cypress *bale;*
Since, whensoe'er all other tokens fail,
In different colours secret thoughts repose;
Since *yellow* jealous pride and envy shews,
And in *green* sprays "hope tells a flattering tale";
So might I — to express devotion true —
Cull flowers of every kind and every hue,
And send to thee the unassorted wreath;
For thou my joys, my hopes, my griefs may'st claim,
My love, my truth, my jealousy, my fame;
To thee I dedicate my life and death.

XV. An Apology.

Whate'er in songs I oftentimes indite
Of kisses at endearing eventide,
Of love by warm embraces testified,
Alas! is all a dream, a poet's flight.
And *now*, thou questionest my minstrel-right,
And sternly wouldst my boastful language chide;
"If thus he dare to speak of bliss untried,
Let him be silent, feeling *real* delight!"
Belov'd one, moderate thy serious tone,
Smile at such dreams as poet's fancy sees
Of shadowy shapes, and sports he ne'er hath known.
In shadows cool the minstrel oft doth lie,
The whilst his harp hangs 'neath the swaying trees
And through the strings the whispering breezes sigh.

XVI. A Proposal.

Oft as the poet views her portrait blest,
The distant fair one's form delights his mind:
And though life's tangling cares around him wind,
The lov'd one's picture is his bosom's guest.
Again — his lays, inspired by sweet unrest,
The fair one reads, at evening hour reclined,
And many a fervid thought so dear doth find
That deep it lies engraved within her breast.
Thus while her cherished picture soothes *his* pains,
And by his songs *her* griefs are oft allayed,
The pain of *separation* still remains!
Then deign, O Fate, the lot of *both* to bless;
Restore the poet to the beauteous maid;
Then might the miniature the songs caress!

XVII. The Critic Converted.

Thou who but lately from thy critic's stool
  Us luckless sonneteers didst so torment;
  Thou who with poisonous gall hast so besprent
And doomed us to the lowest Stygian pool;
Thou cleanly ermine of the olden school,
  How hast thou soiled thy white integument!
  For now thyself hast to thy lady sent
A creaking sonnet, rough beyond all rule!
Thy late fierce scoldings hast thou quite forgot?
  Forgot what, half in jest and half in passion,
    The critic Voss enjoined, that veteran elf?
Thou'rt like the righteous pedagogue, I wot,
  Who, whilst he chid the lad in wrathful fashion
    For stealing cherries, munched them up himself!

XVIII. A Concluding Sonnet.

As, when a funeral bell hath ceased to toll,
The sound yet lingers ere it dies away;
As he who down a mountain takes his way
Too hastily, can scarce his course control;
As from apparently extinguished coal
An unexpected flame will brightly play;
As oft, upon an almost withered spray,
Bursts forth a blossom, desolate and sole;
Or as the shepherd, thrilled with sweet delight,
Pours forth in artless song his fair one's praise
Which thoughtless echoes far and wide extend;
So fares it now with me who sonnets write;
Though neither thought nor purpose it bewrays,
I write one sonnet more, to make an end.

XIX. To the League-detectors.

A. D. 1816.

Ye who with scent so keen smell out a throng
Of secret leagues kept up by dang'rous foes,
Forgive me if I now one league disclose
That hath not vexed you yet with fancied wrong.
I know what makes you grieve your whole lives long —
The plague — the dreadful crime that spreads and grows;
'Tis this: the fervent wish our country shews
To be well-governed, free, united, strong!
I know yet more, which if ye bid me tell,
A mighty, secret league I gladly shew,
That hath been woven close in silent nights;
'Tis the great league of stars innumerable;
And — as keen spies have lately made me know —
The sunbeams vie not with their myriad lights.

Note to Sonnet XIX. Austria and the leading powers of Germany were at this time alarmed at the existence of secret associations. To these belonged most of the professors and students of the universities, who were most strenuous in their efforts to obtain the establishment of constitutional governments, and to defeat despotism. The poet here explains that the men who were said to be "dangerous foes" to government, and to be united in a "league" against it, were really those who were freedom's best defenders. By way of illustration, he suggests that the researches of astronomers have shewn that there are many stars far brighter than our sun, and that therefore the whole light of all the stars very far surpasses the solar brightness. In like manner, the combination of many true men, however apparently humble each may seem to be, far surpasses in real strength the power of the most despotic ruler.

POEMS IN OTTAVA RIMA.

To K. M.

(Perhaps Karl Mayer, to whom he dedicates his ballad of "Merlin". See note to that ballad.)

When Nature would her various works renew,
She loves to travail in some secret lair;
None but her favour'd votaries may view
How her quick hands Spring's ornaments prepare,
How she in concord sweet and order due,
Nurtures in secret haunts her children fair.
But when she would subvert and waste outright,
In storms and hurricanes she bursts to sight.

So also Love delights to exercise
Throughout the spirit-world his wondrous might;
He draws his viewless ring in magic wise
At golden evening, or in starlit night;
And by soft lays and plaintive melodies
Awakens kindred choirs of spirits bright.
He knows how souls in his perennial tie
Are knit by glances from the silent eye.

If in the billows of a boisterous tide
  A youth should fling himself in venturous play,
Full soon will he, returning shoreward, ride
  Upon that wave that swept him fast away.
But I — methought a glassy lake I spied,
  Wherein heav'n's vault, earth's sheen reflected lay.
There sank I down, with softest raptures drunken,
There sank I down, and am for ever sunken.*

One Evening.

The tolling ceased, the last hymn died away;
  No sound recalled the loss that wrung my breast.
My heart was lighter, 'mid my grief's dismay,
  Since she by pious hands was laid to rest.
As if the white shroud in the house yet lay,
  I still was doubtful where to seek her best;
She seemed with gestures sad, without a home,
To hover 'twixt the earth and heaven's high dome.

---

* The meaning is that whoever plunges headlong into love, may soon be free from it again; but whoever sinks into it slowly, will surely sink down wholly and irrecoverably!

The setting sun shone bright; I sat in shade,
And looked afar, across the meadows green;
Methought two children in the distance played
In life's full bloom, as *we* had blooming been.
Then sank the sun, gray mists a curtain made,
The vision fled, dark shadows veiled the scene.
Then — upward gazing — in the Fields on high*
The sunset's glow and her I loved could spy.

Living Backwards.

Beside her grave, fast rooted there, I knelt,
My spirit sought the kingdom of the dead;
My sight reached not to heaven; alas! I felt
The thought we *there* should meet, small comfort shed!
In looking *forward*, naught but sorrow dwelt,
To you, bright dreams of former days, I fled;
I raised the coffin from the grave's dull night
And bore her back again to life and light.

* The Elysian fields or Paradise.

Soon oped her eyelids pale — with sight renewed
  Her eyes toward me shot their kindling glance;
Soon moved her limbs with youthful strength endued;
  She joined her sisters in the mazy dance.
Love's golden hours returned, with bliss imbued,
  Love's first fond kiss, and passion's sweet romance;
Till at the last I lost my life and thine
'Mid childhood's fragrant flowers and noonday shine.

Song and Warfare.

Doth yonder Northern storm its lightnings dart
  To wither e'en the minstrel's garland green?
Hath Poetry become a coward's art,
  And only sword and lance fresh honours glean?
Must poets, clothed with shame, far hence depart
  While warlike hosts advance their weapons keen?
May not the harper, as i' the olden tide,
E'en through the hostile camp, full welcome, stride?

Must Poetry in wood and cave abide
Till War disturbs no more the nations' rest?
Till all volcanic fires have waned and died
That can be nurtured in the earth's deep breast?
If so — no song hath ever yet been tried,
Nor e'er can be in future times expressed.
No! lasting peace, with dews of song endowed,
Broods o'er long warfare like a golden cloud.

Each thing of earth its season doth possess;
But song within the heart hath alway power,
As lasting in exalted nobleness
As in deep love and every generous dower.
As lasting in its gloom of deep distress
As in its mirthful sports and joy's bright flower.
Though rolls the thunder — tho' the whirlwinds scream,
The sun stands steadfast and the stars yet beam.

While hosts prepare their murderous trade to ply,
Fair spring prepares herself for mirth and play;
The drums are beat, the startling trumpets cry,
While winter's storms aside their fury lay.

Fierce war would seek the earth with blood to dye,
That decks herself with many a bud and spray.
If thus the earthly spring fair buds displays,
Let Poetry's fair spring put forth her lays.

Song and Warfare. No. II.

Ne'er clothed with shame shall minstrels hence depart,
Tho' warlike hosts advance their weapons' sheen;
Not yet the bard's is deemed a sordid art,
He dares by sword and lance fresh honours glean.
That Northern storm doth awful lightnings dart,
Yet makes him for the strife more fresh and keen.
Wouldst thou thro' hostile camps, O harper, stray,
Thou still — with sword in hand — mayst force thy way!

When "Freedom!" "Fatherland!" around him ring,
No sound falls sweeter on the brave man's ear;
Where Freedom's holy flag is fluttering,
Fresh life and strength within the minstrel peer.
Did Æschylus*, who of Vict'ry loved to sing,
Or Dante† e'er this glorious hazard fear?
Cervantés, of his right hand's use bereft,
Could yet indite Don Quixote with his left.§

They too our German Poet-fane that throng,
Have shewn what warlike fire within them reigned;
Full oft are heard these joyous sons of song,
And many a one a ruddy wreath hath gained;

---

* Æschylus fought at Marathon, Salamis, and Platæa.

† Dante fought at Campaldino, where he served in the foremost troop of cavalry, and was exposed to imminent danger. — *Cary's Dante.*

§ This is a mistake. Cervantes was wounded in the *left* hand, in the sea-fight off Lepanto. See *Vida de Cervantes;* prefixed to *Don Quijote,* edited by *Don Eugenio de Ochoa.*

Thou, Wehrman Leo, thou, Black Huntsman strong*,
Have both a warrior's glorious death obtained;
And, Fouqué, how thy name my heart doth thrill!
Thou'st dared and fought — yet liv'st and singest still!

As Spring returns, we hear the whirlwinds blow,
Earth quakes as marching hosts pursue their way;
And, as swoln streams beyond their confines flow,
So — far from home — our country's warriors stray.
On through terrific scenes the bard doth go,
And storms and waves alike inspire his lay.
Soon Spring shall bloom and Peace bring golden days
With milder breezes and more tender lays.

---

* Meaning, I suppose, Theodor Körner, who belonged to a cavalry troop called the "Black Huntsmen".

Katharina.

(I am informed that the Katharina here meant was the first wife of William I of Würtemburg, the present king; that she was a Russian princess, much beloved by the people of Würtemburg, and lies buried at a Greek Catholic chapel near Stuttgart.)

The Muse, that aye of Right and Freedom sings,
Remote from palace-halls her way doth steer;
When songs are sung and revelry outrings,
She hath no portion in the courtiers' cheer;
But when loud sorrow comes on brooding wings,
With other mourning guests she then draws near;
Tho' ne'er she named the living in her lays,
The dead that hear not may she freely praise.

With moaning funeral bells the city thrills,
The passers-by in sable garments go;
No features smile, each eye some tears distils,
All men are rivals in unmeasured wo.
For all these signs, the Muse her task fulfils,
And separates the truth from falsehood's show.

The bells will toll whene'er men make them swing,
And tears will fall from shallow depths that spring.

The coffin rich, by skilful workmen made,
  Decked with the purple pall a princess wore,
Decked with a crown with brilliant gems arrayed,
  Declares the land is filled with anguish sore.
Yet though the pall and crown be thus displayed,
  The Muse regards such trifles none the more;
Shall earthly splendour that strong eyesight daze
That on th' eternal sunlight loves to gaze?

She looks from earth to heaven, to earth again;
  Thro' all historic ages peers her sight.
There queens arise to power, ere long to wane;
  Like faces seen in dreams, some vanish quite.

Their names are heard no more in minstrel's strain,
  Their pomp is lost in Fame's surpassing light.
Meanwhile in life still fresh, unfading, sure,
The names of noble burgher's wives endure.

The Muse this weighty question dares not slight —
  "Hath this bright golden crown adorned a head
That wore it worthily, and lent it light?
  Have this soft mantle's purple folds been spread
Above a queenly heart that loved the right?
  A heart with holy aspirations fed,
Filled with an active strength, benevolent,
Spreading good actions o'er a large extent?"

Thus asks the Muse, but in her inner mind
  What answer should be given she fully knows;
She utters much that grieves her, yet doth bind,
  (Pent up within her breast), her deepest woes.
And more — that she an offering too may find
  And of this mournful hour a sign propose,
She thoughtfully — beside the golden crown —
A fruitful wreath of ears of corn lays down.

"Spirit that early fled'st, with this be crowned,
Nor gold, nor priceless gem gleams brightly here;
No flowers within this coronal are bound,
Thy course was done, when days were short and drear;*
Such fruits of earth are here entwined and wound
As thou distributedst when corn was dear;
A wreath like that of Ceres thou didst weave,
Mother and Nurse of men, my praise receive!"

She speaks and, glancing upward, sees divide
The vaulted roof; the clouds asunder flee;
Her sight can pierce to heav'n's dominions wide,
There meekly Katharina bends the knee;
She wears no more the signs of worldly pride,
On earth she leaves earth's hollow 'pomp and glee;
Yet on her forehead, lo! a heav'nly beam
From Light's most holy Source doth purely gleam.

---

* She died Jan. 9, 1819; just three years after her marriage.

BOUTS RIMÉS.

The three poems following are mere specimens of literary skill. A verse of four lines from some well-known author is selected; it is then required to write a poem of four verses, each verse to end with one of the lines aforesaid. These ending lines are italicized, and will be found to correspond with the lines of the quatrain.

I. The Critic.

"Love in music thinketh best,
Thoughts reside too far away;
Only in a tuneful lay
Every mood is well expressed."

Tieck.

Fair one, thou hast bidden me
On this theme to write a rime;
But I tell thee candidly
So to do in waste of time;
As on coals I seem to be.
Didst thou not, O loveliest,
Love at Logic's laws to jest,
Soon would I to thee display,
'Tis but nonsense thus to say,
"*Love in music thinketh best.*"

True! I understand the plot
  Of this senseless kind of play;
But a theme so strange, I wot,
  Such a riddling style of lay
Seems indeed a Gordian knot.
Yet I've pleased thee ere to-day
Often thus, my star-like fay;
  Void of hope I rub my hands,
  Still my verse unfinished stands —
"*Thoughts reside too far away!*"

Shun, my love, the Spanish style,
  Shun the foreign triplets all;
Shun th' Italian stanzas vile,
  Canzonets and sonnets small;
Stick to Sapphic odes awhile!
Fling the modish muse away
Wooed by courtier-minstrels gay;
  Lightly let thy verses skip,
  Only in soft measures trip,
"*Only in a tuneful lay.*"

Not in lines of tinkling sound
  Can the bard his thoughts disclose;
By the ancient metres bound,
  Better may he odes compose
Where the spondee's strength is found.

German-Grecian metres best
Booming, ringing, stand the test;
  Yes! by these the quaintest thought,
  The perversest theme is caught,
"*Every mood is well expressed.*"

II. The Troubadour and the Critic.

"Moon-illumined magic-night
  Such as can the sense ensnare,
  World of legends strange and rare,
Rise, in olden splendour dight!"

Tieck.

Troubadour.

Dark's the night — no moon's soft ray —
  Nowhere gleams one starry spark;
Yet, impelled by love's fond sway,
  Roam I through th' uncertain dark,
With my lute and plaintive lay.
When my love from slumbers light
Waking, lights her taper bright,
  Then with rapt'rous joy elate,
  Gaze I on a star-ornate
"*Moon-illumined magic-night!*"

Critic.

'Would he'd cease his nightly squall,
  Poetaster Helicanus!
What he sings is stolen all
  From the fam'd Octavianus,
Whose deserts are wondrous small.
From the Alps to Denmark's air,
Learnéd men can witness bear
  How I've proved his writings written
  By a *clique* with nonsense smitten,
"*Such as can the sense ensnare.*"

Troubadour.

How that hoarse, rough voice doth bay!
  Is 't the shepherd-lad Hornvilla?
Is 't the butcher's — Clement's — bray?
  From the window of Camilla
Croaker, take thyself away!
All that critics' pens declare
From the Alps to Denmark's air,
  Vent at home, thou void of pity!
  Let thy dreamings spare the pretty
"*World of legends rich and rare.*"

Critic.

Vilely dost thou howl and strum,
  Thou, that cut'st our slumbers short,
Call'st thyself the muses' "chum"!
  Next, when Phœbus holds his court,
All the chimney-sweeps will come!

Age! when every thoughtful wight
Would not — save in Latin — write,
  Age of powdered prim perukes
  Crowned with bays by lords and dukes,
"*Rise, in olden splendour dight!*"

III. The Night-wanderers.

"*One* thing is not fit for *all;*
  What he does, let each take care:
  Where he stays, let each beware:
He that stands, expect to fall."

Gœthe.

The Quarrelsome Man.

Silent through the street I fare
  Where resides my fair-haired she;
Others to this street repair;
  Through the gloom I seem to see
Some one pause and enter there.
Doth it straightway stir my gall
That she others holds in thrall?
  Be it so! but be it known,
  Each should love but one alone,
"*One thing is not fit for all.*"

The Obliging Man.

With her pitchers to the well
  Comes the maid I strive to gain;
Whish! with efforts forcible
  Round the wheel she winds the chain;
Who my bliss — who help — can tell?
Yea! I tugged with vigour rare
Till the wheel was past repair;
  Though no more it round will run,
  Well have we our labour done:
"*What he does let each take care!*"

The Prudent Man.

"Twelve o'clock!" the watchmen cry;
  From my mouth the glass I take;
Shall I rashly homewards hie
  At the hour when ghosts awake,
When patrols each wand'rer spy?
Shall I — for a pastime — bear
All the taunts my wife can spare?
  Then the neighbours! tattlers! Nay,
  In the "Eagle" here I'll stay;
"*Where he stays let each beware.*"

The Reeling Man.

Strangest things at times appear:
  Yesterday 'twas summer's heat,
Now, what slippery ice is here!
  Lest the pavement prove my seat,
Every step I take in fear.

See! how reel the houses all,
Whensoe'er I touch the wall!
  Care, at times like these, should guide;
  He that walks, should fear to slide,
"*He that stands, expect to fall!*"

A NORMAN CUSTOM;

A Dramatic Poem.

Dedicated to Baron De la Motte Fouqué.

Fishermen's huts on the Coast of Normandy.
Balder, a Sailor. Richard, a Fisherman. Thorilda.

Balder.

This to thy welfare, my much honoured host!
Good faith! I have good cause to bless the storm
That drove me hither to this island-bay.
For such good fare beside a quiet hearth
Hath not for many a day my longing fed.

Richard.

No better can be found in fisher's hut.
Hast thou been pleased, much joy and praise is mine.
Most dear to me is such a noble guest,
That comes from the home-country in the north
From whence our ancestors once hither sailed,
Whereof so many things are told and sung.
Yet must I now acquaint thee, worthy sir,
Whoe'er doth enter here, however poor,
Is always asked to offer some small gift.

Balder.

My ship that yonder in the haven lies
Contains much curious ware of divers kinds,
That from the far Levant I hither brought.
Fruits golden-ripe, sweet wines, gay-coloured birds;
Good store of weapons too, the northmen's work,
Two-edgéd swords, rich harness, helms, and shields.

Richard.

Of such I spake not — thou hast missed my drift.
It is a custom in our Normandy,
Whoe'er hath to his hearth a guest received
Expects from him some tale or minstrel-lay,
And afterward requites him with the like.
E'en in my olden days I still hold dear
All worthy legends and time-honoured songs,
And therefore would I fain my claim enforce.

Balder.

A legend oft is sweet as Cyprus-wine,
Fragrant as choicest fruits, gay as are birds,
And many a hero-song of olden time
Sounds like the clash of sword and clang of shield,
And therefore was mine error none so large.

True, that in 'witching tales small skill is mine,
Yet gladly to the custom I accede.
Hear then what lately on a moon-lit night
A shipmate told me on the quarter-deck.

Richard.

Fill up once more; thy health, my guest! Begin.

Balder.

Two northern earls for many a rolling year
Together had o'ersailed the tossing sea,
Together weathered many a fearful storm,
Endured hot combats both on sea and shore,
And many a time in the far South or East
Together rested on the blooming strand.
Now in their castles rested they at home,
Both deeply sunken in a kindred wo.
For each had lately followed to the vault
Where slept their ancestors, a wife beloved.
Yet unto each — e'en from their gloom of grief —
A sweet and fondly-cherished hope upsprung.
The one beheld a blooming, sprightly son,
The other watched with care a daughter dear.
And (their long lasting friendship's bond to crown
And found for it a long memorial)

They twain resolved, on some fair day to come,
These children to unite in holy bands;
And therefore bade they make two golden rings
Which — for they fitted not their fingers small —
Were hung about their necks with ribands gay.
A sapphire, azure as the maiden's eyes,
Was bravely mounted in the young earl's ring.
The other bore a stone all rosy-red,
The colour of the boy's fresh-blooming cheeks.

Richard.

A stone all rosy-red in ring of gold
Hung from the maiden's neck? Saidst thou not thus?

Balder.

'Twas as thou sayest — but of that no more.
Soon tall and slim the rosy youngster grew;
To manly pastimes was he early trained;
Soon managed well a slim and comely steed.
He need not ever — like his father — cross
The foaming ocean on advent'rous quest,
But only well defend with strong right hand
The widely spread domain, the castles high,
The joint inheritance of both the sires.

Meanwhile the future earl's young bride yet lay
Within the cradle in a darkened room,
By trusty waiting-women guarded well.
But on a genial day in early spring
The all-impatient child they gently bore
Down to the sunny, joyous ocean-marge,
And brought her playthings — flow'rs and
glistening shells.
The sea, scarce rippled by a gentle air,
Mirrored the image of the glorious sun,
And cast upon the beach a trembling gleam.
A little skiff was fastened to the shore;
The women deck it round with reeds and
flowers,
And lay therein their beauteous, smiling
charge,
And push her from the shore, and draw her
back.
The happy child laughs out, the women join;
But even as their laughter loudest rang,
The cord by which they drew her in their
play
Fell loose; and when they marked it, not an
arm
Could reach the little vessel from the shore.
All tranquil seemed the sea, all free from
waves,
Yet washed the skiff still farther from the
shore.

Still is the child's shrill laughter faintly heard;
The women gaze at her in wild despair,
Wringing their hands, and shrieking in their grief.
The boy, who but that moment had arrived,
Seeking his love, and o'er the verdant turf
That sloped towards the sea his course impelled,
Hearing the outcry, dashed upon the beach
And boldly urged his courser tow'rds the waves
In hopes to rescue yet the flow'r-decked skiff.
But when the courser felt the chilly flood,
He shivered, and in stubborn mood drew back,
Bearing his rider to the shore once more.
Meanwhile the skiff that bore the hapless child
Already from the creek had drifted forth,
And rising billows on the open main
Soon hid it from their sight.

Richard.

Poor child! poor child!
All holy angels have thee in their care!

Balder.

Soon to the father came the woful tale.
At once he bade each vessel, small and great,
Be quickly launched; himself the swiftest bore.

All vacant is the sea, the evening falls,
The breezes veer, the lowering tempest roars.
After a whole month's search they find at last
And homeward bring the empty, shattered skiff
With withered garlands decked —

Richard.

What troubles thee in speaking, worthy guest?
Thou falterest, thou sighest!

Balder.

I continue.
Since that mischance the boy would never more
Delight in horsemanship, as heretofore,
But rather loved to learn to swim, to dive,
Or hold the rudder with a careful hand.
And now, arrived to man's estate, and strong,
He from his father craved a fleet of ships.
No charm to hold him back the shore had now;
No maid awaits him at the castle's gate;
He seems affianced to the boist'rous sea,
Wherein the maiden and the ring had sunk.
He bade his own swift ship be strangely decked
With purple sails and figure-head of gold,
Like one who o'er the ocean bears his bride.

Richard.

Decked like thine own below there in the bay,
Was't not, my worthy seaman?

Balder.

If thou wilt.
And in that bridal-ship, thus strangely decked,
Oft hath he weathered many a fearful storm.
When to the thunder's peal and tempest's howl
The billows leap, rare bridal-dance is that!
Full many a battle hath he fought by sea,
And therefore in the north is far renowned.
Men gave to him at length a special name;
For when, with lifted sword, he sternly leaps
Upon a boarded ship, then all exclaim —
"Destroy us not, thou Bridegroom of the Sea!"
Here ends my tale.

Richard.

Receive my heartiest thanks.
Most strangely hath it moved mine agéd heart.
And yet, methinks, it seems to want an end.
Who knoweth if the child was really drowned?
Perchance some foreign vessel passed hard by
And quickly caught on board the luckless child,
But on the ocean left the leaking skiff?

Perchance upon some island — like to ours —
Well might the gentle girl be set ashore,
By pious hands be carefully reared up,
And now have blossomed to a beauteous maid?

Balder.

It seems thou knowest well how tales should run;
Then let me list to thine, if such thy will.

Richard.

In days of yore full many a tale I knew
Of our old heroes and our former dukes;
And specially of Richard, Fearless named,
Who saw by night as clearly as by day;
Who wont to ride all night thro' lonely woods,
And many a combat dire with spectres waged.*
But now is my remembrance weak with eld;
All things within my mind are dimly blent.
And therefore let yon maiden take my place,
Who sits so silent and abstracted there,
And by the lamp-light dim strong nets entwines.
She many a moving song hath duly learnt,
And hath a voice as sweet as nightingale's.
Thorilda! fear not thou the stranger-guest.
Sing us the ballad of the "Maid and Ring",

---

* See the legends of Count Richard, near the end of the volume.

Which from an ancient bard thou once didst learn.
A pleasant song — a song I know thou lov'st.

Thorilda sings.

A fair and gentle maiden
Sat by the tranquil sea;
For weary hours she angled,
No fish enticed would be.

A Ring upon her finger
With rosy stone hath she;
Upon the hook she bound it,
And cast it in the sea.

A hand, from depths undreamt of,
Rose — fair as ivory;
Soon on a shapely finger
The ring shone radiantly.

A knight — young, handsome, gallant —
Then issued from the sea;
Rich scales of golden armour,
That brightly gleamed, had he.

"Nay, noble knight, have pity" —
In terror faltered she;
"My golden ring relinquish,
I angled not for thee!"

"Men angle not for fishes
With gold or trinketrie;
The ring I'll ne'er relinquish,
Mine own thou hence must be!"

Balder.

What do I hear — a strange entrancing song?
What do I see — an angel countenance
That, sweetly blushing, peers from golden locks,
Reminding me of childhood's earliest days?
Ha! on her right hand gleams the golden ring,
The rosy gem! My long-lost bride art thou!
And I the "Bridegroom of the Sea" am named.
Here is the sapphire, azure as thine eyes,
And yonder lies prepared our bridal-ship!

Richard.

So much I long have guessed, my warrior brave!
Yea! clasp her close — my favourite foster-child —
See how she clingeth to thy stalwart arm!
Thou claspest to thy breast a faithful heart.
But mark, how thou art taken in the net
Which my industrious child for thee entwined!

———

BALLADS & ROMANCES.

---

1. Renunciation.

Who beneath the pallid starlight
  Through the garden's gloom doth rove?
Seemeth he of bliss expectant,
  Will the night propitious prove?
'Tis the harper — lo! he resteth
  Close beneath the turret gray;
Where the lingering taper shineth,
  Hark! he wakes the tender lay.

"Lady — from thy turret listen;
  'Tis for thee I weave the rime,
Like a gentle dream recalling
  All thy childhood's rosy prime.
As the evening bell was tolling
  Came I — ere the dawn I go;
Never to mine eyes shall sunlight
  This familiar castle shew.

Banished from thy banquet-chamber
  Sparkling with a hundred lights,
Far I roved, whilst all around thee
  Joyous thronged the noble knights.

They, with only joys acquainted,
  Heedless — craved increased delight,
Hearing not love's sad lamentings,
  Honouring not my childhood's right.

Vanish hence — thou dreary darkness!
  Bloom afresh — each gloomy tree;
Place me in the magic kingdom
  Ruled by childhood's lightsome glee!
Let me in the clover tumble,
  Whilst with footfall light as air
Near me steals a winsome fairy,
  Strewing o'er me flow'rets fair.

Yes! tho' childhood's gone for ever,
  Ne'er shall that remembrance fade;
'Tis a glad and glorious rainbow
  'Gainst a sullen sky displayed.
Hence my love avoids the sunlight,
  Lest that sweet remembrance wane.
"Doth thy heart — dear lady, tell me —
  Still thy childhood's love retain?"

Ceased the song — the bard sat silent
  Close beneath the turret gray;
Dropped a ring from out the window;
  Gleaming, in the grass it lay.

"Take the ring — think oft upon me,
  Think of all we held so dear;
Take the ring — a costly jewel
  Gleams there, and a glistening tear!"

---

2. The Nun.

I' the silent convent-garden
  Walked forth a maiden pale;
Sad, 'neath the moon, she seemed;
  Each eyelid's trembling veil
With tears of passion gleamed.

"They tell me that my true-love
  Is dead; 'tis well for me.
Again my love may burn.
  An angel now is he;
Nuns may for angels yearn."

With trembling steps she hastened
  To Mary's sacred shrine;
In sunshine bright it stood.
  With mother-look benign
The maiden pure She viewed.

She, fainting, sank before it
Looked up with face composed
Until her eye-lids pale
At length in death were closed;
Down dropped her streaming veil.

---

3. The Chaplet.

A damsel o'er a meadow fair
Went plucking flow'rets many-hued,
When lo! a dame of beauty rare
Came tow'rds her from the wood.

With friendly look the maid she met,
She twined a chaplet round her hair;
"'Twill blossom, though it bloom not yet;
O wear it alway there!"

And when the damsel older grew,
And wandered while the moonlight gleamed
And wept sweet tears — love's tender dew —
With buds the chaplet teemed.

And when she clasped her bridegroom round
With clinging arms in happy hour,
Then wondrously each bud was found
To yield its full-blown flower.

Ere long upon her breast she nursed
  A lovely babe with rapture mute;
When from the leafy garland burst
    Rich store of golden fruit.

But when within the grave's dark night
  Deep-buried lay her husband dear,
Around her hair with sorrow white
    Waved yellow leaves and sere.

Ere long she too lay pale in death,
  But still her head the chaplet wore;
When lo! the wondrous changeful wreath
    Both fruit and blossom bore!

—

4. The Shepherd.

A youthful shepherd, passing by,
  Beneath the kingly castle came;
A princess from the turret high
    Looked down, with heart a-flame.

"O might I but come down to thee!"
  ('T was thus she spake in accents low),
"What snow-white lambs I yonder see,
    How red the flowerets glow!"

The youth replied in accents low,
"O wouldst thou but come down to me!
How ruddy seem thy cheeks to glow,
What snow-white arms I see!"

And as with silent mournful love
Each morn the castle walls he neared,
He ever gazed till, far above,
His beauteous maid appeared.

Then uttered he a joyful cry —
"Sweet princess, hail! all bliss be thine!"
Her tuneful voice made sweet reply —
"I thank thee, shepherd mine!"

The winter passed, the spring appeared,
The flowerets brightly bloomed around;
Again the youth the castle neared,
His love no more he found.

He called aloud with mournful cry —
"Sweet princess, hail! all bliss be thine!"
A spirit-voice made sad reply,
"Adieu, O shepherd mine!"

5. The Forefathers' Greeting.

Over the heath a warrior old,
Well-sheathed in armour good,
Drew near to an ancient chapel;
In the darksome choir he stood.

The coffins of his fathers brave
Were ranged the halls along;
Afar was heard, like a voice that calls,
A strange unearthly song.

"Ye Hero-spirits! I well can hear
The greeting ye send to earth;
I come — your ranks shall I soon complete,
Ye witness my spotless worth!"

There stood in the shadow deep and cool
A coffin as yet unfilled;
This coffin he chose for his couch of rest,
For a pillow he took his shield.

Over his sword he folded close
His hands, then sank to sleep;
The ghostly voices in silence died,
In silence unbroken, deep.

---

6. The Dying Heroes.

The Danish swords drive down the Swedish host
Towards the coast,
Far off the war-cars roll, the weapons gleam
I' the moon's pale beam.
There, on the fatal field, ere long to die,
Young Sweyn, and Ulf, the grayhaired warrior, lie.

Sweyn.

O father — why should Fate decree my doom,
In youth's full bloom?
My mother never more with loving care
Shall deck my hair;
From her high tow'r my minstrel-girl in vain
Beholds with longing gaze the vacant plain.

Ulf.

Though they will grieve, when in wild dreams by night
We mock their sight,
Be comforted; not long the faithful heart
Endures its smart.
Soon will thy smiling girl — with golden hair —
To thee at Odin's feast the wine-cup bear.

Sweyn.

Once with a festive strain my harp-strings rung;
I blithely sung
Of kings and heroes passed long since from life,
Of love and strife.
Now silent hangs my harp, and yields no tone
Save when the wind draws forth a mournful moan.

Ulf.

Great Odin's hall beneath the sun's bright beams
High-soaring, gleams;
Beneath Him swim the stars, around His throne
The tempests moan.
There with our fathers shall we rest full long,
Then lift thy voice, and end thy broken song.

Sweyn.

O father, why should Fate decree my doom
In youth's full bloom?
As yet no scutcheon, won in well-fought field
Adorns my shield.
Twelve judges, high-enthroned, their judgments deal,
No place they grant me at the hero's meal.

Ulf.

"*One* noble deed may many deeds outweigh,"
The twelve will say,

"'Tis when, to aid his country's sorest needs,
A hero bleeds." —
Behold where flies the foe! lift up thine eyes,
Bright gleams yon heav'n — there, there our pathway lies.

—

7. The Blind King.

Why hasten to the shining sands
The warriors of the north?
Why, with white head uncovered, stands
The blind old monarch forth?
Hark! o'er his staff low-bending,
Loud shouts the anguished king
Till, o'er the straits extending,
The isle's loud echoes ring.

"Give, pirate! from thy rock-retreat
My gentle daughter back!
Her sounding harp, her song so sweet
Were all mine age did lack;
Here once she danced in gladness,
Thou stol'st my child away;
My head thou'st bowed with sadness,
Thyself art shamed for aye!"

Then issues from his rocky cave
  The giant fierce and proud;
His giant sword behold him wave,
  His heavy shield clangs loud.
"Sure thou hadst guards unnumbered,
  But none would dare to stir;
With warriors *thou* art cumbered,
  Will no one fight for *her?*

There steps no champion from the ring,
  But all are mute as stone;
Round turns in grief the aged king:
  "Why mourn I here alone?"
A hand his own is pressing,
  His son claims leave to fight;
"O father, grant thy blessing,
  I feel mine arm hath might."

"O son, a giant's strength hath he,
  Before him none may stand;
And yet — true courage reigns in thee,
  So firm thou hold'st my hand.
Here, take my sword, for slaughter
  Renowned in minstrels' tale,
And let this surging water
  Receive me, shouldst thou fail."

And hark! with keen and rushing prow
  The skiff skims o'er the deep;

The blind old king stands listening now,
  A silence spreads like sleep;
Soon o'er the straits the rattle
  Of sword and shield is sent,
And mingled cries of battle
  With echoes strangely blent.

With anxious glee the old man spoke,
  "Oh say, what have ye seen?
My sword — I know its griding stroke,
  It sounds so sharp and keen!"
The pirate's blood, out-welling,
  Is now his crime's reward.
"Hail thou! in strength excelling,
  Brave prince, heroic lord!"

Once more o'er all doth silence reign,
  The king bends down tó hark;
"What hear I come across the main,
  A rush of oars — a bark?"
"They come to thy caresses —
  Thy son with sword and shield,
And, crowned with sunbright tresses,
  Thy darling child Gunild!"

Blithe welcome from the cliff on high
  The blind old monarch gave:
"Now bliss shall crown me ere I die,
  And honour deck my grave.

My sword, renowned for slaughter,
  O son, beside me lay;
Gunild, my ransomed daughter,
  My dirge shall softly play!"

---

8. The Minstrel.

Oft to the startled echoes
  The beardless minstrel sings;
The fay with listening rapture
  Floats near the trembling strings.
His songs his brows encircle
  As though a wreath he wove;
They go with him like brothers
  Along the leafy grove.

Then comes he to the banquet,
  He sings in kingly hall;
The guests are mute with wonder,
  His songs their hearts enthral.
The loveliest ladies crown him
  With flow'rs that brightly blow;
Then droop his tear-gemmed eyelids,
  His cheeks with blushes glow

---

9. Gretchen's Joy.

"What means yon trumpet's joyous blare?
What mean yon shouts of glee?
From out the window let me gaze,
I guess what it may be.

'Tis he — 'tis he; he home returns,
(The festive tourney o'er),
The king's renowned and gallant son,
My love for evermore!

How rears the horse and curvets high!
How firm the prince's seat!
Good sooth, by this but few would guess
He sings so low and sweet!

How glitters there his helm of gold,
The tourney's hard-won prize.
Ah! 'neath it gleam, more dear than all,
His blue, his piercing eyes!

His breast in rigid brass is bound,
His cloak adown him flows;
Ah! 'neath them beats a gentle heart
That love for love bestows.

His right hand kindly greetings gives,
  His crest he lowly bends;
Then stoop to him the noble dames —
  A roar of shouts ascends.

Why shout ye loud? why stoop ye low?
  He greets but only me.
I thank thee, love — I feel so glad —
  Good sooth, I welcome thee!

Now enters he his father's hall,
  Before him kneels full low;
And there unclasps the golden helm,
  The glittering prize to shew.

At eve, his loved one's door he seeks
  With footstep light and free;
Then brings he kisses fresh and fond
  And ardent love — *to me!*"

---

10. The Castle by the Sea.

"Hast thou beheld the castle
  That looms the sea beside?
Clouds, fringed with gold and crimson,
  Above it softly glide.

It seems as stooping downwards
  The mirrored wave to greet;
It seems as soaring upwards
  The evening clouds to meet." —

"I saw the castle clearly,
  It loomed above the bay;
The moon stood close above it,
  Dull clouds far round it lay." —

"The winds and washing waters —
  Pealed out their voices strong?
And heardst thou from its chambers
  The tones of mirth and song?" —

"Alike the winds and waters
  In tranquil slumber slept;
I heard within its chambers
  A funeral dirge, and wept." —

"And couldst thou on the turrets
  A king and queen behold?
Saw'st thou their waving mantles,
  Their crowns of glistening gold?

And couldst thou not beside them
  Perceive a maiden fair,
Resplendent as the sunlight,
  Beaming with golden hair?" —

"I saw there both the parents
  Without their crowns of pride;
They wore black robes of mourning,
  No maid was by their side."

---

11. Faithful Walter.

On, on towards Our Lady's shrine
  The faithful Walter rode;
Before it kneeled a youthful maid,
  Bowed down by sorrow's load.
"Oh stay, my Walter! Stay, mine own!
Know'st thou no more my voice's tone,
  Which once thou heardst so gladly?

"Whom see I here? the maid untrue
  That once, alas! was mine?
Where hast thou left thy silken robes,
  Thy gold, thy jewels fine?"
"Alas! that e'er I proved forsworn,
From me my Paradise is torn,
  Thou only canst restore it!"

Then up he took the lovely maid,
  With ruth his heart was wrung;
Her clinging arms so lithe and white
  Around his waist she flung.

"Ah, Walter true! my throbbing breast
Against thy breastplate cold is prest,
  It beats not on thine own, love!

To Walter's castle on they rode,
  Its courts were still and lone;
His helmet from his head she took,
  His beauty all was gone.
"Thy cheeks so pale, thy looks distrest
(O faithful heart!) beseem thee best,
  So lovely wert thou never!"

The contrite maid the armour loosed
  From him who mourned her pride;
"What see I here? a garb of black!
  Who, loved by thee, hath died?"
"For her I loved I sorrow sore,
Whom on this earth I nevermore
  Nor after death recover."

Then, sinking at his feet, she knelt
  With arms outstretched in prayer;
"Lo! here — a sinner vile — I lie,
  And crave thy pitying care!
O lift me up, my bliss renew,
Let me upon thy bosom true
  Be healed of every sorrow!

"Arise — poor suffering child — arise,
  I ne'er can thee upraise;

Henceforth mine arms to thee are closed,
  My breast no life conveys.
Like me — for ever make thy moan;
Sweet love has flown, sweet love has flown,
  And back returneth *never!*"

12. The Pilgrim.

A pilgrim, urged by impulse strong,
  To God's Blest City takes his way,
The city of celestial song
  For which the Spirit bids him pray.

"Clear stream, within thy mirror bright
  Its gates shall soon reflected lie;
Ye rocky hills suffused with light,
  E'en now from far its towers ye spy.

I hear a sound like distant bells,
  Eve tints the grove with crimson light;
Had I but wings o'er lonely dells
  And mountain-peaks to waft my flight!"

A lofty joy his thoughts o'erpowers,
  He feels by welcome toil o'ercome;
And, sinking down 'mid fragrant flowers;
  Lies musing on his heavenly home.

"'Too lengthy still the distance seems
To satisfy my hope's fierce fires;
Enfold my spirit, soothing dreams!
Shew me the Vale my soul desires!"

The parted clouds asunder fly,
His angel bright looks down from thence:
"Can I to thee the *strength* deny,
To whom I gave the *hope intense?*

Such hopes, such dreams, with promise rife,
Are to the fainting soul as dew;
But nobler is the strenuous strife
That makes each pleasant dream come true!"

'Mid morning's balms he fades again —
The pilgrim wakes with strength renewed;
O'er hills and clefts he toils amain,
Soon at the golden gates he stood.

And lo! spread out like Mother's arms,
The City opes each folding door;
Its heavenly music soothes and charms
The Son whose toilsome course is o'er.

—— · ——

13. Departure.

What shoutings and songs are rending the air?
Throw open the windows, ye maidens fair!
The student is leaving his native town,
He and his comrades the street go down.

The others are waving their caps in air,
Ribands and flowers they round them wear;
Small joy in the custom the student knows,
Silent and pale in the midst he goes.

The cups are clinking, and gleams the wine.
"Drink all, drink once and again, brother mine!"
"With the parting-cup might the pain but go,
That here within me doth burn and glow!"

And lo! from the very last house of all,
Looks down from the window a maiden tall;
'Mid roses and wall-flowers round her set
She seeketh to hide that her cheeks are wet.

And when to this house he came at last,
Then upward his eyes the student cast;
Then cast them downward with bitter smart,
And layeth his hand on his swelling heart.

"Still hast thou, brother, no flowerets fair?
See those that are winking and waving there!
What ho! thou fairest and best of all!
Now let from thy window a garland fall!"

"My brothers, what use were those flowers
to me?
No kind dear sweet-heart have *I*, as *ye!*
They soon would fade in the sun's hot ray,
The wind would scatter them far away."

Onward and onward with shout and song!
The maiden gazes and listens long.
"Alas! I see him from hence depart
Whom ever I loved in my secret heart.

Here stand I, alas! with this love of mine;
Gay roses and wall-flowers round me shine,
Whilst he to whom I would gladly yield
All, all that I have, is far a-field."

---

14. The Boy's Death.

"Oh seek not the forest so dark and wild,
'Twill cost thee thy life, thou vent'rous child!"
"My light is my heavenly Father good,
He leaveth me not in the darksome wood."

Down, down he goeth — the venturous child —
Beneath him roareth the torrent wild;
Above him the branches are rustling loud,
And the sun, nigh setting, is veiled in cloud.

To the robber's dark hut have his footsteps strayed,
From the window gazeth a winsome maid.
"Poor child, so tender, so young!" she saith,
"Why comest thou down to the vale of death?"

The murderous crew from the door appear,
The maiden veileth her face for fear;
They strike him, they wound him, they strip him bare,
Then wounded and dying they leave him there.

"How dark! how lonely! no sun, no star!
On whom shall I call? Is God so far?
Ah heavenly Maid in thy bright array,
Receive my soul in thy hands, I pray!"

---

15. The Dream.

Hand locked in hand, two lovers
  Strayed through a garden fair;
Two wan and ghostly figures
  Sat in the gay parterre.

On the cheeks they kissed each other,
  Their lips met fondly too;
They clasped each other closely —
  Robust and young they grew!

Two bells were tolling clearly —
  At once the dream was gone!
She lay in the convent-cloisters,
  He — 'neath the churchyard-stone.

---

16. The Three Damsels.

Three damsels from the castle
  Gazed down the winding vale;
Fast rode their father homeward,
  He wore his coat of mail.

"O welcome, welcome, father dear!
  What bring'st thou for thy children,
    Who all thy hests revere?"

"My child i' the yellow garment,
  Of thee I've thought today!
Thy joy is all in trinkets,
  Thou lov'st to make thee gay.
Behold this chain of gold so red!
  From yonder knight I took it,
    For this I struck him dead."

Around her neck the damsel
  The necklace quickly bound;
Then tow'rds the spot she wandered,
  The corse she soon hath found.
"Thou — like a thief — liest murdered here,
  That wast a knight so noble,
    That wast my lover dear!"

Then in her arms she bore him
  To the churchyard's sacred shade;
Where slept his noble fathers,
  The corse she gently laid.
Then tightly round her neck she pressed
  The chain, now doubly fatal,
    And sank upon his breast.

Two damsels from the castle
  Gazed down the winding vale;
Fast rode their father homeward,
  He wore his coat of mail.
"O welcome, welcome, father dear!
  What bring'st thou for thy children
    Who all thy hests revere?"

"My child i' the leaf-green garment,
  Of thee I've thought today;
Thy joy is placed in hunting
  By sun's or moonlight's ray.
By thong of gold this spear is sped;
  'Twas borne by yon wild-huntsman,
    For this I struck him dead."

She took her father's present,
  Her hands the spear embrace;
Then turned she tow'rd the forest,
  Death called her to the chase!
There, 'neath the linden's chilly shade,
  His faithful brach beside him,
    Her love in sleep was laid.

"I promised 'neath the linden
  To meet thee; I am here!"
Then in her breast, despairing,
  She drove the fatal spear.

In slumber cool they rested well;
Above them sang the ringdoves,
Green leaves upon them fell.

One damsel from the castle
Gazed down the winding vale;
Fast homeward rode her father,
He wore his coat of mail.
"O welcome, welcome, father dear!
What bring'st thou for thy darling
Who holds thy words in fear?"

"My child i' the silver garment,
Of thee I've thought to-day;
Thou lovest more bright flowers
Than gold or rich array.
This flower, with silver leaves outspread,
I took from yon bold gardener,
For this I struck him dead!"

"Why, why was he so daring?
Him wherefore didst thou slay?
His care the flowerets tended
That now must droop for aye!
He promised that the fairest flower
That grew within his garden
Should be his true love's dower."

Upon her gentle bosom
  She laid the blossom white,
Then wandered to the garden
  Erewhile her chief delight.
There rose a hillock, fresh and green;
  There, by the snowy lilies,
    She sat with tearful mien.

"O could I like my sisters
  Now cause my life to fail —
How shall this blossom wound me?
  'Tis all too weak and frail!"
She gazed upon it, pale and wan,
  Until its bloom was withered —
    Until her life was gone!

---

17. The Black Knight.

'Twas Pentecost, the joyous tide,
When leaves the forest-branches hide;
  The aged king thus spake:
"So from the ancient walls
Within these palace-halls
  A joyous spring shall break."

The drums are beat, the trumpets sound,
Red banners gaily flaunt around;
  The king looked proudly on,
As in the tournament
Each horseman earthward bent
  Before his stalwart son.

Towards the combat's lists at last
A sable horseman slowly passed —
  "Sir Knight, your crest and name?"
"These should I tell, on all
A dreadful awe would fall;
  Dominion wide I claim!"

As on in swift career he flew,
The vault of heaven all gloomy grew,
  The castle 'gan to rock;
Before his first strong thrust
The prince lay prone in dust,
  Scarce rallying from the shock.

Viol and harp invite the dance,
Along the hall bright torches glance,
  A shadow tall glides in;
He saith with courteous air —
"May I, king's daughter fair,
  With thee the dance begin?"

He danced in sable armour stark,
The guests with awe his movements mark;
She shivers with chill dread.
Down from her breast and hair
To earth the blossoms fair
Drop faded, scentless, dead.

When to the sumptuous banquet came
Each gallant knight and lovely dame,
'Twixt son and daughter fair
Was placed the aged king;
He, inly sorrowing,
Oft scanned the youthful pair.

The children's cheeks were pale as death,
The guest a goblet hands, and saith,
"Red wine can bloom restore."
The cup the children quaffed,
Saying — "so cool a draught
We never drank before."

The children round their father threw
Their clinging arms — the last faint hue
That dyed their cheeks, had fled.
As the poor aged man
Each face in turn doth scan,
He groans to find them dead.

"Alas! my beauteous children twain
Hast thou in youth's fair freshness ta'en;
  Take *me*, their joyless father."
With hollow voice and dead
Replied the phantom dread,
  "In spring I roses gather."

---

18. The Garden of Roses.

Of a beautiful garden of roses
  A lay for your pleasure I weave;
There roved fair maids in the morning,
  There heroes struggled at eve.

"My lord, he is king of the country,
  This garden of roses is mine;
He hath gotten a crown, all golden,
  I, a garland of flowerets fine.

"So listen, ye youthful heroes,
  Mine excellent watchmen three;
Here tender young girls may enter,
  But knights must be bidden to flee:

For if they should spoil my roses,
  My heart were with anguish torn."
Thus the beautiful queen appointed
  As she went from the garden at morn.

The watchmen three at the entrance
  March faithfully to and fro;
The roses in silence scatter
  Their perfume, and brightly glow.

Three tender young girls approach them,
  With gentle and courteous grace:
"Ye watchmen, ye three good watchmen,
  May we thro' the garden pace?"

The damsels some roses gathered,
  Then thus all at once they spake:
"See, see how my hand is bleeding!
  Such scratches can roses make?"

The watchmen three at the entrance
  March faithfully to and fro;
The roses in silence scatter
  Their perfume, and brightly blow.

Three blustering knights, naught fearing,
  Right up to the entrance ride;
"Ye watchmen, ye three vile watchmen,
  Now open the gates full wide!"

"The gates may remain close-fastened,
  Our swords can we nimbly use;
The roses we guard are precious,
  Each rosebud is worth one bruise."

Then struggled the knights and watchmen,
  With the knights did the conquest bide;
They trampled on all the blossoms,
  With the roses the watchmen died.

And when it was now nigh sunset,
  The queen came thither again;
"What? see I my roses perished,
  My trusty young watchmen slain?

Their bodies, o'erstewn with rose-leaves,
  I'll lay in an earthy tomb;
Where once was my sweet rose-garden,
  A garden of lilies shall bloom.

But whom have I left as watchmen
  To shield it from evil plight?
I have none but the sun by day-time,
  The moon and the stars by night."

---

19. The Songs of the Past.

1807.

In boyhood, oft within the towers
  Of ruined fortresses I stood;
Through ancient cities roamed for hours
  And many a vast cathedral viewed.
'Twas then the Spirit of the Past
  Before me stood with pleading looks,
And early bade my mind hold fast
  What afterwards I found in books:

That damsels had their dwelling there
  Named "Ballads", far and wide renowned,
Who, 'mid the ranks of ladies fair,
  With festival and song were crowned,
Till came a troop in ruthless might
  And gave to flames their fair abode;
The Sisters fled, concealed by night,
  Wherever fear a passage shewed.

Of these, alas! some sadly pine,
  Imprisoned in a dungeon drear;
Their gentle voices' accents fine
  Still fail to reach a pitying ear;

Alas! for One who, all forlorn,
  Through ways deserted wandered wide;
She sank, by heavy grief o'erworn,
  Yet sang once more before she died.

In a poor maiden's chamber lone
  Another for awhile abides;
She mingles with her friend's sad moan
  What time in heaven fair Dian rides.
Oft, taking heart, the Martyrs go
  To mingle in the market's din,
And sing sweet tunes to music low,
  In hope the hearts of men to win.

Take comfort! cast your bonds aside;
  The heralds fly from west to east,
Within a town by Neckar's tide
  To bid you to a joyous feast.
Ye Glad Ones, join the happy dance,
  Come dressed in garments rosy-bright;
Ye Sad Ones, veiled as nuns advance,
  Come decked with lilies fair and white.

---

20. The Three Songs.

Enthroned in his hall sat Sifrid the king:
"Which harper a ballad can blitheliest sing?"
And a youth from the crowd drew hastily nigh,
His harp in his hand, his sword on his thigh.

"Three ballads I know, and the foremost song
Is one that has 'scaped from thy memory long.
My brother thou slewest in murderous wise:
Once more: *thou hast slain him in murderous wise!*

The second is one that I thought of first
In a wild dark night, as the tempest burst.
With me thou must battle for life and death:
Once more: *thou must battle for life and death!*"

The minstrel his harp on the table placed;
Then drew they their swords in furious haste;
Long, long they struggled in desperate brawl,
Till the king lay dead in the lofty hall.

"Now sing I the third, and the sweetest lay,
A song I could sing for a year and a day;
King Sifrid lies here in his heart's best blood:
Once more: *here he lies in his heart's best blood!*"

---

21. The Prince and the Shepherdess.

Fytte the First.

In this delicious springtime,
  Here, on this verdant plain,
Here, 'neath the golden sunlight,
  Of what shall be my strain?

Swift glides the azure streamlet,
  O'erhead the cloudlets sail;
And horseman gay are riding
  Along the meadowy vale.

The bending branches quiver,
  Bright glows the flowerets' sheen;
The shepherdesses wander
  In the valley fresh and green.

Prince Goldmar rode rejoicing
  His gallant train before;
A crimson silken mantle,
  And a golden crown he wore.

The youthful prince from horseback
  Sprang lightly to the plain;
The horse he bound to a linden:
  On rode his gallant train.

Amongst the shady bushes
  A sparkling fountain streamed;
There sang the songbirds sweetly,
  There gayest flowerets gleamed.

Why sang the birds so clearly?
  Why gleamed the flowers like gold?
A shepherdess most lovely
  Sat near those waters cold!

He rustles through the brushwood,
  He thrusts the branches by;
To the shepherdess for shelter
  The startled lambkins fly.

"O welcome, welcome, maiden!
  So wondrous fair that art!
If I have caused thee terror,
  'Twould grieve me sore at heart."

"I am not blanched with terror,
  So might I swear to thee;
Methought some straying songbird
  Did through the bushes flee!"

"Wouldst thou revive my spirit
  From out thy pitcher here,
As 'twere the greatest kindness
  I'd hold thy memory dear."

"Drink freely from the pitcher,
To all its use is free;
I'd grant a draught to any,
Though he a prince should be!"

She stoops to dip the pitcher,
She bids him drink his fill;
He gazes on her fondly,
She grasps it tightly still.

He cries, with transport glowing,
"Thou seem'st so sweet a child,
Methinks thou wast created
With the other flowerets mild.

Thou seem'st so pure, so noble,
Such grace doth in thee shine;
Methinks thou art descended
From some imperial line!"

"My father ask — the shepherd —
If he a king hath been;
My mother ask — the shepherdess —
If e'er she ruled as queen."

He clasps his crimson mantle
Around her shoulders fair;
The golden crown he places
Above her nut-brown hair.

The shepherdess looks proudly
  And gaily 'gins to call;
"Ye flowers — ye trees — pay homage,
  Bow down, ye lambkins all!"

And as with merry laughter
  She lays the finery down,
I' the limpid fountain's channel
  He casts the golden crown.

"This crown to thee I render,
  As pledge of fondest love,
Till after many an onset
  Once more I hither rove.

A king fast bound in prison
  These sixteen years hath lain;
A band of foes malicious
  Hath been his kingdom's bane.

His land for him I'll rescue,
  I and my warriors free;
His chains I'll burst asunder,
  Spring's flowers he soon shall see.

Now first I haste to battle,
  My days will sultry be;
Say, wilt thou — if I conquer —
  Draw hence a draught for me?"

"Full draughts I'll draw and hand thee
  While flow the fountain's streams;
To thee the crown I'll render
  As bright as now it gleams."

The first "fytte" here is ended,
  The next begins its flight;
A bird is upward soaring,
  Mark where it next shall 'light!

Fytte the second.

My song must now be telling
  Of swords' and trumpets' play,
Tho' I hear the shepherd's ditties,
  Tho' I hear the skylark's lay.

My muse must now be telling
  Of plains o'erstrewn with dead,
Tho' I see the forest budding,
  And blossoms sprouting red.

To Goldmar turns the legend;
  Perchance ye scarce could tell
That he, in love the foremost,
  Was first in strife as well!

He stormed, he took the fortress,
  His standard o'er it waved;
From death within the dungeon
  The gray-haired king was saved.

"O sun — O distant mountains!
O field, O leafy spray!
How seem ye all so youthful,
And I so old and gray?"

Soon came the joyous banquet
With mirth and festive sheen:
Who sat not at the table
Can scarce describe the scene.

And though I had been seated
Amid the guests' long line,
All things had I forgotten
Except the generous wine!

The aged King to Goldmar
Outspake in lordly wise;
"I hold a splendid tourney,
Say, what shall be the prize?"

"Great king, from kings descended,
Be this the meed of might;
Not spurs nor golden helmet,
But a crook and a lambkin white!"

And that — for which the shepherds
Oft race in flowery field —
For that, brave bands of horsemen
Fought hard with lance and shield.

Where'er he rode, prince Goldmar
  O'erwhelmed each noble knight,
And took — while rang the trumpets —
  The crook and lambkin white.

Once more the king to Goldmar
  Outspake in lordly wise:
"Again I hold a tourney,
  And grant a nobler prize.

No toy, nor idle trinket
  As worthless price shall stand;
My crown shall be the guerdon
  From the fairest princess' hand."

How thronged the guests, all eager,
  When blew the trumpet's call!
Each warrior strove his utmost,
  Prince Goldmar foiled them all.

The king, 'mid lords and ladies,
  Stood in his palace-bower;
He bade them call prince Goldmar,
  Of knights the star and flower.

Then came the tourney's hero
  With shepherd's crook in hand;
The lambkin white beside him,
  Led by a rose-red band.

Outspake the king: "No trinket
  Shall for thy guerdon stand;
For lo! my crown I give thee
  From the fairest princess' hand."

He spake, and from her features
  The flowing veil uptook,
Prince Goldmar to the maiden
  Vouchsafed no slightest look.

"No princess e'er shall win me,
  No crown with glistening sheen;
The shepherdess in the valley
  Remains my bosom's queen.

I give thee for a keepsake
  This crook and lambkin white,
Once more I seek the valley,
  All blessings on thee 'light!"

Then rang a voice so clearly,
  To him at once it seemed
That birds sang near a fountain
  And golden flowerets gleamed.

His eyes he quickly lifted,
  The shepherdess he scanned,
Adorned with costly raiment,
  With glittering crown in hand.

"Here in my father's palace
  I bid thee — traitor! — hail!
Say, must thou still be gadding
  To seek yon grassy vale?

Yet first this crown I give thee,
  Thy pledge of feelings vain;
With usury receive it,
  It rules o'er kingdoms twain."

No longer far asunder
  Those lovers twain could dwell;
What next thereafter happened,
  Perchance ye all can tell!

And would a maiden know it,
  My task should soon be sped,
Might I embrace, and kiss her
  On her lips so rosy-red!

---

22. The Goldsmith's Daughter.

Within his shop a goldsmith stood
  'Mid pearls and jewels clear:
"The fairest gem that ere I viewed
  Art thou, my lovely Helen,
  Mine only daughter dear!"

In came a knight in garments gay:
  "Good morrow, maiden fair!
My worthy goldsmith too, good day!
  Make me a costly circlet
  To deck my bride's dark hair."

And when the circlet fair was wrought
  And gleamed with many a charm,
Then Helen, lost in mournful thought,
  Within her lonely chamber
  'Gan hang it round her arm.

"Ah! wondrous glad the bride will be
  That shall this circlet wear!
Ah! would the knight but send to *me*
  A fragrant wreath of roses,
My bliss were past compare!"

Again the knight doth thither wend,
  The circlet fair he eyed;
"Make me, I pray, my worthy friend,
  A ring with diamonds studded,
To deck my lovely bride."

And when the ring was richly wrought,
  Set round with diamonds rare;
Through it the maid, in mournful thought,
  Within her lonely chamber
  Half thrust her finger fair.

"Ah! wondrous glad the bride will be
  That soon this ring shall wear;
Ah! would the knight but send to *me*
  Of his hair one little ringlet,
  My joy were past compare!"

Again the knight doth thither wend,
  The ring he closely eyed;
"Right well hast thou, my worthy friend,
  Made both these pretty presents
To deck my lovely bride.

But now, their due effect to see,
  Sweet maiden, grant my prayer!
Let me, I pray, behold on thee
  My loved one's bridal presents;
  Her form, like thine, is fair."

'Twas early on a Sunday morn —
  Hence was the beauteous maid
In garments but on Sunday worn
  When churchward folks are wending,
  With special care arrayed.

Before the knight behold her stand
  With modest downcast look;
He placed on her the golden band;
  Then, drawing on her finger
  The ring, her hand he took.

"O Helen sweet, O Helen fair,
The jest is now out-played;
Thou art the bride of beauty rare,
For whom the golden circlet —
For whom the ring was made!

'Mid pearls, and glittering gems, and gold
Thy life did first begin.
A token may'st thou here behold
That thou high rank and honour
One day through me shouldst win!"

---

23. The Hostess's Daughter.

Three students had crossed o'er the Rhine's dark tide;
At the door of a hostel they turned aside.

"Hast thou, Dame hostess, good ale and wine?
And where is thy daughter so sweet and fine?"

"My ale and my wine are cool and clear;
On her death-bed lieth my daughter dear."

And when to the chamber they made their
way,
In a sable coffin the damsel lay.

The first — the veil from her face he took,
And gazed upon her with mournful look.

"Alas! fair maiden — didst thou still live,
To thee my love would I henceforth give!"

The second — he lightly replaced the shroud,
Then round he turned him, and wept aloud: —

"Thou liest alas! on thy death-bed here,
I loved thee fondly for many a year!"

The third — he lifted again the veil,
And gently he kissed those lips so pale;

"I love thee *now*, as I loved *of yore*,
And thus will I love thee *for evermore!*"

---

24. The Mower-girl.

"A fair good morning, Mary! What? so soon upon the move?
Thou art not sunk in sloth, true maid, tho' sunk so deep in love.
Then if thou canst within three days this meadow mow for me,
No more will I withhold my son, my only child, from thee!"

'Twas thus the wealthy farmer spake, with flocks and fields endowed;
How Mary 'neath her bosom feels her heart beat fast and loud!
Through ev'ry limb she feels a new, a bracing influence flow;
How strongly now she sways the scythe, and lays the swathes full low!

Now noonday glows, the mowers tired now cease their tasks to ply;
They seek the brook to quench their thirst, cool shade in which to lie;
But still the bees with busy hum flit o'er the parching field,
And Mary in unresting toil not e'en to them will yield.

The sun sinks down, the vesper-bell bids
men to rest and pray;
Her neighbours all to Mary call — "Enough
thou'st done to-day!"
The mowers go, the shepherds soon drive
home the fleecy ewes,
But Mary whets her scythe once more, and
straight her toil renews.

Soon falls the dew, soon brightly gleam the
moon and many a star,
The swathes smell sweet, the nightingale is
faintly heard afar;
But Mary hath no wish to rest, or hear the
plaintive lay,
She only cares to swing the scythe with
measured forceful sway.

So onward still from eve to morn, from morn
to evening red,
With happy hope alone refreshed, with love's
sweet fancies fed.
When for the third time rose the sun, the
weary task was o'er,
Behold where Mary resting stands, and tears
of joy doth pour!

"A fair good morning, Mary! What? Can hands so nimble be?
The meadow mown? A rich reward I'll surely find for thee;
But as to marriage, girl, thou hast in earnest ta'en my jest,
For *loving* hearts are credulous, and *foolish* hearts at best!"

He spake, he went; but motionless behold poor Mary stay;
She feels her heart grow numb and chill, her trembling knees give way;
Deprived of speech, her feelings dead, her understanding flown,
'Twas thus they found the mower-girl, 'mid swathes but newly mown.

So lives she still these many years, in mute and listless mood;
A few thick drops of honey sweet are now her only food;
Oh keep for her a ready grave in yonder flowery lea,
For never yet poor mower-girl so fondly loved as she!

25. Dirges.

1. The Serenade.

"What strains are these that break my sleep,
  That with my dreams are blent?
O mother, see! what can they be,
  Now night so far is spent?"

"I naught can see, I naught can hear,
  Sleep on in slumber mild;
For thee is played no serenade,
  My poor, my suffering child."

"These strains from earth have not their birth,
  That make my soul so light;
The angels come to call me home;
  O mother dear! good night!"

2. The Organ.

"Once more for me thine organ play,
  My neighbour old and kind;
Perchance, while sounds its solemn tone,
  My soul may feel resigned."

The suff'rer ask'd, the neighbour played,
  So played he ne'er before;
So clearly, softly! Nay, his touch
  Is like his own no more.

It seems a soft and blessèd tune
  That 'neath his hands is sped;
He stops in horror — lo! from earth
  His neighbour's soul hath fled!

3. The Thrush.

"I ne'er would seek the garden more,
  But lie here all the day,
Might I but hear the joyous thrush
  That yonder trills his lay!"

So spake the child — the thrush is caught;
  Within a cage it pines;
It ne'er will sing, but evermore
  Its drooping head declines.

Yet once again with anxious eyes
  The child upon it gazed;
The thrush sang clear and loud — then death
  Its glistening eye-balls glazed.

---

26. The Lode-star.

He who towards the Orient Land
  A light ship guided — not his own,
Now steers towards his native strand
  A bark gold-laden — his alone.

More oft than any other star
  Love's Planet* he hath fondly eyed,
That safely guided him from far
  To where resides his darling bride.

Yet to the goal he hath not come,
  Though now within the gates he strays;
How may he find his darling's home
  Amid the city's wildering maze?

How may his glance perceive her form?
  Walls everywhere his prospect bound.
How, 'mid the market's wordy storm,
  May he detect her voice's sound?

Behold a hand yon window close,
  Perchance she thence but lately gazed;
Behold yon veil that downward flows;
  Conceals it not the face he praised?

Still wanders he from street to street,
  Where now dim twilight's shadow dwells;
He wanders on with weary feet,
  A tireless heart his steps impels.

---

* Venus. *Lode-star* and *Lode-stone* mean a star (or stone) *that leads.* This spelling is preferable to the more usual *Load-star*, *Load-stone*.

15*

What stays his pace, what happy proof?
  What strains are those, what voice divine?
'Twas not for naught that o'er the roof
  He saw love's trusty Planet shine!

27. The Minstrel's Return.

The minstrel on a bier reclines,
  His pallid lips no songs outpour;
Its faded leaves the laurel twines
  Around the brow that thinks no more.

And there, in scrolls rolled neatly round,
  Are laid the songs that last he sang;
His hands still touch — without a sound —
  The harp that once so blithely rang.

Tho' sleeping thus his last long sleep,
  Still sound his songs in every ear,
And feed men's sorrow keen and deep
  For loss of one sublime and dear.

Now many a month and year have fled,
  Above him waves the cypress dim;
And they who mourned the minstrel dead,
  Themselves have sunk to sleep, like him.

Yet as the spring returns, endued
  With verdure fresh and quickening power:
So lives, with fame and youth renewed,
  The minstrel — to this latest hour.

Unblighted by the grave's cold breath,
  To living men he yet belongs;
The age, that once bemoaned his death,
  Survives but in his deathless songs.

28. The Little Ship.

A little vessel smoothly
  Adown the river goes;
The passengers are silent,
  Not one the other knows.

What draws the brawny huntsman
  From 'neath his deerskin guise?
A horn! He blows it clearly,
  The echoing shore replies.

Then from his staff of travel
  A youth unscrews the ends;
And with the horn's soft pealing
  A flute's shrill music blends.

A maid, that sat so bashful,
  She could not speak for fear,
With horn and flute now mingles
  Her voice so sweet and clear.

In measured time the rowers
  Swing back with steady sway;
By melody borne onward,
  The vessel cleaves her way.

In diverse paths they wandered,
  When all had leapt to shore —
Say, friends, on such a vessel
  When shall we meet once more?

---

29. The Passing Minstrel.

Upon a flower-clad hillock
  Beside a path, I slept,
To golden Fable-region
  A dream my senses swept.

Awaked — with dazzled eye-sight,
  As fallen from the sky —
I mark a minstrel playing,
  Who passed but lately by.

On through the grove he saunters,
  I hear the music still;
Was't this, with dreams so wondrous
  That caused my soul to thrill?

---

30. A Dream.

I lately lay a-dreaming,
  I lay upon a steep;
'Twas near the ocean's strand,
I looked across the land,
  And o'er the spacious deep.

Lo! near the beach beneath me
  A vessel trim and strong;
Its pennon gay flew o'er it,
The skipper stood before it
  As though the time seemed long.

Then from the distant mountains
  There came a mirthful train;
They came, like angels shining —
Bright wreaths their brows entwining —
  And drew towards the main.

To lead the train, sweet infants
  In sportive throngs advanced;
Bright cups the rest were swinging,
To music's sound and singing
  They deftly swayed and danced.

Then spake they to the skipper —
"Wilt gladly bear us hence?
Delights and Joys are we —
We seek from earth to flee —
Far, far to wander thence!"

He bade them climb his vessel,
That throng of gay Delights!
He spake — "Ye Pleasures gay,
Do none, yet lingering, stray
In vales, or on the heights?"

"We all are here", they shouted,
"Haste! all thy sails employ!"
Fresh blew the favouring gale,
Far off beheld I sail
From earth each Bliss and Joy.

---

31. The Good Comrade.

I had a gallant comrade,
No better e'er was tried;
The drum beat loud to battle —
Beside me, to its rattle,
He marched, with equal stride.

A bullet flies towards us,
"Is that for me or thee?"
It struck him, passing o'er me;
I see his corse before me
As 'twere a part of me!

And still, while I am loading,
His outstretched hand I view;
"Not now — awhile we sever:
But, when we live for ever,
Be still my comrade true!"

---

32. The Wreath of Roses.

In the merry days of Spring-time
When with flowers the fields are dight,
For the rose-wreath — prize of vigour —
Stalwart youths put forth their might.
Naught they care *themselves* to gather
Garlands from the lavish land;
Nay! they would, as sturdy wrestlers,
Win them from a maiden's hand.

'Neath an arbour sits she, silent,
She whom all with wonder view,
She who in the bloom of beauty
Shews to-day her loveliest hue.

Sprays of roses nod and waver —
  Pleasant arbour — o'er her head;
Round the queen of May and beauty
  Vines their curling tendrils spread.

Lo! a warrior sheathed in armour
  On a flagging steed draws near;
Bows his head as one in slumber,
  Faint with toil, he vails his spear.
Gaunt his cheeks, his locks are hoary,
  Oft his hand the rein forsakes;
Lo! he starts, as starts the dreamer
  When from mournful dreams he wakes.

"Hail to all that throng this meadow,
  Noble youths and lovely dames;
Need is none to fear my presence,
  Fain would I behold your games.
Fain would I, in fierce encounter,
  'Gainst you break a lance or twain;
But mine arms with age are trembling,
  Scarce my knees their load sustain.

Well I know such knightly pastimes,
  Lance and sword my strength have tried;
Still my body wears the breast-plate,
  As the dragon wears his hide.

Strife and wounds by land I've suffered,
  Storms at sea and billows steep;
Calm repose I met with never,
  Save a year in dungeon deep.

Wo! my days and nights are ended,
  Never love my life hath blest;
Thee, O hand in battles hardened,
  Woman's hand hath never pressed!
Never! for from earth's deep valley
  Still yon damsel dwelt afar;
Yon May-queen, who now before me
  Rises like a new-found star.

Wo! could I renew my youth-hood,
  Mine should be the minstrel's art;
Songs of love I oft would warble,
  Striving for my fair one's heart.
In the merry days of spring-time,
  When with flowers the fields are dight,
For the rose-wreath — prize of vigour —
  Gladly would I race and fight.

Wo! for I was born too early!
  Now the golden age is come;
Wrath and envy now have vanished,
  Fadeless spring begins to bloom.

She, in yonder rosy arbour,
  Shall — as queen — the kingdom own;
I to dust and night must hasten;
  Falls on me the burial-stone."

When the knight these words had spoken,
  Close he pressed his pallid lips;
See! his eyes in death are failing,
  Lifeless, from the horse he slips.
But the noble youths sustain him,
  Lay him on the grassy plain;
Ah! no balsam e'er shall heal him,
  Him no shouts shall rouse again!

Then the maid, her arbour quitting
  Gay with flowers, steps slowly down,
Sadly to the old man stoopeth,
  Lays on him the rosy-crown.
"Be thou king of May's rejoicings,
  None like thee his life hath sped;
Though the wreath can little profit
  Twined around a lifeless head."

33. Princess Siegelind.

Young Siegelind, the princess,
  Her lords and ladies fine
Arose at early morning
  To visit Mary's shrine;
In gold and silk she goes,
With flowers and broidered clothes;
Hence grief unlooked-for rose.

Before the church's portal
  Three spreading lindens grow;
There sat the noble Heimé
  And said in whisper low:
"Nor gold nor gems I'd wear,
Had I one floweret fair
From out thy garland rare!"

So spake the youth in whispers —
  The playful Zephyr blows,
And from the flowery circlet
  Drops out the fairest rose.
Young Heimé stooped in haste
To seize the floweret chaste,
And soon his breast it graced.

'Mong Siegelind's attendants
  Is seen a gray-haired knight
Who, chafing at his boldness,
  Steps forth in wrath, to fight;
"I'll teach thee manners, knave!
From honour's garland brave
Dar'st thou one leaflet crave?"

Wo to the garden ever
  That gave those roses life!
Weal to the lindens never
  Where raged that dreadful strife!
How clashed the swords that day,
Till, in the furious fray,
Young Heimé lifeless lay!

Fair Siegelind bent o'er him,
  The fatal rose she hent,
Within the wreath replaced it
  And through the portal went.
In gold and silk she goes,
With flowers and broidered clothes;
Who dares her discompose?

Before Saint Mary's image
  The maid took off her crown;
"Receive it, Pure, Benign One,
  From *this* no flower fell down.

The world I here forsake;
The holy veil I take;
Young Heimé's dirge I wake."

---

34. The Victor.

(In Asonante Verse; the accented vowel being an "o". See the preface.)

Sat a hundred dames above,
  All the tourney's strife beholding;
These were only humble leaves
  Gathered round my queen, the rosebud.
As the eagle views the sun,
  Gazed I on her features boldly;
Burning through my visor's plate
  Seemed mine eyes, with ardour glowing!
How my quickly-beating heart
  Well nigh had my breast-plate broken!
Looks in *her* that softly shone
  Seemed with lightning-flames to clothe me;
Tones from *her* that gently came,
  Turned in *me* to thunder's rolling!
She, a balmy morn in May,
  Seemed, in *me*, a storm explosive.
Forth I burst, by naught restrained,
  Thundering through my conquered foemen!

---

35. The Cavalier by Night.

In the silent, moonless midnight
  'Neath my balcony he stood;
Singing to his lute so sweetly
  Strains with tend'rest love imbued.

Then, by jealous rivals challenged,
  Bravely fought he, fierce and proud;
Till the sparks flashed swiftly, brightly,
  Till the walls re-echoed loud.

Thus, by turns, both arts he practised
  Said to win the coyest fair;
Till my heart with love was glowing
  For the stranger 'neath me there.

Forth I gazed at early morning,
  Fearful what mine eyes might see;
Naught of him my gaze encountered,
  Save his blood, left there for me.

---

36. The Knight of Castile.

I.

"When echoes sound from distant hills, brave knight of fair Castile,
I listen for thy battle-cry, but hear the thunder's peal.
When rosy-bright the hill-tops beam in morning's earliest ray,
I seek afar thy lance's gleam — but see the rising day."

II.

"Once pilgrims', minstrels', pages' feet trod out a pathway wide;
With busy hands a lofty tower was reared the path beside;
Maids watched me from its turrets high with keen and envious sight,
All yearned to see thee pass that way, thou bravest, noblest knight!
Alas! th' expected hour is past! too long I weep and wait;
Alas! the eyes will soon grow dim, that watched thy lordly gait;

The walls will crumble soon, where once thy
charger's trampling rang;
Grass hides the path that echoed once thy
footsteps' iron clang."

III.

No more in him shall love's soft glance excite
a sweet unrest,
Nor stroke of sword nor thrust of lance shall
pierce his noble breast;
The lightning's flash hath struck him on the
lonely wooded height:
A shaft from heaven alone might slay so fair,
so brave a knight!

IV.

Dark clouds go rolling under, brightly shine
the sun's warm rays;
Low growls the distant thunder, twitt'ring
birds renew their lays.
The drenching showers make trees and flowers
seem fresher than before,
And wand'rers from the sheltering wood may
venture forth once more;
Yet ne'er the forest's loftiest oak again its
boughs shall spread,
And close beside its shattered pride Castile's
best knight lies dead!

V.

Fair dames look forth to welcome him, their fairest champion, home:
Swart Moors grow pale and tremble, lest the conquering knight should come;
Fair dames! ne'er hope to greet him more! swart Moors! what cause for dread?
By lightning's stroke, beneath the oak, Castile's best knight lies dead.

---

37. St. George's Knight.

Legend the First.

Through Gormáz, Saint Stephen's city,
Shrilly rings the trumpet's peal;
There his camp holds brave Fernando,
Gallant Count of fair Castile.

Soon the Moorish king, Almansor,
Leading swarthy hosts untold,
From Cordóva's towers advancing
Hastes to storm the Christian hold.

Now full-armed, for battle mounted,
Shines Castile's array afar;
Slowly rides the brave Fernando,
Searching through the files of war.

"Pascal Vivas! Pascal Vivas!
Pride of Spanish chivalry!
All our knights are armed and mounted,
Still the battle waits for thee.

Thou, once first to mount thy charger,
Once in battle foremost found,
Hear'st thou not to-day my summons,
Nor the trumpet's warlike sound?

Failest thou the Christian army
Needing now thine utmost aid?
Shall thy wreath of glory wither?
Shall thy fame's bright lustre fade?"

Pascal Vivas hears no summons:—
Through a wood his path he wound
Tow'rds a smooth and grassy hillock
By Saint George's chapel crowned.

At the portal stands his charger,
Spear and steel cuirass lie there,
Whilst before the holy altar
Kneels the knight in fervent prayer.

Whilst he kneels in deep devotion,
Vainly warning trumpets blow,
Like the moans of distant tempest
Through the woodlands sounding low.

Loudly neighs his steed unheeded,
  All unheard, his armour rings,
As Saint George, the Christian bulwark,
  Prompt to hear his prayer, upsprings.

He, from clouds of heaven descending,
  Dons the champion's armour bright,
Lightly mounts the champion's charger,
  Flies to join the tide of fight.

None but he can charge so fiercely,
  Heav'n-sprung thunderbolt of war!
See! he grasps Almansor's standard,
  Scattering routed Moors afar.

Pascal Vivas now hath ended
  At the sacred shrine his prayer;
Issues from Saint George's chapel,
  Finds his steed and armour there.

Tow'rds the camp he rideth thoughtful,
  Wond'ring as he nears the throng
Why t e trumpets sound to greet him,
  Mixed with bursts of festal song.

"Pascal Vivas! Pascal Vivas!
  Pride of Spanish chivalry!
Thou hast ta'en Almansor's standard,
  Thine the praise, great victor, be!

See! how stained with blood thy weapons,
Hacked with fiercest thrusts and blows;
Wounded is the steed that bore thee
Bravely through the thickest foes!"

Scarce the knight restrains their triumph,
Checks their praise, too freely given;
And, his head in meekness bending,
Mutely upward points to heaven!

Legend the Second.

In the garden's shade, at even,
Whilst the Countess Julia strayed,
Fatiman, Almansor's nephew,
Seized by stealth the beauteous maid.

With his charming prize he hastens
Through the woods by night and day;
With him ride ten Moorish horsemen,
Knights full-armed in rich array.

When the third chill morn was dawning,
In the woods that space they found
Where the verdant hillock rises
By Saint George's chapel crowned.

E'en from far the Countess fixes
On the sculptured stone her gaze,
Which, above the chapel's portal,
Great Saint George's form displays.

Through the dragon's throat the hero
  Drives the lance with furious shock,
While, fast bound, the king's fair daughter
  Watches from the lonely rock.

Clasping tight her hands, the Countess
  Weeping, shrieks in wild affright:
"Help, Saint George, thou warrior holy,
  Save me from the dragon's might!"

See! who spurs his snow-white charger,
  Leaves the shrine, in haste to save!
In the winds his locks are streaming,
  See his scarlet mantle wave!

Sternly is his spear uplifted,
  Struck to earth the robber lies;
Like the wounded, writhing dragon,
  Pierced he struggles, writhes, and dies!

Whilst the ten false Moorish horsemen
  Raise in fear a piercing wail;
Shield and spear in haste abandoned,
  Fast they flee o'er hill and dale.

On her knees the ransomed Countess
  Sinks, nor dares her eyes to raise;
"Great Saint George, thou warrior holy,
  Thrice renowned — receive my praise."

When her eyes once more she raises,
  There the saint no longer stands;
Hence 'twas said that Pascal Vivas
  Saved her from the robber's hands.*

---

38. The Legend of "Little Thumbling".

(Alluding to the fairy-tale of "Tom Thumb", who is here made to have worn the "Seven-leagued Boots", and is identified with "Jack the Giant-Killer". The poem is in *asonante* verse, the accented diphthong being "*ow*" or "*ou*".)

Little Thumbling! little Thumbling!
  Everywhere thy fame resoundeth;
E'en the infant in the cradle
  Listens to thy feats, astounded.
Whose the eye that tears withholdeth,
  When through hideous woods thou boundest,
Whilst the winds of night are roaring,
  Whilst the hungry wolves are howling?
Whose the heart for thee that fears not
  In the giant's house low-crouching,
When thou hear'st the ogre near thee,
  Sniffing for thy flesh around him?

* In the original, Ballads 35, 36, and 37 are all in Asonante Verse.

For thyself and six young brothers
  Thou from death a refuge foundest,
Changing all the crowns and night-caps,
  Slily thus the foe confounding.
On the rock where slept the giant,
  Snoring till the hills resounded,
Slily from his monstrous feet his
  Seven-leagued boots thou stolest, mouse-like!
Courier to a king in trouble,
  Swiftly on thine errands bounding,
Costly was the fee thou askedst,
  E'en a princess, richly dowered!
Little Thumbling! little Thumbling,
  Everywhere thy fame resoundeth;
With the seven-leagued boots it strideth
  Onward still through years a thousand!

---

39. The Legend of the Critic.

Criticus, the valiant warrior,
  Mounts a-horseback, proud and keen;
'Tis no steed of Andalusia,
  'Tis a wooden stool, I ween!

'Stead of sword, a pen well-sharpened
  Draws he forth, prepared for fight;
Spectacles, in place of visor,
  Serve to guard his book-dimmed sight.

Round that worthy dame — "the Public" —
  Countless perils aye increase;
Now a dragon, sought by Siegfried,*
  Fiercely snorting, threats her peace;

Now some sonneteer besets her,
  Twangs his lute, and sweetly wooes;
Now a monk with mystic preachings
  Doth her every sense confuse.

Criticus, the valiant warrior,
  Dragons slays with cheerful air;
Splits the minstrel's lute in splinters,
  Hurls the monk from pulpit-stair.

Yet, in sooth, his mind's so modest,
  He to none his name betrays;
Scarce a sign — enigma-shrouded —
  On his shield the knight displays.

Criticus! the weak who shieldest,
  Be thou friendly, be benign;
So may heav'n's most bounteous blessing —
  Publisher's hard cash — be thine!

---

* Siegfried, one of the heroes of the Nibelungen Lied, distinguished himself (among other things) by slaying a dragon.

---

40. Paris the Knight.

Paris is of knights the fairest,
  Every heart to him is vowed;
Every dame this truth confesses
  'Mid the court's illustrious crowd.

Lo! what boastful proofs of conquest
  Fortune in his bosom flings,
Letters breathing balmy kisses,
  Curls unnumbered, costly rings.

Tokens of too easy cónquests,
  Happiness unsought by pride,
Bonds and fetters Paris calls you,
  Thrusts such glittering toys aside!

Sheathed in steel, he leaps on horseback,
  Glows with lust of glory's bays,
Turns his back on all the ladies,
  Face and breast to men displays.

Nowhere sign of foe appeareth,
  Spring-tide reigns o'er stream and field;
Breezes with his plume are playing,
  Glancing sunlight gilds his shield.

Far and long he thus hath ridden —
  Where begins yon forest drear,
Lo! a knight who, high on horseback,
  Waits him with uplifted spear!

Paris to the conflict rushes,
  Swift as though to dance he hied;
Levels with the earth his foeman,
  Gazes round with conscious pride.

Down he 'lights to raise the fallen,
  Loosens quick the helmet's lace;
Lo! down waver clustering ringlets
  Round a soft and gentle face!

Greaves and breast-plate quick he loosens,
  Ah! how white that bosom bare!
Stretched before him, all unconscious,
  Lies a damsel passing fair!

Should her pale and deathly features
  Blush with beauty's bloom anew,
Should she now unclose those eye-lids,
  What wouldst thou, young Paris! do?

Yes! a deep-drawn sigh she heaveth,
  Softly opes her tender eyes;
She, who died a savage foeman,
  Friendly, kind, to life doth rise!

There, in pieces, lies the casing
  Which but now a warrior seemed;
Here, in Paris' arms, the kernel
  From the steely shell redeemed!

Paris, comely knight, exclaimeth:
"Here is conquest! here is fame!
Must I ne'er attain a garland,
Never win a hero's name?

Changeth all I fain would grasp at
Into shapes of joy and love?
Fortune kind, my path pursuing,
Shall I thank thee — or reprove?"

---

41. The Robber.

May-day dawns — a houseless robber
Issues from the forest dim;
Lo! along the hollow pathway
Trips a maiden, fair and slim!

"Hadst thou, 'stead of sweet May-lilies",
Spake the forest's lawless son,
"Kingly gems within thy basket,
Scatheless shouldst thou wander on!"

Long the lovely wand'rers figure
Follows he with wistful eyes,
Passing o'er the smiling meadows
On to where the hamlet lies,

Till at length the garden-thicket,
  Rich with bloom, her form conceals;
Then the robber, slow returning,
  Backward to the forest steals.

---

42. The Loves of the Poets.

Introduction.

Since the very God of Numbers
  Pallid grew with love's unrest,
Since the laurel round his temples
  Token gives of love unblest,*

Who can wonder, that but seldom
  Shineth out a star benign
O'er the fate of mortal minstrels
  Circled with the wreath divine?

That their looks are sad and earnest,
  Mournful oft their music's strain;
That of bliss they sing but little,
  Much of grief and longings vain?

Loves of minstrels, deep and mournful,
  Sung in long-forgotten day,
Let me now, in sombre colours,
  Rev'rently your woes pourtray.

---

* Alluding to the fable of Apollo and Daphne.

1. *Rudello.*

'Mid Provence's happy valleys
  First the "Minnesang" appeared,
Child of Spring and sweet Affection,
  (Close companions, long endeared).

Flow'rets' bloom and thrilling voices,
  These its father plainly shew;
Warmth of passion, yearnings restless,
  These its mother taught to glow.

Sweet Provence's happy valleys,
  Aye have ye luxuriant been;
Fairest of thy lovely blossoms
  Glowed the "Love-song's" splendid sheen.

Where have knights so brave and comely
  Dignified the minstrel-race?
Where have dames of rank and beauty
  E'er been praised with happier grace?

Honoured by the race of minstrels,
  Worthiest seemed Rudello's name;
When his harp her praises sounded,
  Blest indeed the honoured dame!

Yet could none that heard discover
  Where the nameless maid was found,
Who with more than mortal sweetness
  Made Rudello's song resound.

Only in night's silent watches
  Drew she near the minstrel's side,
Touching ne'er the ground beneath her,
  Traceless, lithe — as visions glide.

When his arms he stretched to clasp her,
  Fled she to the clouds again;
Then, 'mid tears and soft lamentings,
  Sweetly rose his plaintive strain.

Sailors, pilgrims, bold crusaders,
  All alike the tidings bore,
Saying that the crown of beauty
  Tripoli's fair Countess wore.

When Rudello heard the rumour,
  Swifter grew his pulse's play;
Soon towards the strand he hastened
  Where the ships in order lay.

Sea! uncertain, tost by tempest,
  Fathomless and unexpressed!
O'er thy waste and barren billows
  Well may wander wild unrest!

Far from Tripoli storm-driven,
  Flies the minstrel's vessel fast;
Storm without, and love within him,
  Fails Rudello's strength at last.

Strengthless, spent, he lies unmoving,
  Eastward still he turns his gaze,
Till, upon the shore, a palace
  Rises bright with morning's rays.

Then to the sad minstrel's longings
  Smiling heav'n at length is kind;
Into Tripoli's fair haven
  Flies the ship with favouring wind.

Scarce had heard the lovely Countess
  That a guest so famed had come,
Who, alone, for *her* sake only
  O'er the rolling seas had swum,

Ere, by all her dames attended,
  Came she to the level strand,
As with tott'ring step Rudello
  Stept upon the steadfast land.

She her hand extends to greet him;
  Seems the earth to shake and roll;
Caught by one who stayed his footsteps,
  Breathes he out his wounded soul.

She her minstrel duly honours,
  Buries him with costly state;
Rears a porphyry column o'er him,
  Telling his unhappy fate.

Next she bids his songs be written,
  Every letter wrought in gold;
Costly and embellished covers
  Round the leaves she bids them fold.

Many an hour she reads the poems,
  Reads them oft with grief oppressed,
Till, like his, her soul is smitten
  With that nameless, wild unrest.

Parting from the court's gay splendour,
  Leaving all companions dear,
Seeks she, in the convent-cloister,
  Peace — her wounded soul to cheer.

2. Durand.

Harp in hand, to Balbi's fortress
  Young Durand still upward steers;
Sweetest songs his breast are filling —
  Lo! the happy goal he nears.

There (he knows) a winsome damsel
  Waits, in breathless silence bound;
Waits with downcast eyes, deep blushing,
  Listening for his music's sound.

From the court by lindens shaded
  Upward now the music streams;
Clear and full, his voice outpoureth
  Whatsoe'er he sweetest deems.

From the window high above him,
  Friendly flowers towards him bend;
Nowhere can his eyes discover
  Her whom all his lays commend.

Slowly strides a man to meet him,
  Sad the tones in which he saith —
"Vex not thou the silent sleeper,
  Fair Bianca sleeps in death!"

Young Durand, the peerless minstrel,
  Word of answer never spake!
Lo! his eyes are dimmed already:
  Grief his heart that instant brake.

Yonder, in the fortress-chapel,
  Where unnumbered tapers glare,
Where the lifeless damsel resteth
  Decked with garlands fresh and fair,

Falls on all a joyous trembling,
  Falls a strange and wondrous fear;
Lo! they see the fair Bianca
  Rising from her funeral bier!

Naught she knows what things have happened,
  Dreamy thoughts still round her cling;
Softly, longingly she asketh,
  "Heard I not Durando sing?"

Yes! Durand sang sweetly, clearly,
 Nevermore he now shall sing;
He to life the dead hath raiséd,
 Him to life shall no one bring!

In the realms of bliss awaking,
 Roams he through its regions fair,
Anxiously he seeks the lov'd one
 Whom he deems already there.

Far before his sight extended,
 Views he the celestial halls;
Through the lonely courts of Eden
 Vainly he "Bianca!" calls.

3. *The Castellan of Couci.*

How the Castellan of Couci
 To his side pressed close his hand,
When the beauteous Dame of Fayel
 First his wondering glances scanned!

Ever from that happy instant
 Through his songs there gently thrilled
Something of the blissful rapture
 That his heart had wholly filled.

Ah! his art could little aid him,
 Vain his songs, his music sweet!
Never hoped his wildest dreamings
 That his heart on hers should beat.

Even though at times she listened
  Gladly to a tender song,
Close beside her haughty husband,
  Silent, stern, she moved along.

Then the Castellan, despairing,
  Clad with coat of steel his breast;
O'er his heart the Cross displaying,
  That its beatings soon might rest.

When in Holy Land the warrior
  Oft had borne a gallant part,
Flies a shaft thro' Cross and breast-plate,
  Piercing through his noble heart.

"Hear me now, my trusty servant,
  When this heart no more shall beat,
Bear it to the Dame of Fayel,
  Lay it at the lady's feet."

Buried lay the noble body
  'Neath the chilly, sacred soil;
Still his heart, his heart so weary,
  Finds as yet no rest from toil.

Soon it lies, 'mid fragrant spices,
  Hid within an urn of gold;
Soon the servant climbs on shipboard,
  Clasping it with careful hold.

Tempests bluster, waves encounter,
  Lightnings flash, the masts are cleft;
Anxiously all hearts are beating,
  All — save one of fear bereft.

Brightly shines the sun returning,
  Gleams in sight the Gallic shore;
Joyously all hearts are beating,
  All — save one that beats no more.

See! through Fayel's darksome forest,
  Urn in hand, the servant hies;
Hark! a lusty horn is sounded,
  Loud each huntsman's voice replies.

Darts a stag from out the thicket,
  Through its heart an arrow flies;
Bounding up — it falls before him,
  Stretched before his feet, it dies.

See! the gloomy knight of Fayel,
  (His the hand the bow that drew),
Hastens up, by huntsmen followed;
  Closely all the stranger view.

Coveting the golden vessel,
  Many hands to seize it fly;
But the servant, back recoiling,
  Speaks, with hand upraised on high.

"This a minstrel's heart containeth,
  Famed for many a daring deed;
'Tis the Castellan's of Couci,
  Let this heart in peace proceed;

Dying, this command he gave me,
  When this heart hath ceased to beat,
Bear it to the Dame of Fayel,
  Lay it at the lady's feet."

"Well I know that winsome lady",
  Answer made the huntsman stern,
Quickly from th' astonished servant
  Catching up the golden urn.

Bearing it beneath his mantle,
  Brooding hate, he rides apart;
To his own, with vengeance boiling,
  Clasping close the dead man's heart.

Through the castle-gateway spurring,
  Summons he the cooks in haste,
Saying — "When ye dress the ven'son,
  Be this heart beside it placed."

Soon, with garlands gay surrounded,
  Borne upon a dish of gold,
At the board where sit together
  Knight and Dame, the heart behold!

Gaily to the fair he hands it,
  Saying with a smiling air:
"Whatsoe'er mine arrow slayeth,
  Thou the heart shalt alway share."

Scarce the dame the heart had tasted,
  Ere, beset by sudden fears,
Seemed she as from sight dissolving
  Into founts of streaming tears.

Then the gloomy Knight of Fayel
  Speaks with laughter wild, unholy;
"Tis of pigeons' hearts asserted
  That they make one melancholy!*

How much more, O spouse belovéd,
  This that now to thee belongs!
'Tis the Castellan's of Couci,
  His — that cooed such tender songs!"

When the Knight these words hath spoken,
  These and many jests beside,
Proudly then the Dame, uprising,
  Slowly, solemnly replied:

---

* It may be observed that, in German, *to have a pigeon's heart* means *to be a coward.*

"Gross injustice, Knight, you shew me;
  Thine was I, nor sought to change;
Yet, of such a heart partaking,
  Thoughts o'erwhelm me, new and strange;

Many a thought my soul remembers
  Sung by him in earnest tone;
Living, he was aye a stranger,
  Dead, he claims me for his own.

Yes! to death am I devoted,
  Never meal henceforth I eat;
Since this heart I now have tasted,
  Other food were all unmeet.

May to thee the Judge Eternal
  Pardon at the last impart." —
See! how much of pain and sorrow
  Sprung from out a poet's heart!

4. *Don Massias.*

Don Massias of Gallicia
  Named "the Passionate" in song,
Sat in Arjonilla's fortress,
  Mourning her he loved so long.

To a Count, renowned and wealthy,
  Wedded was the beauteous maid;
Far from her the minstrel languished,
  Banished, and in prison laid.

Sadly at the lattice singing,
  Oft he made the wanderer stay;
Oft from thence fell rustling downward
  Leaves that bore some tender lay.

Whether by some wanderer's message
  Or by winds the tale was borne,
Well the dame he loved so fondly
  Knew he never ceased to mourn.

Jealously her husband watched her,
  Chafing, to himself he said:
"Shall a minstrel prove my terror
  Even when in dungeon laid?"

Hastily he leapt on horseback,
  Armed as if for battle-hour;
Rode to fair Granada's frontier,
  Rode to Arjonilla's tower.

Don Massias, passion-stricken,
  Close behind the lattice stood,
Sweetly sang his fair one's praises,
  Struck the strings in rapt'rous mood.

In the stirrups rose his foeman,
  Hurled his lance with effort strong;
Pierced is Don Massias' bosom,
  Swanlike — he expired in song.

Then the Count, assured of conquest,
  Hastens to Gallicia's shore;
Vain the thought — though dead the minstrel,
  Live his ballads more and more!

Far through every Spanish province
  Fly his tuneful lays of love;
Nightingales they seem to others,
  Harpies dire to *one* they prove.

Often at the festive banquet
  Suddenly they wound his ear;
Often from his midnight slumbers
  Wakes he with a start of fear.

In the street, and in the garden,
  Plaintive tones are heard around;
Yea! like wailing ghostly voices,
  Don Massias' songs resound.

5. *Dante.*

Was it but the gate of Florence,
  Was't the gate of Paradise,
Whence, upon a fair May morning,
  Poured a troop in festal guise?

Children, fair as troops of angels,
  Richly dight with garlands gay,
Hastened tow'rd the vale of roses,
  There to join in dance and play.

Dante, who nine years had numbered,
  Stood beneath a laurel's shade;
Straight his glance discerned an angel
  In the loveliest youthful maid.

Rustled not the laurel's branches
  When the Zephyr caught the grove?
Trembled not young Dante's spirit,
  Breathed on by the breath of love?

Yes! within his heart that instant
  Forth the fount of music brake;
Soon in Canzonets and Sonnets
  Tenderly his love outspake.

When once more she met the poet
  In her prime of maidenhood,
Like a tree that raineth blossoms,
  Firm and fair his glory stood.

See! from out the gates of Florence
  Pours once more a num'rous train;
Slowly, mournfully, it issues
  To a sad and plaintive strain.

'Neath a pall of sable velvet
  Which a silver cross doth wear,
Plucked by Death in bloom of beauty,
  Beatricé forth they bear.

Dante in his chamber rested
  Lonely, still, till sunlight failed,
Heard afar the death-bell booming;
  Silently his face he veiled.

Through the forest's deepest shadow
  Paced the noble bard alone;*
Like the death-bell's distant booming,
  Sounded then his music's tone.

But within that dreary desert
  Full to him of grief and fear,
From the band of souls departed
  Came a God-sent messenger,

Who his steps securely guided
  Far through Hell's remotest gloom;
Where his earthly grief was silenced,
  Seeing souls fulfil their doom.

Soon, his gloomy path pursuing,
  Came he to the blessèd light;
Then, from Heav'n's wide-opened portals
  Came his love, to greet his sight.

---

* In the first Canto of the "Inferno", Dante describes himself as lost in a dreary forest; where, as he wandered about in terror, he was met by Virgil, the "God-sent messenger", who guided him safely through the realms of Hell.

Far through Heav'n's delightful regions
  Soared on high the favoured ones;
She, with eyes intent, unblinded,
  Gazing on the Sun of Suns;

He, with eyes aside directed
  Tow'rds his loved one's countenance,
Which, all-glorious, like a mirror,
  Shewed him the Eternal's glance.*

Shrined in an immortal poem
  Is the splendid vision shewn,
Written with such fiery traces
  As the lightning writes on stone.

Rightly was this poet honoured
  With the title — "the Divine" —
Dante, who could earthly passion
  To celestial love refine.

---

* "Beatrice tutta nell' eterne rote
  Fissa con gli occhi stava; ed io, in lei
 Le luci fisse" —
Paradiso. Canto I. 64.

"Her eyes fast fixed upon th' eternal wheels,
Beatricé stood unmoved; and I with ken
Fixed upon her" —
Cary's Dante.

43. Love-songs.

1. The Student.

As I once in Salamanca,
  (Whilst the nightingales o'erhead
Sweetly in the trees were singing),
  Eagerly in Homer read:

How, arrayed in rich apparel,
  Helen to the rampart went,
Shewing to the Trojan senate
  Grace with bloom so sweetly blent,

That distinctly this and that one
  Muttered in his hoary beard:
"Sooth, she comes of race immortal,
  Ne'er hath form so fair appeared!"

As I thus was pond'ring deeply,
  (How it happened, ne'er I knew),
Through the leaves was borne a rustling,
  Round my searching glance I threw;

Glancing at a neighbouring terrace,
  Lo! what wonder saw I there!
There, arrayed in rich apparel
  Stood a girl, as Helen fair!

Close beside her stood a gray-beard,
  Who her form so fondly scanned
That "I might be sworn, (I muttered),
  Thou art of the Trojan band!"

I myself was an Achæan,
  I, who ever since that day
Troy (my arbour) close besieging,
  Watchfully before it lay.

Or, in tropes to speak no longer,
  Often, all the summer long,
Thither I at eve resorted —
  Haunted it with lute and song,

Sang in various strains and fashions
  All my love's distress and pain,
Till at length from far above me
  Rose a plaintive answering strain.

Thus with answering words and music
  Wore away full half a year;
Even this her spouse had grudged us,
  Had not deafness numbed his ear.

Oft as from his couch he started
  Sleepless, filled with jealous fears;
All unheard remained our voices,
  Like the music of the spheres!

Once, when dark the night and dreary,
Starless, gloomy as the grave,
Answer to my wonted signal
Never voice or music gave.

Only an old toothless maiden
Woke I by my ceaseless cry;
Echo — ancient maiden — only
To my song vouchsafed reply.

Vanished was my love for ever,
Every room seemed empty now;
Empty the well-ordered garden,
Waste the vale and mountain-brow.

What her home, her rank, her station,
I, alas! could ne'er discern;
She by voice and hand protested
These I might not hope to learn.

Then determined I to seek for —
Near and far — the fairy elf;
Homer I no longer needed,
Was not I Ulysses' self?

Making then my lute my comrade,
Wandered I thro' every street;
Underneath each latticed window
Oft would I the strain repeat;

Sang in town and field the ballad
  Which in Salamanca's grove
Every eve, by way of signal,
  Sang I to my vanished love;

But the long-expected answer
  Evermore is hushed and mute;
Echo only — ancient maiden —
  Mocks me with her fond pursuit.

2. *The Huntsman.*

As I once behind an oak-tree
  In a thick and leafy wood,
Listening, often forwards leaning,
  Gun in hand, expectant stood,

Suddenly the branches rustled,
  Warning paw my pointer raised;
Quickly I my rifle pointed,
  Cocked it, and intently gazed;

Lo! 'twas neither hare nor roebuck,
  Game of better kind was there;
Through the bushes tripped a maiden
  Young and lissom, fresh and fair.

Such a strange and wondrous impulse
  Suddenly my fancy swayed
That well nigh, for very fondness,
  Fired I at the beauteous maid!

Evermore this game pursuing,
  All her steps I track with care;
Every eve still finds me standing
  Watchfully before her lair;

Or, in tropes to speak no longer,
  'Neath my loved one's window high
Every eve still finds me standing,
  Gazing up with wistful eye.

Vain is all such mute complaining,
  Sure, she thinks the time too long;
Sounds of flute and lute would please her,
  Plaintive airs and tuneful song;

In the art of girl-decoying
  What can huntsman's craft avail?
Naught can I but mock the cuckoo,
  Or, at best, the chiding quail!

---

44. Bertran de Born.

(This warrior and minstrel was among the foremost of those who instigated the sons of Henry II (of England) to rebel against their father. The remorseful death of the eldest of these, Henry, is beautifully described in the sixth stanza. By way of revenge, King Henry besieged and took the castle of Autafort, Bertran's stronghold. The following ballad describes the interview between Henry and Bertran after the surrender of the castle. Compare the ballad entitled "Bernardine du Born", by Mrs. Sigourney.)

Autafort on yonder summit
  Smokes, a shapeless ruined mound,
Whilst before the King's pavilion
  Stands its lord, with fetters bound;
"Art thou he, whose sword and ballads
  Tumult raised in all the land,
Who the children's minds enkindled
  'Gainst the father's strict command?

Stands before me he who boasted,
  (Yielding to audacious pride),
That by only *half* his spirit
  All his needs were well supplied?
Now the *half* hath failed to help thee,
  Summon up the *whole* again;
Bid it build anew thy castle,
  Bid it break thy bonds in twain!"

"As thou say'st, my lord and master,
  Standeth here Bertràn de Born,
He who with a song enkindled
  Perigord and Ventadorn!
He who to his mighty master
  Ever seemed an irksome thorn;
Loving whom, that master's children
  Bore their father's hate and scorn.

Sat within the hall thy daughter,
  Gaily dight, a prince's bride;*
Sent from me, one sang before her,
  Sang a strain I oft had tried;
Sang her bard's impassioned ballad
  Loved by her in former years,
Till her shining bridal trinkets
  Wholly were bedewed with tears.

Slumbering 'neath the olive's shadow,
  Lightly woke thy fav'rite son,
When with stormy songs of battle,
  Stirring wrath, his ears I won.
Soon his horse was girthed and saddled,
  I his standard bore elate,
Till he met the fatal arrow
  Smiting him by Montfort's gate.

---

* Maud, daughter of Henry II, married Henry, duke of Saxony.

Bleeding in my arms I held him —
  Not the cold and piercing steel,
But to die by thee accursèd
  Caused him deathly pangs to feel.
He his hand stretched out to clasp thee
  Over valley, sea, and hill;
Since thy hand was still so distant,
  Clasped he mine more closely still.

Then — like Autafort up yonder —
  All my strength and pride was o'er;
Not the *whole* nor *half* was left me,
  Song and shaft were mine no more.
Easily mine arms were fettered,
  Since my spirit prisoned lies;
Only for a song of sorrow
  Gloomy power it still supplies."

Then the king bows down his forehead,
  "Thou my son hast wiled away;
Once *my daughter's* heart thou charmedst,
  Mine thy words have moved to-day.
Take my hand, my son's dear comrade,
  Due to *him* in sign of grace!
Loose his bonds — of thy great spirit
  Even I have caught a trace."

---

45. The Pilgrim.

On the highest cliff, a chapel
  Crowns Gallicia's rocky shore;
There the holy Virgin-mother
  Blessings endless keeps in store.
To the wanderer in the desert
  Gleams a golden lode-star there;
To the storm-tost on the ocean
  Opens wide a haven fair.

When the vesper-bell is pealing,
  Far it sounds the country through;
In the towns and in the cloisters
  All the bells are chiming too;
Then the ocean-wave is silenced
  That, but now, was heard to roar;
At the rudder kneels the seaman,
  Humbly says his "Ave" o'er.

On the day, by men kept holy,
  When the Virgin rose on high,
In the Son She bare beholding
  God's all-glorious majesty;
Then within the holy chapel
  Wondrous works are yearly shewn;
Where before She seemed an image,
  Makes She then her presence known.

Coloured flags, the cross displaying,
  Mark the pilgrims' onward way;
Greets the shore with painted streamers
  Every skiff that nears the bay.
Pilgrims, clad in festal garments,
  Move the rocky path along;
Up the steep — a Jacob's ladder —
  Climbs the heav'n-ascending throng.

After those that triumph, others
  Soiled with dust, bare-footed fare;
Shirts of hair are round their bodies,
  Ashes on their heads they bear.
These from Christian men's communion
  For a time are thrust away;*
Unto whom 'tis but permitted
  In the porch to kneel and pray.

Last of all a pilgrim panteth,
  Hopeless seem his wandering eyes;
Long his beard, and foul and tangled,
  Wild his hair that scattered flies.
See! a hoop of rusty iron
  Round his body clasped, he wears;
Round his legs and arms are fetters
  Clanking as he onward fares.

---

* I. e. excommunicated. These stanzas are vividly descriptive of a Romish pilgrimage.

For that he had slain his brother
  In his anger's reckless haste,
From the sword he bade them fashion
  Penance-ring to gird his waist;
Far from home and hearth and household
  Roams he, ne'er to rest again
Till some wonder wrought by heaven
  Break at last his bonds in twain.

Had his feet, now bare and bleeding,
  Been encased in iron shoon,
Long had these been cut to fragments —
  Rest is still a hopeless boon.
Saint benign he findeth never,
  None will grant him sweet release;
Every shrine he suppliant seeketh,
  None vouchsafes him hope of peace.

E'en as he the rock had mounted,
  Whilst before the porch he bowed,
Sweetly pealed the vesper-summons —
  Silent prays the kneeling crowd.
Enters not his foot the chapel
  Where the Virgin's form appears,
Glowing in the sun's bright glory
  As the sea he slowly nears.

O'er the clouds, the sea, the landscape
  Streams a glory richly blent;
Stood the golden gates asunder
  As the Virgin upward went?
Still upon the rosy cloudlets
  Glows her footsteps' radiant trace?
Casts She through the gleaming azure
  Gentle looks of healing grace?

All return consoled, rejoicing —
  One alone forbears to rise;
Still upon the chapel-threshold
  Pallid, motionless, he lies.
Closely round his limbs and body
  Clings unsnapped the fetters' might;
Free from bonds his soul ascendeth,
  Floating in the Sea of Light!

46. The Bridge over the Bidassoa.

"In 1836, on the 24th December, died at Narbonne, aged 55, general *Mina*, a distinguished Spanish constitutional commander, who first commenced his military career in Navarre against the French, in 1810."

Wade's English History, p. 1014.

(The Bidassoa, flowing down from the Pyrenees, divides France from Spain.)

On the bridge of Bidassoa,
Gray with age, an abbot stands;
With his left hand France he blesses,
With his right the Spanish lands.
Great the need that bounteous heaven
Comfort sweet should here outpour,
Where from native soil so many
Issue, to return no more.

On the bridge of Bidassoa
Magic spells delude the sight;
Where, to one, dark shadows lower,
Sees another golden light.
Where to one gay roses waver,
Sees another barren sand;
This beholds a land of exile,
That, his welcome Father-land.

Peaceful flows the Bidassoa
  To the sheep-bell's tinkling song;
Yonder in the mountains thunder
  Cannon-peals the whole day long,*
Till, at evening's fall, descendeth
  Tow'rds the river's bank a band;
Slow their steps, and torn their banner,
  Tracks of blood bedew the sand.

On the bridge of Bidassoa
  Down awhile their guns they lay,
Strive to bind their wounds yet bleeding,
  Count who still survive the day.
Long they 'wait each missing comrade,-
  None to swell the ranks appears;
Once again the drum is beaten,
  Speaks a warrior, gray with years:

"Furl again the tattered banner
  That for Freedom ever flew;
Once again across the frontier
  Moves our band of warriors true.
Once again behold us seeking
  Freedom's glorious rest afar;
Here we meet — not poor in honour,
  Not without some favouring star.

---

* Battle of the Pyrenees, September, 1813.

Thou who dost of former battles
  Honourable scars retain,
Thou, when all to-day are bleeding,
  Mina! dost unscathed remain!
Whole and sound is our preserver,
  Still secure the weal of Spain;
Glad at heart, we cross the river,
  Homeward we return again!"

Mina from the stone arises
  Where he sat so spent and still,
Slowly tow'rds the sun he turns him
  Sinking now behind the hill.
Ah! his hand, his breast compressing,
  Can no more the blood restrain;
On the bridge of Bidassoa
  Olden wounds brake out again!

---

47. Unstern.

(The word "unstern" answers to the English "ill-starred", and means *luckless*. It is here used as a proper name.)

Unstern, bold and luckless youngster,
  Often was by fate undone;
Many a time he *nearly* prospered,
  Many a prize he *nearly* won.

Every star that rules propitious
  Of success a plenteous store
Would have brought him, had his mother
  Borne him but an hour before!

Fame in war, a hero's glory
  Soon had been his own by right;
No one, through the countless army,
  Fought with more courageous might;
Only — as to storm a castle
  He his band impetuous led —
Comes a herald who, exhausted,
  Waves a flag of truce o'erhead!

Fixed was Unstern's day of marriage,
  Fair and lovely glows the bride;
Lo! there comes a wealthier suitor,
  Truckling to her parents' pride.
Later, she who thus was stolen,
  Widowed, would have eased his pain;
Had not he whose death was rumoured
  Suddenly returned again!

Unstern would have rolled in riches
  Gotten in the Newer World,
Lo! a raging storm his vessel
  (Now in port) to ruin hurled!

He himself had 'scaped by swimming,
  Grasping tight a floating plank;
But — as near the beach he drifted —
  Slipped the board, and down he sank!

Soon had he arrived in heaven,
  (Upward to the skies he flew),
But, by chance, a blundering demon
  Crossed him on the way thereto.
"Surely this — so thought the demon —
  Seems the soul I came to seize;"
Unstern by the throat he catches;
  Like a madman, off he flees.

Lo! to save him comes an angel,
  From the clouds he flashes down;
In the deepest pit infernal
  Swiftly hurls the swarthy clown;
Unstern bears he, upward soaring,
  Tow'rds the heights where dwell the blest;
Far o'er good and evil planets
  Finds he now eternal rest.*

---

* Although this poem is written in a strain of banter, it has a significant moral, viz. that what is called "ill-luck" is, after all, under the control of Providence, and that none can reasonably complain of "misfortunes" in this life, if they have a hope of eternal rest hereafter.

---

48. The Ring.

One morn across the meadows
  A Knight full slowly went;
On one most dear, most lovely,
  His anxious thoughts were bent.

"My golden ring so cherished!
  E'en thou perchance canst tell —
Thou pledge which once she gave me —
  If still she loves me well?"

But whilst he closely viewed it,
  Aside it slipped, and see!
How fast, how far 'tis rolling
  Adown the grassy lea!

With hands outstretched to seize it,
  To where it stopped he flew;
But golden flowers confuse him,
  And grasses bright with dew.

Hard by was perched a falcon
  That watched with glistening eyes;
Down swooped he from the tree-top,
  And seized the golden prize.

But whilst on lusty pinions
  Aloft he bore his prey,
Fast came some brother-falcons
  To snatch the prize away.

Of all, not one could gain it,
  For down, fast down it slipped;
The knight beheld a ripple
  As in the lake it dipped.

The nimble fishes darted
  To catch the trinket bright;
But still the ring sank downward,
  Far down, till hid from sight.

"O Ring! that in the meadow
  'Mid flowers I vainly sought;
O Ring! for which the falcons
  Aloft so vainly fought;

O Ring! that 'neath the waters
  The fishes failed to gain;
My Ring! are these the tokens
  I trust her faith in vain?"

---

49. The three Castles.

Three castles in my district rise,
Whereon I gaze with loving eyes;
And I, th' appointed minstrel good,
Who freely range through field and wood,
How may I dare their praise to scorn,
When all so well the land adorn?

The First scarce claims a castle's place,
Small are the ruined heaps you trace;
It lies beneath a wooded steep,
Its very name long buried deep;
For since its towers no longer last,
The wanderer's queries too are past.
Yet onward through the thickets pace,
Tho' supple twigs should lash your face;
There, where the axe's strokes resound,
Strange notes of elfin bugles sound;
There may'st thou wondrous legends hear
From towers that now no more appear.
Yes! if (when shines the moon) alone
Thou sitst upon some fallen stone,
Soon will some wondrous tale, unsought,
Before thy silent soul be brought.

The Second of the Castles Three
Is less than what it seems to be;
Thou see'st it on the mountain-height
Gleam proudly in the sunshine bright,

With towers and battlements bedight,
With fosses deep surrounded quite;
Filled everywhere with statues great;
Two marble lions guard the gate.
But all within is waste and still,
Tall grass the lonely court doth fill;
Ne'er water in the fosses flows;
Within, nor step nor room it shews;
Round it the ivy-branches creep,
Swift swallows through the windows sweep.
There once, gold-crowned, enthroned on high,
Stern rulers sat in days gone by.
Thence heroes rushed to fight and bleed,
Whose names in History's page we read.
The rulers rested in the grave,
In fight had fall'n the heroes brave,
The hum of men had died away,
When flashed from heav'n a fiery ray;
In flames the treasures met their doom,
In ruin fell each stair and room.
Within, the fort is ruined all,
Without, unscathed is every wall.
When passed away the owner's state,
Ere long the house lay desolate;
But — as old story still records
The names of knights and mighty lords —
So still the towers and walls have stood,
And statues huge of heroes good;

And future ages wonderingly
The brave memorials yet shall spy,
And mark that fort on yonder height
Gleam glorious in the sunshine bright.

Halfway between this ruined pair
Is seen the Third, a Castle fair.
Not proudly perched on mountain-height,
But on a rising hillock pight.
Not 'neath a forest's darksome screen,
But girt with trees of vivid green;
With scarlet tiles, walls dazzling white,
And sunlit windows flashing bright.
Too small 'tis found for History's view,
For legend or romance too new.
Yet I, th' appointed minstrel good,
Who range at will through field and wood,
Must strive that now no longer should
This castle still unknown abide.
At morning and at evening-tide
I wander round it, singing clear;
And whensoe'er my Clœlia dear
To greet me at the window hies,
A hope doth in my heart arise
That soon a tale, where history
With minstrel-verse entwined shall be,
That such a tale the bliss shall prove
Of Clœlia's and her minstrel's love!

---

50. Count Eberhard's White-thorn-bush.

"Eberhard V. was created Duke of Würtemburg by the Emperor Maximilian at the diet of Worms. July the 21st, 1494."

English Cyclopædia; Art. Würtemburg.

Count Eberhard-im-Bart
From Würtemburg's fair land
Went on a pious pilgrimage
To Palestina's strand.

As through a leafy wood
He took his lonely way;
He cut from off a hawthorn-bush
A green and healthy spray.

Upon his cap of steel
He placed it carefully;
He wore it in the battle's brunt,
And o'er the flowing sea.

And when he reached his home,
He placed it in the earth;
Where soon to many a swelling shoot
The genial spring gave birth.

The Count, good knight and true,
As year by year went by,
Would mark how strong, how tall it grew
With well-contented eye.

The Count was old and weak,
The sprig was now a tree;
Beneath its shade he oft would sit
And dream deliciously.

The arching boughs o'erhead,
Low-murmuring, softly bore
Sweet memories of the olden time
And that far-distant shore.

---

51. The Elm-tree at Hirsau.

(Near Hirsau are the roofless ruins of a convent, containing a fine elm-tree. In the eighth stanza there is an allusion to Luther, who was for awhile a monk at Wittemburg.)

At Hirsau, 'mid the ruins
An elm-tree may be seen;
High up above the gable
Peers out its summit green.

Girt by a cloister's ruins
It deeply strikes its roots;
A roof high-vaulted forming,
Right up to heaven it shoots.

Because the ruin's closeness
  Denied it air and sun,
It mounted high and higher,
  Till light and air it won.

'Twould seem the cloister-ruins
  Were destined there to rise
To shield the growing elm-tree
  While climbing tow'rd the skies.

When down that verdant valley
  I took my lonely way,
Oft to that lofty elm-tree
  My changeful thoughts would stray.

When 'mid the silent ruins
  I sat in listening mood,
Above, the rustling breezes
  Its towering branches wooed.

Full oft I marked it gleaming
  In morning's earliest ray,
And still beheld it shining,
  When darkness round it lay.

In Wittemburg's old cloisters
  A Tree yet fairer grew,
That with its giant branches
  The cloister-roof brake through!

O ray of light! thou piercest
  To every cave of night;
O soul of man! thou forcest
  Thy way to air and light!

---

52. A Legend of Strasburg Cathedral.

(On one of the stones in the tower of Strasburg Cathedral may be seen, carved by his own hand, the name of *Gœthe.*)

On Strasburg's Minster-turret
  The names of great and small
Are carved; the stone with patience
  Receives and keeps them all.

The windy staircase climbing,
  A poet thither came;
Looked round in every corner,
  Then 'gan to carve his name.

Struck out by those firm touches,
  Bright sparkles crack and fly,
The tower appeared to tremble
  From base to turret high.

Within his grave are stirring
  Erwin's, the Master's, bones;
The tracery seems to rustle,
  The echoing belfry moans.

A movement stirred the building
  As though itself would fain
Produce unhelped the letters
  That yet unhewn remain!

At length the name was written
  That then to few was known;
There stays it, read by many
  With reverential tone.

Who wonders that the turret
  Beneath *his* fingers thrilled,
Whose voice for fifty summers
  The realms of song hath filled?

---

53. The Roe.

A huntsman chased, from break of morn,
  A roe o'er meadows wide,
When lo! behind a garden-thorn
  A blushing maid he spied.

What is it checks the gallant horse?
  Say, can its foot be sore?
What is it stays the huntsman's course,
  That now he shouts no more?

The timid roe, by none pursued,
  O'er hill and dale doth flee;
Stay, foolish roe! the huntsman good
  Hath long forgotten *thee!*

A translation of mine of the same poem, in alliterative verse, may be found in the Gentleman's Magazine for June, 1861. It runs as follows:

A huntsman on horseback
  Full hotly was hasting;
O'er field and thro' forest
  He followed a roebuck.
When lo! his eyes lighted
  On a lovely young lady,
Who gazed from her garden
  With tenderest glances.

What harm can have happened?
  His horse must be ham-strung!
What harm can have happened
  Alas! to the horseman?
Why cease on a sudden
  His shouts of excitement?

Fast raceth the roebuck
  O'er rock and through forest:
Why flee'st thou so frightened,
  Thou foolish young creature?
No longer 'tis likely
  He'll look for thy foot-tracks!

---

54. The White Hart.

Three huntsmen set out with their guns one day,
The milk-white hart they would hunt and slay.

They laid them to rest 'neath a fir-tree tall;
A wonderful vision had each and all.

First Huntsman.

I dreamt, as I beat at the brushwood thick,
Out rushed the white hart in hot haste — quick! quick!

Second Huntsman.

As off, followed close by the hounds, he sprang,
I scorched him well on the hide — bang! bang!

Third Huntsman.

And when he lay on the earth, ha! ha!
I lustily blew on the horn, trara!

While thus they lay and conversed, these
three,
The white hart rustled hard by, scot-free;

For ere the three hunters had seen him aright,
Away was he gone over dale and height!
Quick! quick! bang! bang! trara!

---

55. The Hunt in the New Forest; or, The Death of William Rufus.

King William dreamt a hideous dream;
He left his couch in fear;
His knights he bade to the forest's shade
Ride forth to hunt the deer.

And when they to the forest came,
Awhile the king stood still;
A cloth-yard shaft to each he gave,
The goodly deer to kill.

The king rides past a lofty oak,
  A hart springs full in view;
His trusty bow in haste he draws —
  The string is snapped in two!

Sir Tyrrel* may shoot with better luck:
  Sir Tyrrel his bow soon bends;
The shaft the king so lately gave
  To the giver's heart he sends.

Sir Tyrrel through the forest flees,
  Flees over sea and shore;
Like a startled deer he flees, but finds
  No rest for evermore!

Prince Henry rides thro' the forest shade,
  Both hind and hare he sees;
"The shaft a king hath given should find
  Some nobler game than these!"

Full soon a train of noble knights
  Ride up in eager haste;
Tidings they bring of the murdered king;
  The crown on the prince they placed.

---

* Called by Uhland "Herr Titan".

"In this sad chase 'tis thine to gain,
Great prince! the choicest prey;
The Leopard* proud thou hast chased and ta'en;
Fair England's thine this day!"

---

56. Harold.

(The following translation I have ventured to make in alliterative verse, in imitation of the old Saxon. This kind of verse is suitable for old legends, and is so thoroughly accordant with the genius of our language, that it seems wonderful it is so completely neglected.)

Heading his heroes
Hardy king Harold,
Marching by moonlight
Moved through the forest.
Banners their hands bare
Taken in battle;
Wildly their war-flags
Waved in the wind;
Wildly their war-songs
Rang through the woodland.

---

* The Lion passant, seen in the arms of England, is sometimes called a Leopard.

What bodeth yon bustle
  That's heard in the brushwood?
What swings there, close-swarming,
  And sways in the tree-tops?
What drops from the dark cloud,
  And darts from the fountain?
What flings to them flowers,
  While fluently singing?
What whirls round each warrior,
  And leaps on each war-horse?
What clasps them so closely,
  And clings to their armour?
Draweth their daggers,
  And drags them from horseback,
Conquers their calmness,
  And keeps them unquiet?

'Tis the army of elfins!
  No aid can avail them;
The fairies have found them,
  And force them to Fay-land!

But hardy king Harold,
  Brave hero, was left there;
From steel-cap to stirrup
  In steel was he cased.
Shields sees he and swords,
  Tho' the swordsmen have vanished;
Bereft of their riders,
  Steeds rush thro' the forest.

Heavy at heart
  The hardy king Harold
Mused as he moved
  Through the forest by moonlight.

Down from a dark cleft
  A fountain is dashing;
Lightly down-leaping
  He loosens his helmet;
Lightly down-leaping
  He lappeth the cool wave.
He feels that his forces
  Wax faint, as he drinketh;
He slumbers and sleeps
  As he sinks on the boulders.
He rests on his rock-bed,
  Naught recking, for ages;
His head, with its hoar locks,
  Still heaves with his breathing.

When flameth and flasheth
  The flare of the lightning;
When rustle the rain-drops
  And rolleth the thunder,
Lo! Harold the hero
  Still handles his sword-hilt,
Seeking to seize it
  Tho' sunk in his slumber.

---

57. The Elves.

The First.

Hither come! my sister-fairies!
  Lo! a child of earth is here!
Nimble are such winsome witches —
  Haste! before she disappear.

All.

Maiden, join the elfin-dance
'Neath the stars' and moonlight's glance!

The Second.

'Sooth, thou art a lightsome darling,
  Scarcely fifty pounds dost weigh;
Small thy foot, yet deft and nimble,
  Join us in the dance, we pray!

The Third.

Just while three is being counted,
  Freely in the air thou'lt leap,
Stamping in between a little,
  Just enough the time to keep.

All.

Be not angry, darling wight!
Dance beneath the moonbeams' light.

The Fourth.

Canst thou laugh, belovéd darling?
  Weep'st thou 'neath the moon's soft ray?
Weep yet more — so shalt thou, melting,
  Soon become a lightsome Fay!

The Fifth.

May we, dear, industrious call thee,
  Art thou of thy labours proud?
Are thy bridal coverings woven,
  Spinnest thou as yet thy shroud?

The Sixth.

Know'st thou yet the lore important,
  How with pastry lard to blend?
How much salt — and how much pepper —
  Hast thou at thy fingers' end?

All.

Darling, be our questions heard;
Answer not a single word.

The Seventh.

Hast thou not upon thy conscience —
  Like so many a child beside —
Thoughts of sweet but stolen kisses,
  Trespasses thou fain wouldst hide?

The Eighth.

Is thy faith already plighted?
  Hast thou, dear, a lover true,
One who takes thee out a-walking
  Every day from one till two?

The Ninth.

Lies a ring around thy finger,
  Golden, with a gem bedight?
Truth it means, and deep devotion,
  When it clasps the finger right.

The Tenth.

Art thou, darling, still so angry,
  Is thy spirit always high?
Pray, subdue that hasty temper,
  Ere thou seek the marriage-tie!

All.

Darling, join the elfin-dance
'Neath the stars' and moonlight's glance.

---

58. Merlin the Seer.

(Dedicated to Karl Mayer, born in 1786, the year before Uhland's own birth. He was a political friend of Uhland, and himself the author of some songs, which are alluded to in the first stanza below.)

Sweet songs to me thou sendest
  Of woodland joys that tell,
Within my breast exciting
  Poetic fires as well;
Of shady slopes thou singest
  Beside a reedy pool;
A timid hart thou lurest
  To taste its waters cool.

O'er some old volume poring
  I while away the hours;
Yet fear not, I am seeking
  Therein no withered flowers;
Methinks — along its pages
  A pathway green extends
Towards the fields, and lastly
  In some lone forest ends.

Beside the lake sits Merlin
  Upon a mossy stone,
And gazes at his image
  In dim reflection shewn.

He marks how toil hath blanched him
  Amid the world's fierce strife;
Here, in the lonely forest,
  He gains new strength and life.

The bright and dewy verdure
  Hath made his sight so keen,
His eye can pierce the future,
  And see whate'er hath been;
At dead of night, the branches
  Have rustled round his ear,
Till nature's deepest meanings
  Around him echo clear.

A hart that near him lingered —
  (The sage it did not fear) —
Dashed off in terror, hearing
  A horn ring loud and clear.
Amid the press of huntsmen
  Is Merlin borne away
E'en to the king's far castle,
  Who'd sought him many a day.

"A blessing on the morning
  That Merlin hither brings,
The man who, men forsaking,
  To beasts of wisdom sings.

Full fain are we to challenge
  That wondrous learning's aid,
Which many a year hath taught thee
  In yonder forest's shade.

Not of the planet's courses
  Shall be my first request;
A lesser proof will serve me
  Thy boasted skill to test.
Thou com'st to me thus early
  As though invited here:
My brain is sorely puzzled,
  Thou'lt soon make all things clear.

Beneath yon linden's shadows
  I heard this very night
A murmur and a rustling
  Like lovers' whispers light;
To catch the tones more clearly,
  My head I downward bowed;
But ere I knew the voices,
  A nightingale sang loud.

And now, O sage! I ask thee
  Who stood beneath the tree?
All secret things thy spirits
  Can manifest to thee;

To thee birds' voices sing them,
  Leaves sigh them forth to thee;
Speak fearlessly! conceal not
  The truth, whate'er it be."

Still stood the king, surrounded
  By many a knight and dame;
His rosy-blooming daughter
  To bid good morrow came.
Then Merlin who, undaunted,
  Had viewed the circle there,
A tender leaf of linden
  Took from the maiden's hair.

"This leaflet let me hand thee —
  What saith it, king! to thee?
Who fails to read this token,
  Let him but answer me:
If e'er in kingly palace
  Leaves raining down he spied?
Where linden-leaves are falling,
  The tree not far doth bide!

How great my secret knowledge
  Experience hast thou gained,
And may'st thou deem it worthy
  The praise it hath obtained.

If thus thy riddle's answer
  One leaf can soon evolve,
Think what mysterious secrets
  The thick-leaved wood can solve!"

The king stands awed and silent,
  The princess glows with shame;
The aged seer re-seeketh
  The wood from whence he came.
A hart that well he knoweth
  Awaits him at the bridge,
He mounts, and fast it bears him
  O'er stream and grassy ridge.

On couch of moss sat Merlin;
  His voice's wondrous song
From out the wood's recesses
  Resounded far and long.
There all things now are silent,
  Yet, friend! I make no doubt
That in thy pleasant ballads
  Sage Merlin yet speaks out!

---

59. The Statue of Bacchus.

Callisthenes, a wild Athenian youth,
After a night in revelry misspent,
With faded ivy-garland round his hair,
Drew homewards, stumbling in the twilight dusk,
Himself — as was the twilight — wild and pale.
And as a servant through the gallery
Of statues lighted him towards his chamber,
Behold! before them in the torch-light's glare
The marble form of Bacchus, prince divine,
Framed by the artist's master-hand, stands out.
In bloom of youth the stately statue stands;
And through his full and downward-streaming locks
His rounded shoulders gleam, an ivory pair;
While 'neath the shade of a luxuriant wreath
Of vine-leaves and full purple clusters twined,
Peers out his rounded and full-blooming face.
Callisthenes in terror backward starts,
Seeing the vision's majesty and sheen.
It seemed to him as though the god in wrath
Had struck his temples with his thyrsus-staff —
As though in wrath the living mouth thus spake:

"Why hauntest thou this spot, thou reeling ghost,
Thou shade of Erebus, distraught in mind?
My sacred ivy thou hast dared profane,
And impiously dost call thyself my priest!
Hence from my sight! I know thee not for mine.
I am the Fulness of Creative Nature,
Who specially make known my godlike power
In the luxuriant vine's heart-gladdening juice.
If then thy senseless deeds desire a god,
Dare not to seek him on the vine-crowned slope,
But seek him rather in dark Hades' gloom!"
Here ceased the god — the torch's light expired;
Ashamed the youngster to his chamber slunk,
Snatched from his head the withered ivy-wreath,
And in the secret chambers of his heart
Sware solemnly a wise and sacred vow.

---

60. The Seven Boon-Companions.

Sev'n boon-companions, jovial men,
(The thirstiest in the land are they),
Have sworn an oath, that ne'er again
Their lips a certain word should say —
In no manner — no!
Not in loud tone, nor low.

Sure "*Water*" is a gentle word,
  Small harm or hurt therein can be;
How came it that the topers heard
  This little word so loathingly?
      Now list, while I tell
      How this wonder befell.

Once some drink-loving stranger-wight
  Assured these thirsty souls 'twas true,
That on a neighbouring wooded height
  An inn was opened, large and new,
      Where flowed, pure and fine,
      The most excellent wine.

Now, though to hear a sermon preached
  Not one would from his place have stirred,
Yet, if good liquor might be reached,
  These brethren started at a word.
      "Let's prove it, my brothers",
      Said each to the others.

Away at early dawn they marched,
  The sun arose with angry frown;
Their tongues grew dry, their lips were parched,
  Large heat-drops rolled their faces down.
      How sparkling, how bright
      Leapt the streams from the height!

What copious draughts they swilled in haste!
  Yet ere their thirst was wholly drowned,
Disgust in every look was traced
  That water there — not wine — was found.
    "What tap have we here,
    What detestable cheer!"

As onward up the height they press,
  The wood receives them on their way;
At once they're placed in sad distress,
  Entangled shrubs their steps delay;
    Perplexed more and more,
    They wrangled, they swore.

Meanwhile behind a gloomy cloud
  The sultry sun his face concealed,
Rain through the leaves came pattering loud,
  The lightning flashed, the thunder pealed;
    The torrent, increasing,
    Poured down without ceasing.

The wood a thousand isles was made
  By countless streams that burst to view;
Here groans are vain, or shrieks for aid,
  They cannot choose but flounder through.
    O baptism meet!
    O drenching complete!

Full oft of old in founts and streams
  Were converts made the sons of heaven,
And such a holy ending seems
  To threaten these poor sinners seven;
    All dripping, each seems
    To be several streams!

At last to that long forest's verge,
  More swimming than on foot, they come;
No inn doth anywhere emerge,
  They see a path that leads them home.
    Still sparkling and bright
    Dash the streams from the height!

They seem a mocking voice to hear,
  "You're welcome, brethren undefiled!
Ye stigmatized as evil cheer
  The water that your thirst beguiled;
    Now, soaked in it wholly,
    Remember your folly."

Hence came it that these worthy men
  Feared water from that very day,
And sware an oath that ne'er again
  Their lips that vilest word should say.
    No, never, no, no!
    Not in loud tone or low.

---

61. The Ghost's Wine-press.

At Weinsberg, town well known to fame,
That doth from "Wine" derive its name,
Where songs are heard of joy and youth,
Where stands the fort, hight "Woman's Truth" —
Where Luther e'en, 'mid women, song,
And wine would find the time not long —
And might perchance find room to spare
For Satan and an ink-horn there;
(For there a host of spirits dwell) —
Hear what at Weinsberg once befel.

The watchman, seeing all was right,
Commenced his round upon the night
Wherein one year exhausted dies,
And straight another year doth rise.
The clock proclaimed that moment near,
The watchman 'gan his throat to clear,
When, 'twixt the warning and the stroke,
Just as the day and year awoke,
He hears a crash that makes him start;
The house before him falls apart;
The wall dissolves — within doth seem,
Firm fixed on high, a winepress-beam;
Around it dance with shouts of glee
A mixed and noisy company;

While from the pipes all purple bright
Rich must, out-flowing, seeks the light.
The songs like mill-wheels' hum resound,
Whose paddles streams of wine drive round.
The watchman knows not what to do,
He turns him round the hills to view;
When lo! tho' hid the town in night,
The hill-side gleams with noonday light.
The golden sun of autumn shines
Around the rich luxuriant vines;
Fair troops who cut the vines are seen,
Half-hidden by the foliage green.
Some through the rows ripe clusters bear
In baskets large up-piled in air.
He scarce, for foam that spurts o'erhead,
Can see the boys the grapes that tread.
Blithe songs and jests are echoed back,
The lath-swords clash, the pistols crack;
Soon fades the setting sun's soft light;
Then fiery sheaves burst out to sight,
From whence unnumbered sparkles fly,
Flung upward tow'rd the evening sky.
Just then, within the gray church-tower
The hammer strikes the midnight hour.
The songs are hushed, fades every ray,
Winepress and vines are whisked away,
And from the chamber-window dark
Glimmers a lamp's expiring spark.

As was his wont, in tones full clear,
The watchman straight proclaims the year;
Though, 'midst his cries, his lips at times
Pour forth a store of honeyed rimes,
Wherein aloud he gladly tells
Of all these strange surprising spells;
For when the phantom-winepress hums,
A plenteous vintage always comes.

A hand doth on his shoulders light,
It is no spectre's of the night;
A boon-companion, void of faith,
O'ertakes him, shakes his head, and saith:
"Your winepress yielded must, I fear,
Not of the *new* — but *olden* year!"

---

62. Young Rechberger.

Rechberger was a youngster wild
Who travellers of their cash beguiled.
Within a church, as best he might,
He thought to while away the night.

At last, when midnight came, he rose;
To seize th' expected prize he goes;
He knew that ere the break of day
A merchant-train would pass that way.

Ere far they rode, he stayed his steed:
"My trusty groom, ride back with speed;
My riding-glove I quite forgat,
'Tis on the bier where late I sat."

Returned the groom with pallid cheek;
"The de'il may go your glove to seek!
A ghost sits on the bier upright,
My hair is bristling yet with fright.

The glove was on his withered hand,
With fiery eyes its shape he scanned;
He stroked it o'er with rapturous leer,
My limbs are quaking yet for fear."

In haste Rechberger wheeled about,
He fought the ghost with courage stout;
The ghost perforce he backwards bore,
The glove is on his hand once more.

Then spake the ghost in eager tone:
"Tho' naught you grant to be mine own,
Yet for a twelvemonth let me wear
This nice, this soft, this pliant pair?"

"I'll lend them for a year to thee,
To prove how true the de'il can be;
They will not burst, I dare opine,
Upon such withered paws as thine."

Thence rode Rechberger, fearing naught;
His man and he the forest sought.
Far off, the cock is crowing clear;
When hark! the tramp of horse they hear.

The youngster's heart beat fast and strong:
Along the road a sable throng
Of horsemen masked all slowly ride;
Awhile the youngster draws aside.

The last of all the train doth lead,
All riderless, a coal-black steed;
Bridle and saddle both he wears,
A sable saddle-cloth he bears.

Then up Rechberger rode, and said:
"Say, who commands this cavalcade?
Pray tell me, lad, for whom you lead,
All riderless, this noble steed?"

"For one whom men Rechberger call,
Who serves my master best of all;
If he within the year be slain,
This steed shall then his weight sustain."

The cavalcade had passed away —
Rechberger to his groom 'gan say:
"Now let me from my horse descend,
I fear my life draws near its end.

If, then, my horse will own thy hand,
If thou canst use my shield and brand,
Receive them as thy share of gain,
Serve God, and quit thy follies vain."

Rechberger to a convent went:
"Abbot, though for a monk ne'er meant,
Yet let me as a layman here
Serve thee in penitence sincere."

"To judge thee by thy spurs, I ween,
Thou hast a fearless horseman been;
Then be it thine the steeds to mind
That rest within our stables find."

But when a year had run its course,
The abbot bought a wild black horse;
'Twas given to Rechberger's care,
It madly reared, and pawed the air.

It struck him near the heart amain
That down he sank in mortal pain;
Then in the forest-depths it ran,
And ne'er again was found by man.

At midnight, by Rechberger's tomb,
Clothed all in black, appeared a groom;
A mettled steed he held, a pair
Of gloves the saddle-bow doth bear.

Rechberger from his coffin breaks,
The gauntlets from the saddle takes,
And straight into the saddle flies;
The grave-stone serves to help him rise.

This lay should make young men beware
That of their gloves they take good care;
And that they ne'er should deem it right
To prowl about about the roads by night.

---

63. The Count of Greiers.

The youthful Count of Greiers before his house doth stand:
He views, in morning's glimmer, the distant mountain-land.
He sees the rocky summits i' the sunlight's golden glow,
And, dimly stretched between them, the Alpine vale below.

"O Alps, O Alpine valley — ye lure me like a spell;
How blest the maids, the herdsmen that 'mid your pastures dwell!
I oft have gazed upon you, and felt nor joy nor smart,
But now a quenchless yearning constrains my inmost heart."

A sound of pipes falls clearer, and clearer on the ear,
The shepherd-lads and maidens the lonely castle near;
Now, on the turf before it, begins the circling dance,
The white sleeves wave and shimmer, the wreaths and ribands glance.

The youngest of the maidens, lithe as a branch in May,
The County's hand she seizes — he too must join their play;
Ere long the dance enfolds him in wild and whirling glee,
And "Ho! young Count of Greiers! our prisoner must thou be!"

Far, far from thence they lead him with dance and roundelay,
They dance thro' many a village that swells the glad array.
They dance across the meadows, beyond the forest's bounds,
Till far up on the mountains the merry shout resounds.

Soon came the second morning, the third is
rising bright;
Where stays the Count of Greiers — say,
hath he vanished quite?
Again at eve descending, the sultry sun hath
gone —
There's thunder on the mountains, a mighty
storm comes on.

The cloud hath burst, the streamlet a roaring
torrent flows,
A sudden glare of lightning the darkened
landscape shews;
Lo! struggling in the torrent, a man floats
swiftly past,
Till, grasping at a sapling, he wins the bank
at last.

"Lo! here am I, abruptly from your mountain-
hollow torn,
A storm that burst above us, me hitherward
hath borne.
Ye all in huts and caverns escaped its rushing
sway,
Me only hath the tempest swept forcefully
away.

Farewell, ye Alpine pastures, ye herdsmen blithe and true,
Farewell, three days of rapture, when shepherd-life I knew;
For such a blissful Eden I ne'er, alas! was born,
Whence heav'n, with sword bright-flaming, hath thrust me forth forlorn.

O Alpine rose so blooming, press never-more my hand!
Tho' e'en the chilly torrent hath quenched not passion's brand;
And ye, enchanting dances, ne'er tempt me hence again!
Receive me home, my castle, where solitude doth reign."

---

64. Count Eberstein.

In Spires' wide hall is a tumult gay,
'Mid torches and tapers they dance and play:
Count Eberstein
Is first in the line
With the Emperor's daughter so comely and fine.

As round in the dance together they spin,
She whispers a warning she cannot keep in:
"Count Eberstein!
Some heed should be thine!
This night is imperilled thy fortress fine."

"Many thanks for the Kaiser's care" — thinks he —
"For *this* I was asked at the dance to be!"
For his charger he hied;
For no one would bide,
But fast to his jeopardized fort did ride.

To Eberstein's fort the warriors sweep,
With ladders and hooks thro' the mist they creep.
Count Eberstein
Gives them greeting fine,
And tumbles them down in the moat to pine.

And when on the morrow the Kaiser came,
He fully expected the fort to claim;
But lo! on the wall
With noise not small
Are dancing the Count and his merry men all.

"Ha! Sire! when you creep into castles again,
Take heed lest you happen to dance in vain!
That daughter of thine
Dances so fine,
To *her* shall be opened this fort of mine!"

I' the Count's castle-hall is a tumult gay;
'Mid torches and tapers they dance and play,
And Count Eberstein
Is first in the line
With the Emperor's daughter so comely and fine!

---

65. Suabian Intelligence.

As, to redeem the Holy Land,
King Barbarossa led his band,*
He needs must, with his pious crew,
A barren mountain-tract pass through.
Among them soon a scarceness spread,
There's many a stone, but little bread;
And many a cavalier is forced
Awhile to be from drink divorced.

---

* Frederick I. of Germany (1152—1190) was surnamed Barbarossa or *Red-beard,* in German *Rothbart.* He undertook a Crusade in 1188, to which this ballad refers.

Each famished steed so droops and flags,
'Twere best the riders bore the nags!
A knight was there from Suabia's land,
Of giant frame and stalwart hand,
Whose horse so lean and weak had grown,
He by the bridle dragged him on.
He never would have left its side,
E'en though to save its life he died.
Soon had he dropped some little way
Behind the host's compact array,
When suddenly appeared in sight
Full fifty Turkish horsemen light.
At first from far their shafts they sent,
And hurled their darts with fell intent.
The gallant Suabian would not budge,
But onward marched with steady trudge,
Caught on his shield the arrowy shower,
And scanned them with disdainful lower;
Till one, who scorned to fight afar,
'Gan raise his crooked scimitar.
Then too the Suabian's blood waxed hot,
The Pagan's horse he fiercely smote;
The swaying sword so fiercely dropped,
The two fore-legs in twain were lopped;
And as the creature forward fell,
Again his sword he swung right well;
Full on the head it smote the foe,
Cleft downward to the saddle-bow,

The saddle next in twain did hack,
And wounded deep the horse's back.
His brother Turks saw earthward glide
Just half a Turk on either side.
Chill terrór seized on all the rest,
Each fled where'er he deemed it best;
Each felt that sword, in shuddering fear,
Through head and trunk descending sheer.
A Christian troop came next in view,
Who by the way had lingered too;
They marked the cloven horse and Turk,
And marvelled at our hero's work.
The news reached Barbarossa's tent,
Who for the gallant Suabian sent,
And said — "Declare, my trusty knight,
Who taught thee such a stroke of might?"
At once the hero answered thus:
"Such strokes are common, Sire, with us;
Where'er the simple Suabian's found,
The "Suabian trick" is far renowned."

---

66. Retribution.

The squire his master hath foully slain;
The rank of a knight the squire would gain.

His lord he hath stabbed in the dusky wood;
The body he sank in the Rhine's deep flood.

The armour he donned, so heavy and bright,
His master's charger he mounted light.

As over the bridge he would briskly ride,
The charger stopped short, and started aside.

With the golden spurs its sides he stung;
In the stream its rider it madly flung.

With arm and with foot he struggles amain;
The *heavy chain-armour* makes all in vain!

---

67. The Sword.

To a smithy there came a youthful knight,
For there had he ordered a broadsword bright;
But when in his hand the sword he weighed,
Too heavy he deemed the sturdy blade.

Then, stroking his beard, quoth the aged wight:
"The sword is neither too heavy nor light;
Too weak, methinks, is your arm, my son!
To-morrow shall all that you wish be done."

"Not so, but *now*, by my word as a knight,
By mine own strength, not the flame's fierce
might;"
So spake the stripling — his nerves he strings,
And high in the air the sword he flings.

---

68. Siegfried's Sword.

The youthful Siegfried was brave and bold;
He hastened away from his father's hold.

In his father's castle he would not bide,
But longed thro' the world to wander wide.

Often he met with a worthy knight
With glittering shield and broadsword bright.

Siegfried only a cudgel bore;
I trow, as he gazed, his heart grew sore.

And as through a darksome wood he passed,
To a glowing smithy he came at last.

There saw he of iron and steel good store,
And heard the flames of the furnace roar.

"O master smith! O master dear!
Let me awhile be thy comrade here!

And teach me, I pray thee, with patient care,
How I may make me a broadsword fair."

Siegfried the hammer swung deftly round;
He hammered the anvil hard into the ground!

He hammered till loudly the forest rang,
And all the iron in pieces sprang.

And then from the last bar, sound and strong,
Made he a broadsword, wide and long.

"Now have I made me a broadsword bright,
Now may I cope with the boldest knight;

Now may I slay, like a hero brave,
Giants and dragons in field and cave!"

---

69. Little Roland.

(Roland, the hero of so many romances, and immortalized by Ariosto by the name of Orlando, was the son of Milo of Anglant and Bertha, the sister of Charlemagne. In this ballad Milo is supposed by Bertha to have been drowned in crossing a torrent, but it is subsequently discovered that he had escaped death. which accounts for his re-appearance in Ballad 70.)

Dame Bertha sat in a rock-hewn cave,
  And mourned her hapless fate.
Young Roland played in the open air,
  His sorrow was nowise great.

"Alas! king Charles, my brother dear!
  That ever I fled from thee!
For love both honour and state I left,
  Now fierce is thy wrath with me!

O Milo, husband so dearly loved,
  The torrent hath strangled thee!
Thy love, for which I forsook my all,
  Hath now forsaken me!

O Roland, young and darling child,
  Be thou my honour and love!
My Roland, hitherward haste to me,
  For thou must my comfort prove.

My Roland, hie thee away to the town,
  Ask alms of drink and meat,
And whoever shall give thee the smallest gift,
  With blessings and thanks him greet."

King Charles at his banquet-table sat
  In his golden banquet-hall;
With platters and goblets the servants haste
  To deck the festival.

The music of harp and flute and song
  Each hearer's ear doth bless;
But the sound so clear came yet not near
  Dame Bertha's loneliness.

And round about in the court without
  Had many a beggar his seat,
Who was more refreshed by the meat and drink
  Than e'er by the music sweet.

The king looks through the open door,
  Beholding the beggar-throng;
When lo! thro' the press a beauteous child
  All fearlessly hastes along.

The child's patched garb is a wondrous sight,
  Four colours together blent;
But not with the beggars he deigns to stay,
  To the hall his looks are bent.

And into the hall young Roland came,
  As though 'twere his home for aye;
A platter he takes from the midst of all,
  Which in silence he bears away.

"What's this I behold?" the monarch thinks,
  "'Tis a custom strange and new!"
But since in silence he lets him pass,
  The others must do so too.

They had but waited a little while,
  When Roland returns more bold;
With hasty step to the king he comes,
  And seizes his cup of gold.

"What ho! there, stop! you saucy imp" —
  Are the words that loudly ring.
But Roland clutches the beaker still,
  With eyes fast fixed on the king.

The king at the first looked fierce and dark,
  But soon perforce he smiled —
"Thou comest", he said, "into golden halls
  As though they were woodlands wild.

A dish thou tak'st from the table royal,
  Like an apple from off a tree!
A cup thou tak'st full of good red wine
  As though from a fountain free!" —

"A peasant girl from a fountain draws,
  Breaks apples from off the trees;
But game and fish and the bright red wine —
  My mother is fed with these!" —

"If then thy mother's so grand a dame
  As thou, fair child, wouldst boast;
She surely must own a castle strong,
  And of vassals a seemly host?

Say! who is her steward, her butler sage,
  And what are their honoured names?"
"My right hand, sir, is her steward true,
  My left to be butler claims." —

"But tell me, who are her watchmen true?" —
  "My two blue eyes are those." —
"And tell me, who is her minstrel blithe?" —
  "My mouth, that's red as the rose." —

"Thy mother hath vassals stout, I ween;
  But yet is her livery strange;
The rainbow's hues methinks it shews,
  Its colours so often change." —

"Eight boys in each fourth part of the town
  Have I brought beneath my sway,
Who have brought for my use four kinds of cloth,
  To make me a garment gay." —

"Thy mother is served by one, methinks,
In all the world most able;
She reigns, I should ween, like a beggar-queen,
And keeps an open table.

A dame so great from my court and state
So far should never be;
What ho! three dames! what ho! three knights!
Go, fetch her in here to me!"

Young Roland, still with the cup in hand,
From the hall doth now retreat;
Three dames and knights, at the king's command,
Close follow his hasty feet.

The king looked out with an anxious glance
When a little while had passed;
And soon the dames and the knights he sees
Towards him hurrying fast.

At once he spake with a startled cry:
"May Heav'n forgive my sin!
In the open hall I have passed my jests
On one who is near of kin!

Dost thou, O Bertha my sister, here
In a pilgrim's garment stand?
So pale and wan, in my hall so rich,
With beggar's staff in hand?"

Dame Bertha fell at the monarch's feet,
  Her frame with terror shook;
Above her erect stood the stern old king,
  And grim was his piercing look.

Dame Bertha fearfully droops her gaze,
  To utter no word she tries,
But loudly Roland his uncle greets
  As he raises his clear blue eyes.

Then spake the monarch with soothing tone:
  "Arise! dear sister mine;
My pardon to thee I freely grant
  For the sake of this son of thine!"

Dame Bertha rises with joyous heart:
  "My brother, my thanks to thee;
My child one day shall well repay
  The good thou hast done to me!

In warfare he, like his king, shall be
  A hero of lofty fame;
The colours of many a conquered land
  On his banner and shield shall flame.

He'll snatch from the board of many a king
  Rich trophies with daring hand,
And honour and weal shall his boldness bring
  To his mourning maternal-land."

---

70. Roland the Shield-bearer.

(Compare preface to Ballad 69.)

King Charles sat at the festive board
Amongst his peers at Aix;
With fish and flesh 'twas royally stored,
Sore thirst on no man lay.
Large golden cups of brightest sheen,
Enriched with jewels red and green,
Were gleaming down the hall.

Then spake king Charles, that hero bold:
"What means this idle show?
The brightest jewel earth doth hold
Is wanting still, I trow!
This jewel, bright as noontide's blaze,
A giant on his shield displays
In dark Ardennes' deep wood.

Archbishop Turpin, Richard keen,
Sir Naims, Bavaria's knight,
Sir Milo, Aymon, Count Guarine,
Sprang up to claim the fight.
In haste they donned their panoply,
And bade their chargers saddled be,
To seek the giant fell.

Young Roland, Milo's son, 'gan speak:
"Dear father, hear my suit;
Tho' deeming me too young and weak
With giants to dispute,
Yet grant me forth with thee to fare,
For thee thy trusty lance to bear,
And eke thy glittering shield."

In haste these six companions good
'Gan all together start,
But when they reached the darksome wood,
They deemed 'twere best to part.
Behind his father Roland rode,
Rejoicing in his glittering load,
The hero's lance and shield.

By sunlight and by moonlight pale
Far rode the warriors keen;
Yet ne'er by rock or wooded dale
The giant's form was seen.
At noon, upon the fourth long day,
The good Sir Milo sleeping lay
Beneath an oak's vast shade.

Young Roland in the distance viewed
A flashing swift and bright,
Whose radiance, piercing through the wood,
Put hart and hind to flight.

He marked it gleaming from a shield,
The which a giant huge did wield
 Descending from the hill.

Young Roland thus 'gan counsel take:
 "What cause have I for fear?
What need with startling cry to wake
 From sleep my father dear?
Awake, his charger crops the field,
Awake are sword and spear and shield,
 Awake young Roland too."

Sir Milo's keen and trusty brand
 Beside him Roland bound:
The lengthy lance he took in hand,
 And seized the target round.
Sir Milo's horse he next bestrode,
And softly through the wood he rode
 His father not to wake.

And when he reached the rocky wall,
 The giant laughing spake:
"What doth this dwarf, this infant small
 On such a charger make?
His sword's far longer than himself,
His spear to earth nigh drags the elf,
 His shield will crush him soon!"

"Come on, come on!" young Roland cried,
  "Thy jests shall cost thee sore;
For if my shield be long and wide,
  'Twill shelter me the more.
A horse that's big, a man that's small,
An arm that's short, a sword that's tall
  Must help each other out."

His staff the giant downward brought,
  Its sweep was swift and wide;
Young Roland swung, as quick as thought,
  His charger far aside.
Against his foe his lance he flung,
But from the wondrous shield it sprung
  Again to whence it came!

In both his hands young Roland grasped
  His sword right speedily;
The giant too his sword-hilt clasped,
  But clumsier far was he.
Young Roland with a flourish deft
His left hand 'neath the target cleft —
  Down tumbled hand and shield.

Then quailed the giant's heart at length,
  When thus the shield was gone;
The jewel, that had lent him strength,
  He mourned with bitter moan.

To seize the target hastened he,
Young Roland smote him near the knee,
  To earth the giant fell.

Young Roland caught him by the crown,
  And hewed his neck in twain;
A gushing stream of blood ran down
  Towards the grassy plain.
Then from the dead man's shield in haste
The jewel bright he soon displaced,
  Rejoicing in its gleam.

Then 'neath his cloak the gem he thrust,
  Next to a spring he goes;
There washed from stains of blood and dust
  The weapons and his clothes.
Then back young Roland rode amain,
His father soon he found again
  Still sleeping 'neath the shade.

He laid him at his father's side,
  And slept beneath the oak,
Till in the chilly eventide
  At last Sir Milo woke.
"Come, Roland, wake! come wake, my son,
Take shield and spear and let's begone
  To seek the giant fell."

Then up they rose in eager haste,
  And wandered far a-field;
Behind his father Roland paced,
  Still bearing lance and shield.
At last they reached the very spot
Where lately raged the contest hot,
  Where slain the giant lay.

The scene with wonder Roland scanned,
  For nowhere could be seen
The giant's head, nor yet the hand
  That late had severed been!
Nor sword, nor cudgel met their view,
Gone was his shield and harness too,
  They found but trunk and limbs!

The giant's trunk Sir Milo scanned;
  "How huge a corse we see!
This stump may make us understand
  How mighty was the tree!
'Tis he we sought — what more's to say?
Success and fame I've slept away,
  For which I aye must mourn." —

At Aix king Charles stood gazing round,
  Before his castle-gate;
"Are all my heroes safe and sound?
  They linger all too late.

Lo! yonder doth at last appear
Sir Aymon, bearing on his spear
  The giant's gory head!"

Sir Aymon rode with downcast gaze;
  His lance he downward bent,
Before his master's feet he lays
  The head with blood besprent:
"This head within the wood I found,
The giant's trunk lay on the ground
  Some fifty paces off."

Archbishop Turpin next displayed
  The giant's glove to view;
The clumsy hand therein was laid,
  Which — laughing — forth he drew:
"A pretty relic this, I ween!
I found it in the forest green
  Already hewn away!"

Sir Naimé of Bavaria then
  Dragged in the giant's stick:
"See what I found in yonder glen —
  A weapon tall and thick.
Its weight doth make me thirst amain,
Right well could I a goblet drain
  Of good Bavarian beer!"

On foot Count Richard came in sight,
  And led his charger on;
It bore the giant's armour bright,
  Both sword and habergeon.
"Who cares to search yon lonely wood,
More bits may find of armour good;
  I could not bring them all."

Next in the distance Count Guarine
  The shield held up to view.
"Who brings the shield is he, I ween,
  Who brings the jewel too."—
"The shield, my worthy sirs, have I;
And would the gem therein did lie!
  But, ah! 'tis broken out."

The brave Sir Milo last of all
  Towards the castle came;
His charger's steps but slowly fall,
  He hangs his head for shame.
Behind his father Roland rode,
Rejoicing in his glistening load,
  The hero's lance and shield.

As nearer to the gate they paced,
  And tow'rds the heroes went,
He from his father's shield displaced
  The central ornament;

Then set the giant's gem thereon;
With wondrous light it flashed and shone
  As brightly as the sun.

And as this flashing lustre flamed
  From Milo's shield afar,
With joyous shout the king exclaimed:
  "Hail, Milo! famed in war!
By thee the dreadful giant bled,
'Tis thou hast severed hand and head,
  And rent from him the gem!"

Amazed, Sir Milo turned to see
  The wondrous gleam intense —
"What, Roland! say, thou stripling wee!
  How hast thou that, and whence?" —
"Dear father, be not wroth, I pray,
That I the monster dared to slay
  While thou wast sound asleep!"

---

71. King Charles's Sea-voyage.

(This poem relates to Charlemagne and the twelve peers of France, who are all mentioned by name in order.)

King Charles with all his doucëperes*
  Across the ocean sailed;
Towards the Holy Land he steers —
  A dreadful storm prevailed.

Out spake Sir Roland, hero brave:
  "I well can fence and fight;
Yet little may such arts avail
  Against the tempest's might."

Next spake Sir Holgar, Denmark's pride:
  "I've skill with harp and song;
What 'vails me this, when thus contends
  The blast with billows strong?"

Sir Oliver felt little cheer;
  He viewed his weapons keen:
"It is not for my life I fear,
  But Alta Clara's sheen!"†

---

* The twelve peers of France were called sometimes "doucëperes", from the French *les douze paires.* Thus Spencer: —

"Big-looking like a doughty doucëpere."
Faerie Queene. III. 10. 31.

† *Alta Clara*, i. e. "tall and bright", was the name of Oliver's battle-sword. Roland's sword was named *Durindana*, and King Charles's *Joyeuse*.

Next spake the treach'rous Ganelon —
  In undertone he spake: —
"Were I but far from hence on land,
  The rest the fiend might take!"

Archbishop Turpin sighed aloud:
  "God's champions stout are we;
Come, Saviour dear, from Holy Land,
  And guide us o'er the sea."

Next Richard — Dauntless named — 'gan say:
  "Ye powers and imps of hell;
Now help me in my need, I pray,
  I oft have served you well."

Sir Naimé next his rede began: —
  "I've counselled much this year;
But water sweet and counsel good
  On shipboard oft are dear."

Then spake Rioul, a veteran brave: —
  "A warrior old am I,
And fain would hope my corse at last
  In good dry ground may lie."

Sir Guy, a young and gallant knight,
  Right gaily 'gan to sing:
"I would I were a lightsome bird,
  I'd to my love take wing!"

Then spake Guarine, that noble knight:
"May God our succour be!
I'd rather drink the good red wine
Than water from the sea."

Sir Lambert next, brave youngster, cried:
"God our protection be!
I'd rather eat the dainty fish
Than that the fish ate me!"

Last spake Sir Godfrey, far renowned:
"What matters what befal?
Whatever fate myself o'ertakes
Shall whelm my brethren all."

King Charles beside the rudder sat,
No word his lips would vent;
With sure control the ship he steered
Until the storm was spent.

---

72. Taillefer.

"Immediately before the Duke rode Taillefer the minstrel, singing with a loud and clear voice the lay of Charlemagne and Roland, and the emprises of the paladins who had fallen in the dolorous pass of Roncevaux. Taillefer, as his guerdon, had craved permission to strike the first blow, for he was a valiant warrior, emulating the deeds which he sung: his appellation, *Taille-fer*, is probably to be considered not as his real name, but as an epithet derived from his strength and prowess: and he fully justified his demand, by transfixing the first Englishman whom he attacked, and by felling the second to the ground." — Quoted from a description of the battle of Hastings, by Sir F. Palgrave.

In German Taillefer is a trisyllable, as it it also in old French, and as it would be even in modern French *poetry*. I have, however, made it a dissyllable, as it is thus that most Englishmen, acquainted with French, would probably pronounce it. It means, "having an iron frame". Compare the surname "Ironside", given to Edmund II.

Duke William the Norman spake out one day:
"Who sings in my court and my room alway?
Who sings from the morning till late at night
So sweetly, my heart seems to laugh outright?"

"'Tis Taillefer, my liege, that so sweetly sings,
In the court, as the windlass around he swings,
In the room, as the fire he fans and rakes,
When at eve he lies down, and at morn awakes."

"'Tis well", quoth the duke, "I've a servant rare
In Taillefer, who serves me with faith and care.
The wheel he turns and the fire makes bright,
And so clearly he sings that my heart grows light."

Then Taillefer answered — "were I but *free*,
Far better I'd labour and sing for thee!
How well on horseback I'd serve my lord,
And sing, as I clashed my shield and sword!"

Soon Taillefer rode to the battle-field
On a war-horse stout, with sword and shield;
Duke William's sister, as down she gazed
From a turret, the knight's bold bearing praised.

And when 'neath her turret he rode, he sang;
Like a breeze, and next like a storm it rang;
She cried — "When he singeth, what joys awake!
The tower is shaken, my heart doth quake!"

Duke William sailed with a mighty host
O'er the rolling billows to England's coast.
He sprang from the ship — on his hands he fell:
"Ha! England!" he shouted — "I grasp thee well!"

As the Norman host to the battle strode,
For a boon, to the duke brave Taillefer rode.
"Many years have I sung, while thy fire I made,
Many years, while the sword and the lance I've swayed.

If I've served thee and sung to thy heart's delight,
At first as a servant, and last as a knight,
Then grant me this boon — when the morn shall shine,
Let the first blow struck at the foe be mine!"

With sword and spear he his horse bestrode,
Before the whole army brave Taillefer rode;
Over Hastings' field his song rang out,
Of Roland he sang, and of heroes stout.

When the "Roland-song" rose loud as a blast,
Many standards waved, many hearts beat fast;
Its notes with courage the knights inspire;
For well, as he sang, could he *fan their fire!* *

Then charging, his first quick thrust he gave,
An English knight to the ground he drave;
His sword he swung for the first swift blow,
An English knight on the ground lay low.

* Alluding to his former menial occupations.

The Normans beheld it, and stayed not long;
With yells and smiting of shields they throng;
Hark! arrows are whirring, swords clash in the fray,
Till Harold is slain and his host gives way.

The Duke on the field his standard spread,
His tent he pitched i' the midst o' the dead;
A golden beaker his table graced,
And the English crown on his head was placed.

"Come, pledge me, my Taillefer brave, this day!
In love and in grief thou hast tuned thy lay,
But on Hastings' field thou hast sung me a song
Shall ring in my ears for my whole life long."

---

73. The Tunic of Proof.

"I must to the field, my daughter dear!
An evil fate from the stars I fear;
Then make me, girl! with thy tender hand,
A tunic that may all blows withstand."

"How shall a maid's weak hand avail
To make thee, my father, a shirt of mail?
O'er the stubborn steel have I no power,
I spin and weave in the maiden's bower."

"Yes! daughter — spin in the silent night
With threads that are steeled by hell's dread
might,
And weave me a tunic, wide and long,
To guard me from harm in the battle's throng."

I' the sacred night, as the full moon shines,
Alone, the maiden the threads entwines;
"In the name of hell" — she mutters low,
Swift doth the whirling spindle go.

From thence to the loom in haste she goes,
With trembling hand the shuttle throws;
As quickly the rustling work she plied
As if spirit-fingers wove beside.

When the host rode out to the battle-press,
The Duke had donned an unwonted dress;
A waving tunic, wide and white,
With awful figures and emblems dight.

All shun his arm as they'd shun a sprite;
For who so bold as to brave his might,
'Gainst whom is shivered the staunchest brand,
And the arrow rebounds to the archer's hand?

Before him standeth a youngster bold:
"Thou frayest me not! hold, murderer, hold!
Not thee shall the arts of hell bestead,
Thy charms are as mist, thy labour dead!"

Stern are the strokes on either side;
The tunic of proof with gore is dyed;
They fight till they fall on the crimsoned sand,
And either curseth the other's hand.

The daughter seeketh the field of blood:
"Where lieth the duke, that hero good?"
She finds the wounded and dying twain,
Shrilly she raises a shriek of pain.

"Is't thou, my daughter, O child unblest?
How didst thou spin the faithless vest?
Didst thou not seek hell's mighty aid?
Is not thine hand the hand of a maid?" —

"I sought, as thou saidst, hell's mighty aid,
But my hand is not the hand of a maid;
Thy slayer is not unknown to me,
So wove I — alas! — but a shroud for thee!"

74. The luck of Edenhall.

(The "Luck of Edenhall" is the name of a goblet in the possession of the Musgrave family, of Eden Hall in Cumberland. There is a tradition that it was the gift of a fairy, and that on its safe preservation depended the safety of the lord of Edenhall. It is still preserved at Eden Hall, and is not so entirely broken as the ballad describes.)

Of Edenhall the youthful lord
Bade summon the guests by trumpet's call;
He rises at the festive board,
And, 'midst the drunken revellers all,
Cries: "Bring me the Luck of Edenhall!"

The steward sighs at his lord's command;
(The oldest vassal was he of all);
From its silken case with careful hand
He taketh the crystal goblet tall —
They call it the "Luck of Edenhall".

"To honour this glass" — was the next command —
"Come fill it with wine of Portugal!"
The old man pours with tembling hand,
And purple light streams over all
From the sparkling Luck of Edenhall.

Then speaks the lord, and the glass doth wave:
  "This gleaming goblet of crystal tall
A water-sprite to my fathers gave,
  And wrote thereon — *If this glass should fall,*
  Farewell to the luck of Edenhall!

'Twas fitting a *glass* o'er the fate should reign
  Of the mirthful race of Edenhall!
The full deep draughts we gladly drain,
  While merrily clink the beakers tall;
  Come, clink with the Luck of Edenhall!"

First, full as the song of the nightingale,
  Its ring on the ear doth clearly fall;
Then loud as the torrent that sweeps the vale,
  And last, like the deafening thunder's brawl,
  The matchless Luck of Edenhall!

"It taketh a race of mickle might
  This fragile goblet to hold in thrall;
It hath lasted longer than seemeth right;
  Then cling! with the hardest blow of all
  Will I prove the Luck of Edenhall!"

As the ringing goblet in pieces flies,
  Cracked is the roof of the vaulted hall;
Bright flames of death from the rift arise;
  Dashed to the earth are the feasters all
  As breaketh the Luck of Edenhall!

In storms the foe, with fire and sword,
  Who in the night had scaled the wall;
By the sword-stroke dieth the youthful lord,
  His hand still holding the beaker tall,
  The shattered Luck of Edenhall.

Early at morn the butler came,
  The old man, to the ruined hall;
Alone he seeketh his lord's burnt frame;
  And, 'midst the hideous ruin's fall,
  The shards of the Luck of Edenhall.

"Stone walls" — saith he — "must in pieces go,
  The lofty pillar at last must fall;
Of glass is this world's wealth and show;
  One day in atoms this earthly ball
  Must burst, like the Luck of Edenhall!"

---

75. The Last Palgrave.

I, palgrave Götz of Tübingen,
  Sell fortress, town, and hill,
With servants, rents, inclosures, woods;
  Of debts have I my fill.

Two freeholds only sell I not,
  Two tenures old and good,
I' the cloister one, with steeple fair,
  One in the leafy wood.

The cloister we've endowed till poor,
  There built till plunged in need;
And therefore I the abbot charge
  My hound and hawk to feed.

At Schönbuch, near the cloister-walls,
  A hunting-ground I hold;
And, having this, I little care
  Tho' all the rest be sold.

And when one day your monkish crew
  No more my bugle hear;
Then toll the bell, and seek my corse
  Beside the fountain clear.

Then lay me 'neath the shady oak
  Which birds frequent with song,
And o'er me read a hunter's mass
  That lasteth not too long!

---

76. Count Eberhard der Rauschebart.

(Ulrich, Count of Würtemburg, who reigned from 1246—1265, was the founder of the family now on the throne of Würtemburg. From his death, Würtemburg was governed by *Counts* of his family till the latter end of the fifteenth century, when the Emperor Maximilian conferred the title of *duke* upon Eberhard V. Amongst these counts, one of some distinction was Count Eberhard, surnamed der Greiner (the Growler), and also der Rauschebart (Flowing-beard), who died in 1392, and who, together with his son Ulrich (who died four years earlier), is interred in the choir of the collegiate church at Stuttgart. The four following ballads relate to the exploits of the Eberhard and Ulrich last mentioned.)

Introduction or Prologue.

Are then in Suabia's province hushed all
heroic lays,
Where once the harps of knighthood rang out
the Staufen's praise?*
And if they be not silenced, why fail they to
recite
How fought our gallant fathers, how gleamed
their weapons bright?

---

* Some of the old dukes of Suabia belonged to the house of Stauffen, or Hohenstauffen. Suabia partly included Würtemburg.

Men lisp their vapid numbers, teach epigrams to scold,
But scorn fair woman's beauty, the Light of ballads old;
Where heroes wait th' enchanter, in dismal silence bound,
Men o'er the spot trip lightly, and shudder at a sound.

Then break from out thy coffin, rise from the dusky choir,
(With brave and dauntless Ulrich), thou Rauschebart, the sire!
Thou foughtest all unconquered, thro' many a rolling year;
Burst forth and stand before us with clash of sword and spear!

Legend I. The Surprise at Wildbad.

(Eberhard, bathing in the natural bath at Wildbad, is surprised by his enemies, the Schlegels and the Wolf of Wunnenstein, but escapes with the assistance of a shepherd.)

I' the beauteous days of summer, when breezes warmly blow,
When woods are clothed with verdure and gardens gaily glow,

There rode from Stuttgart's portals a knight of stalwart mould,
Count Eberhard der Greiner, hight Rauschebart the old.

But scantily attended, on rides the noble knight,
He wears nor helm nor breastplate, nor seeks the stormy fight.
Right on he rides to Wildbad, where wells a tepid spring,
That to the old fresh vigour, to sick men health can bring.

At Hirsau, with the abbot awhile abides the knight,
And drinks, while peals the organ, the convent-wine so bright;
Then threads the dark pine-forest, and rides the vale along,
Where down its rocky channel the Enz rolls fierce and strong.

At Wildbad, near the market, a lofty house is seen,
The sign that hangs before it — a lance of brightest sheen;

There 'lights the Count from horseback, there seeks from care to rest;
And daily to the fountain repairs the noble guest.

There having doffed his garments, awhile he pausing stood;
A prayer to Heav'n he uttered — then plunged within the flood:
He ever took his station where from their craggy spout
The fountain's healing waters rushed fullest, hottest out.

A wild boar sorely smitten, that washed his wound of blood,
First shewed the eager huntsmen where rolled the hidden flood;
There now the aged hero oft whiles an hour away,
And bathes the limbs where linger the scars of many a fray.

One day in haste came thither a page, with terror pale:
"Sir Count! a troop of horsemen come down the upper vale;

They swing right heavy maces — a Wild
Boar to the gaze
Beneath a Golden Rosebud the leader's shield
displays."

"My son — those are the Schlegels, well-
known for mighty deeds;
Give me my tunic, youngster — 'tis Eberstein
that leads.
Full well I ken the Wild-Boar — his foes in
wrath he tears,
Full well I ken the Rosebud — a piercing
thorn it bears."

Just then a watchful shepherd draws near,
and pants for breath:
"Sir Count, a troop of horsemen ride up the
vale beneath;
Three Axes bears the leader — his armour
brightly gleams;
Till, like the flashing lightning, to daze mine
eyes it seems."

"'Tis then the Wunnensteiner, the Gleaming
Wolf y-hight,
Give me my mantle, youngster — I know his
scutcheon bright;

But little joy he brings me — the Axes cleave
amain —
Come bind my sword beside me — my blood
the Wolf would drain.

A maid surprised in bathing, who cowers in
quick alarm,
Some raillery must suffer, but 'scapeth free
from harm;
But if they thus discover a chief grown old
in strife,
'Twill cost him much in ransom, if not
perchance his life."

Then answer made the shepherd — "Be by
my counsel swayed,
I know a secret footpath, where warrior ne'er
hath strayed;
No horse could ever follow, there goats alone
can flee —
I'll bring thee hence in safety, if thou but
follow me!"

Right through the tangled brushwood they
clamber up the steep;
The Count with trusty broadsword his onward
way must reap;

He ne'er till then had tasted the bitterness of
flight —
The bath had lent him vigour; he longed to
turn and fight.

Tho' noontide's heat glowed fiercely, right up
the hill they pressed,
Upon his broadsword's pommel ere long the
Count would rest;
The shepherd viewed with pity the old and
valiant lord,
And on his back he takes him: — " 'Tis done
with free accord."

Then thinks the gray-haired Greiner: "I hold
it passing good
So gently to be carried by one of trusty
blood;
In dangers and distresses the people's faith is
shewn;
Then let their ancient charters aside be never
thrown."

Within his hall at Stuttgart in safety sits the
knight;
He bade them coin some medals, memorials
of his flight;

Of these the trusty shepherd a goodly share receives,
Whilst others to the Schlegels, in scorn, he freely gives.

He next some sturdy masons to Wildbad sends apace,
To build protecting ramparts around the open space,
That each one who in future, age-stricken, thither goes,
May gain fresh health and vigour, secure from fear of foes.

Legend II. The Three Kings of Heimsen.

(Three brothers of the Schlegel family, who had attempted to surprise Eberhard in the bath, dub themselves the "Three Kings of Heimsen". They are plotting further designs against Eberhard, when he turns the tables upon them as is here described.)

Three kings at once in Heimsen! who *could* have thought it true?
By mounted knights attended with state and honour due!
The three, who ruled as captains the Schlegel brotherhood,
Now claim a kingly title to make their conquests good!

Enthroned they sit together and eagerly take
rede,
Devising and concocting a great and warlike
deed,
How with a gallant army the Greiner to
surround,
And (better than at Wildbad) his every wile
confound;

How next they may immure him and break
his castles small,
Until he free the nobles from irksome feudal
thrall;
Then, Peace! farewell for ever; then, Feudal
rights, good night!
Then shall the lawless soldier treat all the
world with slight!

At length the night hath fallen, the kings
have sought repose;
E'en now the cocks were crowing, as morning's
light arose,
When loudly from the turret the sentry's
warning swells:
"Awake! awake! ye sleepers!" — that sound
a siege foretells.

There, 'mid the mists of morning, appears a surging tide
That round the little township draws near on every side.
Hark to the low-voiced murmurs, the tramplings and alarms,
The sound of hoofs and snortings, and hollow clash of arms!

And as the morning lightens, and sink the shades of night,
Lo! morning-stars* and lances shine brighter and more bright!
The peasants of the province the township close enfold,
And 'midst them, high on horseback, sits Rauschebart the old!

The Schlegels fain would struggle to guard their fort and town,
A flight of stones and arrows they hurl unceasing down;

* Visitors to the Tower of London may perhaps remember a formidable iron weapon, consisting of a short bar, a piece of chain, and a ball full of spikes, which was pleasantly termed by our ancestors a "morning-star".

"Now softly" — quoth the Greiner — "to
warm your bath I'll try!
It needs must steam and simmer till waters
every eye!"

Around the ancient outworks are wood and
straw up-reared,
Brought thither in the darkness, and well with
tar besmeared.
They shoot in burning arrows — how blazed
the crackling straw!
They hurl in flaring torches — what sheets
of flame they saw!

And now from every quarter is fuel swiftly
brought,
Which far and wide the peasants with eager-
ness have sought;
And higher still and higher the flame ascends
and turns
Till now with merry crackle the castle-roof it
burns.

One gate was left unguarded — for so the
Count approved —
Hark! how the bolts behind it are softly,
slowly moved!

Thence burst the Schlegels fiercely, with
courage of despair?
Ah no! they walk demurely, as in a house
of prayer.

First come the Kings of Heimsen, on foot, in
humble wise,
Their heads — once crowned — uncovered,
with sad and downcast eyes;
Next many lords and servants pace forth by
twos and threes,
That all may well behold them, and number
them at ease.

"Now welcome" — quoth the Greiner — "nor
deem that ye intrude,
I've caught you cooped together, much honoured
brotherhood!
Ye sought me once in Wildbad — *my* visit,
friends, is this;
One only, (and 'tis pity), the Wunnenstein I
miss.

A peasant who right nimbly had helped the
flames to feed,
Now leant upon his halberd, of all that passed
took heed;

"Three kings at once" — he muttered —
"'tis plenty, by my fay!
Were but a fourth here present, a game at
cards we'd play!"

Legend III. The Battle at Reutlingen.

(Whilst Ulrich, Eberhard's son, is besieging Reutlingen, the townsmen by a night-sally burn a hamlet in the Urachthal, and drive off the herds. Ulrich, attempting to intercept them, is surrounded, his band of knights nearly cut to pieces, and himself severely wounded; by which disgrace his father is deeply affected.)

Upon the crags at Achalm fierce birds of prey
abide,
Der Greiner's son, Count Ulrich, and many
a knight beside;
Round Reutlingen they hover, and flap their
wings in scorn;
Soon must the town surrender, by constant
toil outworn.

But suddenly the townsmen have risen up by
night,
Down Urachthal they hasten, a band of mickle
might;
And soon from mill and homestead shoots up
a flame blood-red,
The herds away are driven — the herdsmen
lie for dead.

Sir Ulrich marked their doings, he cries in lofty scorn:
"Within your town shall enter no hoof and eke no horn;"
His knights are up and ready, they clothe themselves in mail,
Bound lightly on their chargers, and ride adown the vale.

Below the town there standeth a church — St. Leonard's hight —
A grassy plot adjoins it, where knights can freely fight;
They 'light from off their chargers, they stand in stern array,
Their threatening lances bristle — who dares to pass that way?

From Urachthal the townsmen at length 'gin homeward hie,
Far off are heard their shoutings, mixed with the herd's hoarse cry;
The host comes slowly onward, equipped with warlike gear,
How proudly float their pennons, how glimmer sword and spear!

Now close your ranks together, ye brave and
knightly band,
Against so stout an army ye had not thought
to stand.
Their troops in countless numbers roll onward,
one and all,
The knights stand fast in silence, like rock or
rampart-wall.

In Reutlingen's old outworks is found an
ancient door,
With boughs of thickest ivy 'tis closely woven
o'er;
The knights had clean forgot it, but now 'tis
opened wide,
And through it groups of townsmen roll like
a rising tide.

Upon the knights to rearward they rush in
furious mood,
To-day for once the townsmen shall bathe in
knightly blood;
The tanners tan more soundly than e'er they
tanned a hide,
Nor e'er before the dyers so crimson-red had
dyed.

To-day are ta'en no captives, each strikes his foeman dead,
To-day blood flows in fountains, the grass-plot blossoms red.
Hemmed round still close and closer, by fierce attacks condensed,
All round by brothers' corpses the knightly band is fenced.

Their standard droops — 'tis taken — Count Ulrich's wounded sore —
His few surviving comrades are wearied to the core;
They seize their horses' bridles, upon their backs they leap,
They burst through all their foemen, they gain their moated keep.

Once, pierced by an assassin: "Ach Allm—" groaned out a knight;
He would have said "Allmächt'ger"; the castle hence was hight;*

---

* I. e. the castle of Achalm was so called from a wounded knight's exclamation, when he was endeavouring to say "Ach Allmächtiger!" or, "Ah Almighty Lord!"

There Ulrich from the saddle sinks wounded, faint with pain:
Were it not named already, its name it now might gain.

Next morn in slow procession to Reutlingen there crossed
A sorrowing troop of pages, who sought their masters lost.
In rows before the Town-Hall are ranged the pallid dead,
And thither, closely guarded, each trusty page is led.

There slumber more than sixty, so stained with gore and pale,
To recognize his master each page at first doth fail;
At last each trusty servant hath found his dear-loved knight,
Hath washed the corpse and wound it in grave-clothes fair and white.

In waggons some are carried, on biers are others borne,
With ivy-leaves encircled, as men the brave adorn.

So tow'rds the olden portal adown the street they roll,
While slowly from the belfries the funeral knell doth toll.

Götz Weissenheim, the bravest, goes all the rest before,
'Twas he who in the battle the County's standard bore;
Not once his hold he quitted, but reared it high till slain,
In death he still is worthy to head the funeral train.

Three noble Counts next follow, whose fame afar had rung,
From Tübingen, from Zollern, from Schwartzenburg outsprung;
O Zollern! round thy temples is twined a radiant wreath!
Thy house's future glory beheldest thou in death?

From Saxony two heroes, gray sire and son, draw nigh,
With lilies crowned and poppies, in close embrace they lie.

Round their ancestral castle a spectre stalked
of old,
Who long with sad lamentings a coming wo
foretold.

A certain Lord of Lustnau, deemed dead,
awoke to life;
By night in funeral garments returned he to
his wife;
Thenceforth in jest his offspring were as the
"Dead Men" known,
But now, one forth is carried as void of life
as stone.

The lay proceeds no farther, no more the
Muse will mourn;
Wouldst know of all the heroes, who thence
were sadly borne?
Go, view the Town-hall windows; in colours
bright and fair,
Each warrior's name and scutcheon is duly
blazoned there.

Till from his wounds recovered, awhile Count
Ulrich stayed;
Then rides he straight to Stuttgart, but little
haste he made;

He meets his aged father at dinner-time
alone;
A frosty welcome, truly! he hears no word,
no tone.

Just opposite his father sits Ulrich at the
board,
Thereon, abashed, he gazes; with wine and
fish 'tis stored;
A knife the old man seizes, speaks not, but
sad at heart,
He slowly cuts between them the table-cloth
apart.

Legend IV. The Battle at Döffingen.

(The burghers of Reutlingen, Augsburg, and Ulm attack the peasants of the hamlet of Döffingen. Eberhard and Ulrich come to the rescue, and the burghers are defeated. Ulrich is slain in the battle, which is gained partly by the courage of Eberhard, and partly by the opportune arrival of the Wolf of Wunnenstein, who (although Eberhard's old enemy) came on this occasion to assist him. Eberhard is consoled for the loss of his son by the birth of a grandson.)

Within the quiet churchyard men wont to
wander lone,
And hear but Paternosters by cross and
burial-stone;

At Döffingen 'twas *not* so; for all the livelong day
The churchyard rang with warcries, loud raged the furious fray.

The burghers come on foray — the peasants there secure
Their few poor goods and chattels, and strive to make them sure;
With pike and hoe and sickle their foes they long defy;
Whoe'er to death is wounded may find a grave hard by.

Count Eberhard der Greiner perceived the peasants' need;
A band of knights he summons and comes with hottest speed;
Around him soon are gathered the flower of German knights,
The chieftains whom in friendship the "Löwenbund"* unites.

There comes a hasty message from Wolf von Wunnenstein,
"Erelong to-day my master will join his host with thine."

---

* Lion-band or Lion-confederation, the name of a confederation of German chiefs.

The Count makes answer proudly — "'Tis not by my request;
Had he in vain the medal I sent him once in jest?"*

Count Ulrich sees before him the troops of burghers brave,
Of Reutlingen, of Augsburg, of Ulm the banners wave;
Fierce thoughts of olden rancour awake within his breast:
"Too well I know, ye proud ones, what so exalts your crest!"

He hastens to his father: — "Old debts 'tis time to pay,
Please God — I'll here recover my fathers' fame to-day:
Though with thee *at one table* I may not dine, brave knight!†
Yet *on one field of battle* I still may dare to fight!"

They 'light from off their horses, the noble Lion-band,
They dash upon the foeman, like lions fierce they stand;

* See the *first* of these ballads, last stanza but one.
† See the preceeding ballad, last stanza.

Ho! how the lion Ulrich so grimly roars and
slays;
He keeps his word sincerely, his debts in full
he pays.

On oaken stump supported, whom bear they
off perforce?
"God pity me, a sinner" — he cries in
accents hoarse;
Thee hath the lightning shattered, thou proud
and princely oak?
Thee hath the sword, brave Ulrich! hewn
down with sweeping stroke?

Then shouts the aged hero, whom naught
could e'er dismay:
"Fear not — he is as others whom fate hath
slain to-day;
Press on! the foes are flying!" he shouts,
like thunder's roar;
How streams his beard beside him, how deeply
bites the Boar!*

These words, in cunning spoken, the wondering
burghers scare:
"Who flies?" saith one to other — recoiling
here and there;

---

* Alluding to his surname Rauschebart (flowing beard) and to his cognizance, a Boar.

As though a spell were uttered, their hearts
within them sank,
Amid his knights, the Greiner bursts through
them, rank on rank.

What gleams and glitters yonder, and flames
like lightning's shine?
See, 'mid his sturdy horsemen, the Wolf of
Wunnenstein!
He darts upon the burghers, sweeps out an
ample bay,
The conquest is accomplished, the foes flee
fast away.

I' the harvest-month it happened — in sooth,
a sultry day!
Full ripe upon the cornfields the sheaves all
thickly lay;
How many a sturdy reaper his wearied arms
let fall!
In blood the knights have holden their
harvest-festival.

The peasant long thereafter that ploughed the
fertile vale,
Oft struck on rusty sword-blades, bent spears,
or hauberk's mail;

And as a hollow linden was once condemned
and felled,
Behold! a suit of armour and skeleton it
held.

When now the fight was ended 'mid victory's
noisy shout,
To Wunnenstein, the Greiner his right hand
reaches out:
"I thank thee, valiant hero; now homeward
ride with me,
This desperate battle ended, we'll feast right
merrily!"

"Ha!" — spake the Wolf, loud-laughing —
"dost like these merry pranks?
I fought from hate of townsmen, and not to
get thy thanks!
Good night, and prosperous journey — my
olden rights shall stand";
He spake, and galloped homeward with all
his valiant band.

In Döffingen's small chapel all night the Count
delays,
Beside his Ulrich's body — his only son's —
he prays;

Beside the bier he kneeleth, and closely veils his face,
And if he weeps in silence, his tears may no one trace.

Count Eberhard next morning soon mounts his horse again,
And hies him back to Stuttgart with all his martial train;
From Zuffenhaus a shepherd hath met them by the way —
"The man looks sad and drooping, what news hath he to say?" —

"I bring you evil tidings — among our flocks last night
The Gleaming Wolf descended, and took what pleased his sight!"
Then laughs the aged Greiner and shakes his beard: "My friends,
Poor sheep the wolfling hunteth — that way his nature tends!"

They ride in order onward, and from the valley green
See Stuttgart's castle peering, illumed by morning's sheen;

When lo! a trim retainer comes riding by the way —
"The lad looks bright and joyous, what news hath he to say?" —

"I bring thee happy tidings; come, wish thy grandson joy!
To Ulrich fair Antonia hath borne a beauteous boy!"
Thereat the aged hero his hands on high doth raise:
"Still hath the Finch* a fledgeling — to God be thanks and praise!"

---

77. The Cupbearer of Limburg.

A noble Count, at Limburg,
Dwelt in the castle fair;
But none of all that sought him
Could ever find him *there:*
For always he delighted
O'er hill and dale to roam;
Nor threatening storm nor tempest
Could keep him pent at home.

---

* This seems to intimate that Ulrich's cognizance was a Finch.

He wore a leathern doublet,
  A hat adorned with care
With many a gallant feather,
  E'en such as hunters wear.
A drinking-cup of boxwood
  He carried at his side;
He was of lofty stature
  And walked with rapid stride.

He owned a sturdy courser
  And serving-men to boot,
Yet left at home his servants
  And roved abroad on foot.
He had but one companion,
  A boar-spear stout and long,
Wherewith he lightly bounded
  O'er torrents wide and strong.

At Castle Hohenstaufen*
  The Kaiser then abode;
Who, by gay troops attended,
  One day a-hunting rode;
A nimble hind he followed
  So hotly and so fast,
That 'mid the tangled forest
  From sight of all he passed.

* The Hohenstaufen dynasty of the German emperors or kaisers sometimes resided at a castle of the same name.

At length he stops exhausted
  Beside a fountain cold;
The spot was painted gaily
  With blossoms manifold.
Here purposed he to rest him
  And slumber by the fount;
When hark! the brushwood rustles —
  Before him stands the Count.

At once he 'gan to chide him —
  "Meet I my neighbour here?
At home he bides but seldom,
  The court he comes not near.
Whoever hopes to catch him
  Must roam o'er dale and hill;
And tightly must one hold him,
  Else keeps he never still."

As sat the Count to rest him
  In unsuspecting mood,
And in the turf beside him
  Drave deep his boar-spear good,
With both his hands the Kaiser
  Caught up the pole with speed:
"Thy spear I take as hostage,
  Some pledge I sorely need.

This spear, which oft I longed for,
  Is mine at last perforce;
For which I here present thee
  With this my swiftest horse;
A man like thee should never
  Go walking through the wood,
Who, in the chase or warfare,
  Might render service good."

"My liege, I crave thy pardon,
  Thou mak'st my heart full sore;
Leave me my life of freedom,
  My hunting-spear restore.
I have — indeed — a palfrey,
  For thine my thanks are told;
I mean to mount on horseback
  When once I'm faint and old."

"I see 'tis vain to parley
  With one so flown with pride;
Yet hold! a cup of box-wood
  Thou bearest by thy side;
The chase hath made my thirsty:
  Now by thy favour, Count,
A draught would much revive me
  From out this sparkling fount."

At once the Count arises,
  And rinses out the cup,
Right to the brim he fills it,
  And slowly hands it up.
The Kaiser quaffs with relish
  The water cool and fine,
And deems the draught as pleasant
  As 'twere the choicest wine.

Then by the hand, half-smiling,
  The drinker takes the knight —
"Well hast thou rinsed the beaker
  And filled it to the height;
Sweet was the draught thou gavest,
  Fresh life it lends, I vow;
Henceforward to thy Kaiser
  Lord-Cupbearer art thou!"

———

78. The Vale of Song.

The Duke, far in the forest,
  Sat 'neath an oaktree's shade;
Whilst near him, gathering berries,
  A maiden singing strayed.
The fresh and fragrant berries
  She to the graybeard bore;
Her dulcet tones around him
  Still floated evermore.

Then spake he — "Gentle maiden,
  At thy sweet voices sound,
Of huntsman's toil a-weary,
  My spirit peace hath found.
The strawberries thou bringest
  Are fresh and cool, y-wis;
But sing again — thou soothest
  My soul with dreams of bliss.

When 'neath this oaktree's shadow
  My ivory horn is blown,
Where'er its sound re-echoes,
  The vale is all mine own.
Where'er from yonder birch-tree
  Thy thrilling song shall sound,
I give to thee in guerdon
  The land that lies around."

The gray-beard's horn resounded
  Adown the pleasant vale,
In distant rocky gullies
  It pealed like thunder's wail;
Then from the birch-crowned hillock
  Was heard the maiden's strain,
As though the wings of angels
  Swept o'er the peaceful plain.

His seal-ring, as an earnest,
He laid within her hand: —
"My hunting here is ended,
Thine own is all the land."
The maiden bowed to thank him,
And home, rejoicing, went;
Fresh strawberries she carried
I' the golden circlet pent.

What time the pealing bugle
There reigned with sombre might,
The wild-boar fled to hide him
I' the forest's deepest night;
Then loudly bayed the beagles,
The startled hind dashed out,
And, as the prey fell bleeding,
Arose a lusty shout.

But since the maiden's carol,
There flourish meadows green,
The playful lambs are frisking,
And cherry-groves are seen;
There dances are enwoven
In springtide's golden light,
And — won by song — the valley
The "Vale of Song" * is hight.

* In German, *Singenthal.*

79. The Battle of the Larks.

"Larks are we, as free as ether,
'Neath the sun we blithely fly;
Rising from the waving cornfield,
Soar we through the azure sky."
Larks a thousand singing hovered
O'er the wide and even plain;
None that heard their joyous carol
Pent at home could long remain.

Wallerstein's proud castle leaving
Rode the Count, his son beside;
Who, before the Kaiser kneeling,
Soon shall win his spurs of pride.
Gladly hears the Count their carol,
Token of a numerous brood;
Whilst with beating heart beside him
Rides the youth in dauntless mood.

From the town with time-worn turrets,
Through the dark defiant gate,
As the golden Sunday dawneth,
Issue young and old elate.
Whilst the town-guard's youthful captain
Tow'rds a garden leads his bride;
Bids her list the larks' gay carol,
Plucks for her the violet's pride.

Soon, alas! these vernal mornings
  Rife with bloom, fly quickly past;
E'en the months of summer-glory
  Yield to winter suns at last.
"Larks are we, as free as ether,
  Wherefore pine we lingering here?
Naught remains for song to utter,
  Wander we o'er land and mere!"

In the misty autumn evening
  From the gate the burghers steal;
Spread the nets in careful silence,
  Listening as they crouching kneel.
Hark — a whirr! the larks are coming —
  Hark — a rush! a louder flight!
Tow'rds the nets a troop is riding,
  Loudly clash their weapons bright.

Shouts the aged Count from horseback:
  "Aid us, Mary, purest Dame!
Whilst this saucy rout we punish,
  Seizing thus our lawful game!"
Answering shouts the youthful captain:
  "Draw the sword — thrust home or fall;
Larks may each at pleasure capture,
  Little birds are free to all!"

As the cold gray morn is dawning,
  On the field a youth lies dead;
O'er him, by his sword supported,
  Stoops the Count in silence dread.
Yonder — o'er the captain's body
  Sadly bends his lovely bride,
Whilst her long dishevelled tresses
  Serve the bleeding corse to hide.

Once again, before departure,
  Rise a thousand larks on high,
Fluttering in the sun of morning,
  Warbling as they blithely fly:
"Larks are we, as free as ether,
  Flying far o'er land and flood;
They that sought to snare and slay us
  Welter in their oozing blood!"

---

80. "Ver Sacrum."

("Ver Sacrum" means the firstlings of all that grew or was brought forth in the spring, which were sometimes devoted to the gods. In this instance the offering is made to Mars, who requires further that the youths and maidens should be devoted to him also; not that they should be slain, as the people at first supposed, but should emigrate and found a distant colony in his honour.)

When in Lavinium erst the Latin crew
No more against their foes' fierce shock could stand,
They to their country's last defence withdrew,
The Spear of Mars, uplifting eye and hand.

Then spake the aged priest the lance who bore:
"I tell you, prompted by your angered King,
A favouring flight of birds* he sends no more,
Except to him ye consecrate the Spring!"

---

* The words "auspice" and "augury" are both derived from words relating to the custom of divination by means of *birds*.

"To him the Spring be sacred" — cried the crowd,
"To him be brought whate'er the Spring shall boast;"
A rush of wings was heard; the spear clanged loud,
O'erwhelmed with panic, fled th' Etruscan host.

With shouts of victory they homeward went,
E'en while they triumphed, grew the landscape green;
With flowers, beneath each hoof, the fields are sprent,
Where lances graze the trees, fresh buds are seen.

Beside the altar, and before the gates,
To welcome them with song and mirth unchecked,
A troop of matrons and fair maidens waits,
With flowers, that blossomed but that morning, decked.

And whilst around the joyous welcome spread,
The priest the hill ascended; in the ground
The sacred Spear implanted, bowed his head
In reverent wise, and spake to all around:

"Hail, Mars! who savedst us 'mid death's alarms,
What we have promised will we freely bring;
Across this land I stretch abroad mine arms,
And consecrate to thee this teeming spring.

Whate'er you pasture, rich in herds, doth hold —
The lambs, the kids upon thy hearth shall flame;
The bullock for the plough shall ne'er grow old,
Nor conquering bit the mettled courser tame.

Whate'er you garden yields of ripened fruit,
The corn, now waving green on yonder lea,
No touch of human hand shall e'er pollute,
All, all we consecrate, great god, to thee!"

Still knelt the multitude in silent prayer,
Deep silence spread the sacred landscape round;
None e'er beheld a vernal scene so fair;
A strange portentous awe all senses bound.

Again the priest outspoke — "Yet deem ye not
Yourselves from debt released, your vow complete;
Have ye the statutes of old time forgot,
Nor on your promise made reflection meet?

The scent of flowers — the corn but newly sprung —
The pastures that the new-born flocks receive —
Do these to spring belong, and not the young,
Your sons and maids, who through them dances weave?

More than the yearling lambs, your guardian loves
The maiden sweet, who youth's first garland wears;
More than young foals untamed, the God approves
The youth, when first his shining blade he bares.

Oh not for naught, ye sons, 'mid battles tide,
Were ye with energy divine endued;
And not for naught, ye maids, when home we hied,
We found your bloom so wondrously renewed!

A people, Mars! hast thou preserved from shame,
From badge of servitude hast kept us free;
All that this year attains its prime thou'lt claim;
Receive it, Mars! we offer it to thee!"

Again the people bowed themselves in prayer,
 The dedicated ones stood close around;
Tho' white their lips, they shone with beauty rare,
 And deep mysterious awe all senses bound.

Still silent as the grave the people lay,
 Trembling before the god to whom they prayed,
When lo! from heav'n there flashed a lustrous ray
 That struck the spear, and round it flickering played.

Thereat the priest looked up with mien inspired,
 Down waved his shining beard and silver hair;
With heavenly light his kindling eyes were fired,
 And thus their guardian's will he 'gan declare.

"His sacred spoil the god will ne'er forego;
 Their death he asks not, but their strength and life;
He loves not blossoms that have ceased to blow,
 But those with sap still green, with vigour rife.

26*

A colony must quit old Latium's towers
To serve in distant lands the god of war;
And from this Spring, so rich in germs and flowers,
Rich store of future fruit shall rise afar.

Let each devoted youth then choose his bride,
Bright wreaths amid their locks already twine;
Let each fair maiden, by her loved one's side,
Depart, where'er your guiding star shall shine.

The corn, which waving green ye yonder view,
That take for seed-corn when the land ye share;
And from yon trees, that now their shoots renew,
Preserve the kernels and the seeds with care.

There shall the bullock plough th' unbroken land,
The playful lamb o'er new-found pastures stray;
There the young colt shall feel your conquering hand,
Ere long to bear you through some desperate fray.

For frays and future strife your fates portend,
From these the homage claimed by Mars is wrung;
Himself amongst you shall ere long descend
From him your future race of kings be sprung.*

Within your temple shall his spear abide,
Which there your captains tremblingly must smite†
Whene'er they wander forth o'er land and tide
To spread o'er all the world their conquering might.

Ye hear the destiny for you decreed;
Depart, prepare you for your glorious task;
Ye are a future world's most precious seed;
Such is the "sacred spring" your god doth ask!"

---

* Mars was the reputed father of Romulus; and the Romans were descended from the old Latins, according to some traditions.

† Referring to a custom connected with a declaration of war by the ancient Romans.

81. The King's Son.

I.

The old, grayheaded monarch sits
  On the throne his fathers won;
His mantle gleams like the evening's glow,
  His crown as the setting sun.

"Come hither, my first and my second sons,
  For you shall the kingdom be;
My third dear son, my favourite child,
  What pledge shall I leave for thee?"

"Give me no treasure except thy crown,
  (Tho' rusty and old it be),
And three strong vessels, and bid me seek
  A kingdom beyond the sea!"

II.

The young prince stood at the vessel's prow,
  And watched it onward fare;
The sun shone bright and the breezes played
  With his radiant golden hair.

The rudder creaks, the sails swell out,
  Far stream the pennons gay;
Around the keel with a low sweet song
  The mermaids flash and play.

"Behold my kingdom", the prince exclaims,
"Far-stretching without a bound,
That sweeps with its billows fresh and blue
The sluggish earth around!"

But heavy clouds come rolling up,
Fierce gales and storms they bring;
The lightning flashes athwart the gloom,
And the masts in pieces spring.

The mountain-waves 'gainst the vessel's side
Break with a thunderous roar;
Whirled in the depths is the daring prince,
His dream of empire o'er!

III.

Fisherman.

"Alas! 'tis sunken, mast and keel,
And the seamen's cries are o'er;
But see! who hither so stoutly swims
As the waves around him roar?

He smites the flood with a sturdy arm,
Right little the waves he fears;
High lifts he his head with a golden crown,
Like a king's his mien appears!"

Youth.

"A king's son I — but my childhood's home
Have I lost beyond recal!
The earthly mother was faint and weak
That bare me first of all;

A second mother, the mighty sea,
Hath borne me now again;
With her giant arms she wildly rocked
My brothers and me amain!

The others, alas! survived it not;
But me she hath borne astrand,
And chosen for me a kingdom fair,
This broad and welcome land!"

IV.

Fisherman.

"Why watchest thou thus thy fishing lines
From early morn till night,
And yet, with all thy wondrous care,
Bring'st never a fish to sight?"

Youth.

"I angle not for a paltry fish,
But gaze in the depths below,
And see, too deep for the fisher's art,
Much kingly pomp and show."

V.

"How like a monarch the lion stalks!
His mane in the air he shakes;
And utters laws with a despot's voice
Through woods and forest-brakes.

Yet with my spear in my stalwart hand
I'll lay him before me dead;
And proudly o'er my shoulders broad
His golden garment spread.

How like a monarch the eagle soars!
He rises on joyous wing,
As though he would seize the golden sun
To crown himself a king.

But far aloft to the distant cloud
Shall soar my arrow fleet,
Shall reach him there and shall pierce him through,
And lay him beneath my feet."

VI.

A wild horse through the forest runs,
That never hath felt the rein;
Its colour like cream; its hoofs strike fire,
It tosses its long thick mane.

The young prince seizes its flowing mane,
  Himself on its back he swings;
Its tail it lashes, its chest dilates,
  Loud-neighing, it forward springs.

And all that down in the valley dwell
  In listening wonder throng,
And seem to hear, on the hills above,
  Hoarse thunders roll along.

Then, wrapt about with the lion's hide,
  Before them the prince doth dash;
Out streams the mane of the savage steed,
  And sparks from its foot-tracks flash.

The people cluster around him soon
  With jubilant shout and song:
"All hail! 'tis he, 'tis the mighty prince
  We have waited for all too long!"

VII.

Behold yon steep and lofty crag,
  Round which the eagle flies!
There's none will dare to its peak to climb,
  For there the dragon lies!

There lies she within the mouldering walls;
  Her crest like gold doth gleam;
She rustles along with her scaly skin,
  And her breath, it is flame and steam.

The youth, unarmed with a sword or shield,
  Hath boldly attained the height;
His arms he around the serpent casts,
  And grasps her with conquering might.

Then thrice he kisseth her ghastly mouth,
  For thus must he break the spells;
In his arms he claspeth a lovely maid,
  The fairest on earth that dwells.

Now crowned is his young and lovely bride,
  And close to his heart she lies;
From the ruins old, self-built, behold
  A regal castle rise!

VIII.

The king and queen stand side by side
  By the throne he hath boldly won;
The throne shines bright as the morning's glow,
  Their crowns as the rising sun.

A knightly band doth around them stand,
  Their swords in their hands they hold;
And ne'er can they turn their eyes away
  From the throne of gleaming gold.

A blind and aged minstrel leans
  On his harp, as he rests from song;
He feels that the time at length is come
  He hath waited for all too long.

At once by the throne's bright sheen is burst
  The veil that dimmed his sight;
Around him he gazes, and ne'er can tire
  Of the pomp so royally bright.

He seizes his harp, he smites the strings;
  With clearest tones it rang;
And, flushed with the light and rapt with joy,
  Like a swan ere it dies he sang.

---

82. The Minstrel's Curse.

There stood in former ages a castle high and large,
Above the slope it glistened far down to ocean's marge;
Around it like a garland bloomed gardens of delight,
Where sparkled cooling fountains, with sunbow-glories dight.

There sat a haughty monarch, who lands in
war had won;
With aspect pale and gloomy he sat upon
the throne;
His thoughts are fraught with terrors, his
glance of fury blights;
His words are galling scourges, with victims'
blood he writes.

Once moved towards this castle a noble
minstrel-pair,
The one with locks all-golden, snow-white the
other's hair;
With harp in hand, the graybeard a stately
courser rode,
In flower of youth, beside him his tall
companion strode.

Then spake the gray-haired father — "Be
well prepared, my son;
Think o'er our loftiest ballads, breathe out
thy fullest tone;
Thine utmost skill now summon, joy's zest
and sorrow's smart,
'Twere well to move with music the monarch's
stony heart."

Now in the spacious chamber the minstrels twain are seen,
High on the throne in splendour are seated king and queen;
The king with terrors gleaming — a ruddy Northern Light,
The queen all grace and sweetness — a full moon soft and bright.

The gray-beard swept the harp-strings, they sounded wondrous clear;
The notes with growing fulness thrilled through the listening ear;
Pure as the tones of angels the young man's accents flow,
The old man's gently murmur, like spirit-voices low.

They sing of love and springtime, of happy golden days —
Of manly worth and freedom, of truth and holy ways;
They sing of all things lovely, that human hearts delight,
They sing of all things lofty, that human souls excite.

The courtier-train around them forget their
jeerings now,
The king's defiant soldiers in adoration
bow;
The queen, to tears now melted, with rapture
now possessed,
Throws down to them in guerdon a rosebud
from her breast.

"Have ye misled my people, and now my
wife suborn?"
Shouts out the ruthless monarch, and shakes
with wrath and scorn;
He whirls his sword, like lightning the young
man's breast it smote,
That, 'stead of golden legends, bright life-
blood filled his throat.

Dispersed, as by a tempest, was all the
listening swarm;
The youth sighs out his spirit upon his master's
arm,
Who round him wraps his mantle, and sets
him on the steed,
There tightly binds him upright, and from
the court doth speed.

Before the olden gateway — there halts the minstrel old,
His golden harp he seizes, above all harps extolled:
Against a marble pillar he snaps its tuneful strings;
Through castle and through garden his voice of menace rings.

"Wo, wo to thee, proud castle! ne'er let sweet tones resound
Henceforward through thy chambers, nor harp's nor voice's sound;
Let sighs and tramp of captives and groans dwell here for aye,
Till retribution sink thee in ruin and decay.

Wo, wo to you, fair gardens, in summerlight that glow,
To you this pallid visage, deformed by death, I shew,
That every leaf may wither, and every fount run dry,
That ye in future ages a desert heap may lie.

Wo, wo to thee, curst tyrant! that art the
minstrel's bane;
Be all thy savage strivings for glory's wreath
in vain!
Be soon thy name forgotten, sunk deep in
endless night,
Or, like a last death-murmur, exhaled in vapour light!"

The graybeard's curse was uttered; heav'n
heard his bitter cry;
The walls are strewn in fragments, the halls
in ruins lie;
Still stands one lofty column to witness olden
might,
E'en this, already shivered, may crumble
down to-night.

Where once were pleasant gardens, is now a
wasted land;
No tree there lends its shadow, nor fount bedews the sand;
The monarch's name recordeth no song, nor
lofty verse;
'Tis wholly sunk — forgotten! Such is the Minstrel's Curse!

---

83. The Sunken Crown.

High up on yonder hillock
  A little cottage stands;
A pleasant view its threshold
  O'er happy fields commands.
There sits a free-born peasant,
  At eve, upon the sod;
His ringing scythe he sharpens,
  And praises sings to God.

Far down within the valley,
  Where darkly yawns the ditch,
There lies, sunk deep within it,
  A crown, superb and rich.
There carbuncle and sapphire
  In secret twilight gleam;
There hath it lain for ages,
  And troubles no man's dream.

---

84. The Death of Tell.

"On quitting Altorf, the road crosses the mouth of the vale of Schächen, traversing by a bridge the stream in which, according to tradition, William Tell lost his life (1350) in endeavouring to rescue a child from the water-fall of Bürglen. He plunged in, and neither he nor the child was seen after."

Murray's Swiss Guide. p. 107.

According to Uhland, however, the child was saved and Tell's body recovered.

Green grow the Alpine pastures,
The avalanches cease;
The flocks ascend the mountains,
As yielding snows decrease.*
When, by the South-wind melted,
The ice in pieces falls,
Your struggles fierce for freedom,
Ye Swiss! the scene recals.

Down foams the roaring Schächen
From yonder cloven height,
And rocks and pines are shivered
Before its headlong flight.

---

* In Switzerland, in the spring, the cattle are sent up from the vallies to the lower pastures of the Alps.

Its stream hath swamped the foot-bridge
  That o'er the torrent hung,
And swept away the stripling
  That on the plank had sprung.

A man was fast approaching
  The foot-bridge, as it gave;
The grayhaired wanderer stays not,
  But dives the lad to save,
Grips him with eagle-swiftness,
  Seeks out a shallow bay;
The boy escapes the billow,
  The man is whirled away!

But when ashore the body
  Was drifted by the flood,
Around it men and women
  In speechless sorrow stood;
As though a shock had cloven
  The Rothstock's* rocky bed,
One mouth (it seemed) shrieked loudly —
  "Brave Tell — our Tell — is dead!"

Roved I o'er snows eternal,
  A mountain-shepherd free,
Were I a daring sailor
  O'er Uri's** emerald sea;

* The Uri Rothstock, a mountain 10,376 feet high.
** One of the bays of the lake of Lucerne.

And saw I Tell's dead body —
  By heart-felt sorrow wrung,
My arms should fondly clasp him,
  My lay should thus be sung:

"Thou wast the life of all men,
  Now here thou liest dead;
Thy gray hair still is dripping
  Around thy pallid head.
A ruddy boy stands near thee
  Recovered from the stream,
And round thee, clothed in sunshine,
  The land thou didst redeem.

The love that late within thee
  For that poor boy did glow,
Once woke in thee the impulse
  That laid the tyrant low.
Intent to save, thou knew'st not
  Of slumber or dismay,
Or when thy locks were auburn,
  Or when thy hair was gray.

Hadst thou in youth's full vigour
  Plunged in this lad to save,
And hadst thou 'scaped in safety,
  Not sunk beneath the wave,
We might from thence have augured
  Thy future glorious deeds;

But now the less achievement
  The greater one succeeds.

Although a nation's praises
  Conspired thine ears to fill,
A faint appeal for succour
  At once could reach them still.
That hero's breast is kindled
  With freedom's purest glow,
Who, crowned with victory's garland,
  Loves rather use than show.

In safety thou returnedst
  From that destructive deed,
'Twas in a work of mercy
  Thou couldst no longer speed;
'Twas not to save a people
  Heav'n asked thy life's dear price,
But deemed thee for a stripling
  A fitting sacrifice.

Where, by thine arrow stricken,
  The ruthless Gessler fell,
A house of prayer stands open
  Of God's revenge to tell.
But here where thou didst perish
  A stripling's life to save,
A simple cross of stonework
  Denotes thy humble grave.

All lands shall hear the story
  How Switzerland was freed,
And tongues of famous poets
  Shall celebrate thy deed;
But shepherds by the Schächen,
  At purple eventide,
Shall tell the rocks around them
  How nobly thou hast died."

85. The Bell-cavern.

I know a curious grotto
  With crystals vaulted round,
'Tis by some God invested
  With wondrous powers of sound;
Whate'er one sings, whate'er one tells,
Re-echoes like a peal of bells.

Two blest ones there are standing,
  (Like hopes their spirits move),
Their pent desires outpouring,
  Avowing mutual love;
Meanwhile a clear-voiced bell keeps time
With one of deeper, stronger chime!

There lie some boon-companions
  The stony bench along;
Full cups of wine they brandish,
  Sing scraps of drunken song;
Ne'er rang the echoes louder, higher —
Like bells that warn of storm or fire.

Two men, sedate and earnest,
  Linked by pure freedom's band,
Are anxiously discussing
  Their German Fatherland;
Hark! from the farthest nook a bell
Booms deeply, like a funeral knell.

86. The Lost Church.

Oft, yonder forest's depths within,
  Is faintly heard a chiming peal;
None know from whence the sounds begin,
  E'en legends scarce the spot reveal.
The church hath passed away, but still
  The chimes come softly on the wind;
Once pilgrims would the pathway fill
  Which now none knoweth where to find.

The forest's depths I lately sought,
  From every track of man retired;
To quit the ills this age hath wrought
  And yearn for God, my soul aspired.
Where silence all around was poured,
  I heard this pleasant chime again;
The more my aspirations soared,
  The nearer, louder seemed the strain.

My soul was so absorbed in dreams,
  My mind so ravished by the sound,
That still a mystery it seems
  How I such heights of fancy found;
Methought a hundred years had fled
  Whilst still I mused in dreamy mood,
When in the parting clouds o'erhead
  A sunny opening space I viewed.

The sky was there so deeply blue;
  And, 'neath the cloudless sun's full gleam,
A fair cathedral rose to view
  All glorious in the golden beam.
Methought light clouds, fringed round with fire,
  Like wings, the stately pile upbore,
And lo! its turret's topmost spire
  To heaven itself appeared to soar.

The bell's melodious cheerful sound
  Rang quivering from the lofty tower;

The rope no human hand drew round,
'Twas moved by some mysterious power.
Methought that impulse strange and strong
Seemed too my beating heart to draw;
The spacious nave I paced along
With tottering step and holy awe.

What felt I in that blest abode
Is past the power of words to paint;
The windows deeply, purely glowed
With forms of many a martyred saint.
Behold! with wondrous glory bright,
Each pictured form awoke to life;
I saw where reigned the saints in light,
Made conquerors in the holy strife.

O'ercome with holy fear and love,
I knelt before the altar fair;
I glanced upon the roof above,
Heav'n's glories were depicted there.
But when I glanced aloft once more,
The vaulted roof asunder flew,
Wide open stood heav'n's golden door,
No veil obscured the dazzling view.

The thousand glorious sights that stirred
My soul with silent rapt amaze,
The sweet melodious sounds I heard,
More sweet than organ's tones of praise;

All these no words have power to tell —
  But he that such delights would feel
Must list to that entrancing bell
  That in yon wood doth faintly peal.

---

87. The Sunken Convent.

A convent lies deep-sunken
  Beneath the tranquil wave;
The sisters and the father
  Have found a watery grave.
A troop of laughing mermaids
  Go swimming round and round,
In every corner peering
  For what may there be found.

Through dormit'ry and chapel
  A splashing rabble steers,
The locutorium's prattle
  Again the convent hears.
Right blithely peals the organ,
  Song through the choir resounds,
And — when it suits the ringers —
  The bell for vespers sounds.

The verdant beach invites them,
  When gleams the moon o'erhead,
Decked out in sacred garments
  A merry round to tread;
Black stoles stream out and flutter,
  White veils, swift whirling, glance;
The flaming tapers splutter
  As though they joined the dance.

In yonder cave, a goblin —
  Behind a stony mound —
A father's cowl wraps round him
  Which on the shore he found;
In haste — to scare the dancers —
  He joins the motley rout;
But down into the abbey
  They dive with jeering shout.

88. A Fairy Tale.

(The poet here ingeniously applies a well-known tale to describe the growth of German b a l l a d poetry; its displacement by poetry of a more artificial kind; and, finally, its revival.)

Thou oft hast heard the story
  Of her who, hidden deep
Within a wood's recesses,
  For ages lay asleep.
This wonder's name was never
  Till now, revealed to thee;
I found it out but lately —
  'Tis — **German Minstrelsy**!

At birth — two potent fairies
  Approached this princess fair,
Each stood beside her cradle
  And brought her presents rare;
The first one quickly muttered —
  "Why smilest, child, at me?
From pricking of a spindle
  Thy death thou soon shalt see!"

Then spake in turn the other,
  "Dost smile, my child, at me?
I give thee, dear, my blessing,
  From death that sets thee free;
So well shall it protect thee,
  Thou shalt but slumber take;
Four hundred years thereafter,
  A prince shall bid thee wake."

Thereon strict charge was issued
  Where'er the king bore sway;

In every street 'twas published,
'Twas death to disobey: —
"That whosoe'er had spindles
Should yield them up apace,
To burn them all together
I' the open market-place."

Not in the wonted manner
They trained this future queen;
Ne'er pent her in dull chambers
Where spinning-wheels are seen;
In gardens bright with roses,
Or 'neath the forest's shade,
With laughing, blithe companions
She freely romped and played.

And when her years were ripened,
Oh! she was fair to view,
With streaming golden tresses
And eyes of deepest blue!
In gait and gesture modest —
Her tones all hearts would win;
Well skilled in every labour
Excepting — how to spin.

Proud knights appeared in numbers
The beauty's grace to crave,
Heinrich of Ofterdingen,
And Wolfram, hero brave;

They came in mail and armour,
  Their hands held harps of gold,
How fortunate the princess
  By knights like these extolled!

With sword or lance in tourneys
  They fought right readily,
Held women all in honour,
  And sang in rivalry:
They sang of God's affection,
  Of men renowned in fight,
Of thoughts that lovers cherish,
  And gardens of delight.

From walls of olden townships
  The echoes rolled along;
The burghers and the peasants
  All joined the cheerful song;
The herdsman lone hath sung it,
  Above the clouds who dwells,
E'en from the mine's recesses
  The chorus faintly swells.

The stars, one fair May even,
  Shone out so wondrous bright,
The princess thought they asked her
  To seek the turret's height.
To gain the roof she hastened —
  A beauty fair and lone —

When from a turret-chamber
  A lamp's dim lustre shone.

With hair as white as silver,
  A dame sat there and span
Who ne'er had heard that spindles
  Were put beneath a ban;
The princess, who had never
  That art beheld till now,
Cries, as the room she enters,
  "Thy pardon — who art thou?"

"They call me, fairest maiden,
  "**Domestic Minstrelsy**;"
For from my dear-loved chamber
  I never seek to flee.
This garment deftly weaving
  I sit, nor care to rove;
My blind old cat oft aids me,
  Nor from my lap will move.

Long, long didactic poems
  I spin with industry;
Like flax — heroic ballads
  I weave right rapidly.
My cat's deep whine is Tragic,
  My wheel hath Lyric sound;
Rare Comedy my spindle
  Plays, as it dances round."

As thus she spake of spindles,
  The princess pallid grew;
In haste to fly she turned her,
  The spindle tow'rds her flew;
Upon the time-worn threshold
  She tripped as she withdrew;
Her heel the cruel spindle
  Immediately pierced through.

Next morning when they found her,
  What cause had they to weep!
In vain they sought to rouse her,
  She slept the magic sleep!
Within a lofty chamber
  A couch they straight prepare;
With cloth of gold 'twas covered,
  And decked with roses fair.

So slept she in the chamber,
  A princess royally dight;
Ere long on all the others
  A sleep like hers did 'light.
The minstrels, e'en in dreaming,
  Still sought the strings to sway,
Till through the roomy castle
  The last sound died away.

The dame within the turret
  Sits spinning soon and late;

In every room the spiders
  Are spinning, small and great;
The shrubs and sprays more closely
  Twine round the princely tower;
Gray clouds, together woven,
  Above it alway lower.

* * *

Four hundred years had ended,
  When lo! a prince of might
By huntsmen keen attended,
  Drew near the wooded height.
"What battlements and turrets,
  Grown gray with age, are these,
Of curious mould and structure,
  That peer above the trees?"

At once an aged weaver
  Stood in the pathway near —
"Illustrious prince, thy pardon!
  My words of warning hear;
Huge cannibals, 'tis rumoured,
  Within yon castle wait,
Who oft with knives inhuman
  Dismember small and great."

But still the prince rode onward,
  With him three huntsmen stout;
Soon with their trusty broadswords
  They hewed a pathway out;

They found the drawbridge lowered,
  The gates stood wide apart,
Whence (as they boldly entered)
  Ran out a frightened hart;

For in the castle's precincts
  A forest tall had grown,
Where many a bird was singing
  With ever-changing tone;
But yet the huntsmen stayed not,
  But daringly pressed on
To where, amid the branches,
  A pillared gateway shone.

Before the gate's tall columns
  Two sleeping giants lay;
Their halberds, crossed together,
  Appeared to bar the way,
But still the sturdy huntsmen
  Pressed forward one and all;
With daring steps they entered
  A large and lofty hall.

All round in deep recesses
  Were dames in rich array;
Knights sheathed in mail between them,
  Who seemed on harps to play.
Tall silent stalwart figures
  With eyelids closed, they see,

Who seem like graven statues
  Of gray antiquity.

A couch with gold embroidered
  High in the midst is seen,
Where slept in rich apparel
  A maid of loveliest mien;
The fair one was surrounded
  With roses fresh and bright;
On mouth and cheeks there rested
  A tender rosy light.

The prince, to learn more surely
  If life had wholly fled,
His own warm lips pressed closely
  To hers so rosy red.
The truth he soon discovered,
  Her breath was sweet and warm,
And even as she slumbered
  She clasped him with her arm.

Her long and golden tresses
  Aside she gently threw,
And oped, in sweet amazement,
  Her eyes so heavenly blue;
In all the deep recesses
  Each knight and dame awakes;
With olden songs and ballads
  The princely building shakes.

A morning red and golden
  Sweet May to us hath brought;
To 'scape the forest's darkness
  The prince and princess sought.
Like proud gigantic spirits
  The minstrels stride along,
With solemn steps and stately,
  And sing a wondrous song.

The joyous song awakens
  The vallies sunk in sleep;
Whoe'er within his bosom
  A spark of youth doth keep,
Exclaims with deep emotion —
  "This morn aye praised shall be,
To us that now restoreth
  Our **German Minstrelsy!"**

Still sits the aged beldame
  Within her chamber small,
The roof hath sunk in ruin,
  Therein the rain doth fall.
She scarce the thread can handle,
  A stroke hath made her numb;
God send her rest — in mercy —
  Till judgment-day shall come!

BALLADS FROM THE OLD FRENCH.

---

1. The King's Daughter.

The king of Spain's fair daughter
Would some employment know,
Both how to wash a garment
She'd learn, and how to sew.

But ere the first fine garment
Washed wholly white could be,
The ring from off her finger
Hath fallen in the sea!

The damsel fell a-weeping,
A tender heart had she;
When lo! a knight rode near her
Right worshipful to see.

"What wilt thou give me, fair one,
If I thy ring restore?" —
"I scarcely can deny thee
One kiss — or even more."

The knight soon doffed his armour
And plunged beneath the sea;
But when his dive was ended,
With naught returnèd he.

Again he dived — before him
The ring shone bright and round;
But when he dived the third time,
The luckless knight was drowned!

The damsel fell a-weeping,
A tender heart had she;
She trembling sought her father:
"Henceforth no work for me!"

---

2. Count Richard the Fearless.

Legend I.

Brave Richard, Count of Normandy,
Ne'er frightened in his life was he;
He roamed abroad by day and night,
Encountering oft a ghost or sprite;
But naught could touch his soul with fear,
By daylight, or at midnight drear;
And, since by night so oft he rode,
A common rumour went abroad,

He saw more clearly in the night
Than others could in sunshine bright.
He wont, whene'er he roved around,
As often as a church he found,
(If open) through the porch to stride,
If shut, at least to pray outside.
One night he found — it so befell —
A chapel in a lonely dell.
Quick from his men he turned aside,
And, musing, let them onward ride.
His charger near the porch he bound,
Within the choir a corpse he found.
Close by the bier he fearless passed,
Himself before the altar cast,
Threw on a bench his gloves with speed,
And kissed the earth with pious heed.
But scarce had he an "Ave" said,
Ere (close behind his back) the dead
'Gan from the trestle to descend.
The Count looked round, and cried, "My friend,
Thou may'st mean either good or ill,
Turn on thine ear and keep thee still."
At last his prayers were ended well,
(What time they took I cannot tell),
Then as he crossed himself, said he,
"Lord, I commend my soul to Thee!"
He seized his sword and rose to go,
When lo! the ghost with movement slow

Rose up before him threateningly,
And stretched its skinny arms on high
As though 'twould keep him prisoner there,
Nor let him to his friends repair.
Small time for counsel Richard took,
The spectre's head in twain he strook;
I know not if it shrieked or no,
At least it let Count Richard go.
He found his charger tethered fast,
Already is the churchyard past,
When to his thoughts the gloves arise;
'Twere shame to lose them — back he hies,
And takes them from the bench — good lack!
How few would e'er have ventured back!

Legend II.

Within a cell at St. Ouan
Whilome there dwelt a sacristan;
A pious character he bore,
All to his right behaviour swore.
But ah! to souls of higher worth
Sets Satan strong temptation forth.
Once went the monk, of whom I spake,
His wonted place in church to take,
When lo! he spied a lovely dame,
For whom he straight conceived a flame;
'Twill be his death if she demur,
He'd gladly risk his soul for her.
So much he promised her and prayed,

At last his words the dame persuade.
She whispers him a time and place,
Where he by night may gain her grace.
So, when the shades of night fell deep,
And all the rest were sunk in sleep,
Forth on his way the brother fared,
For company he little cared.
Her house was on a streamlet's bank;
He needs must cross a narrow plank;
In haste he sought across to go;
(I know not how it happened so —
Whether he tripped, or stept aside,
Or took in haste too long a stride),
But, toppling headlong in the wave,
He sank, beyond man's power to save.
His soul at once a demon hent,
As newly from the corse it went,
And hastened tow'rd the fiery flood —
When in the way an angel stood.
About the soul a strife began,
And thus the sharp encounter ran:
The demon spake — "'Tis ill for thee
To snatch at what belongs to me;
Thou know'st the soul to me is bound
That doing sinful deeds is found.
I found the monk to evil prone,
As by the path he took is shewn;
That path his final doom hath sealed,
For this, thou know'st, hath God revealed,

E'en as I find thee, so I judge." —
But here the angel answered — "Fudge!
A spotless life the brother spent
When in the convent-walls y-pent;
And scripture makes it understood,
A sure reward awaits the good.
For good that he hath done on earth
Must he receive its tenfold worth.
The sin was not committed quite,
For which thou 'dst punish him outright.
He past the convent-gate had gone,
Thence to the plank he hurried on,
But had he not mista'en the track,
Who knows but he had yet *gone back?*
For evil he did ne'er commit
To punish him is hardly fit;
And — for a little evil *thought* —
It hath not his perdition wrought.
No longer let us wrangle — no!
But rather to Count Richard go;
Let him the best solution tell,
He evermore decideth well." —
"Content am I" — the fiend replied —
"Count Richard should our strife decide."
So to his chamber swift they sped;
He late had slept, and lay a-bed;
Of many things he 'gan to take
Good counsel, as he lay awake.
They straight related him the whole

Of what had happened to the soul,
And prayed him judge betwixt them two,
To which of them the soul was due.
Not long the Count his rede delayed,
But briefly thus his answer made.
"Unto the corse its soul restore,
Then place him on the bridge once more,
Just where he late was overthrown,
Then both must leave him quite alone.
Then, if he hold an onward course,
Nor glance behind, nor feel remorse,
Then fall he into Satan's toil
Without revoke or further coil!
But if he homeward turn to flee,
He — for his penitence — is free!"
They hearken to Count Richard's rede,
To try the plan are both agreed.
They to the corse its soul restore,
And place him whence he fell once more.
But when the monk his senses found
And on both legs stood safe and sound,
He backward drew in greater dread
Than one who on a snake doth tread.
As soon as they had set him free,
To say farewell ne'er waited he,
But home at utmost speed he goes,
Concealed himself, and wrung his clothes.
He thought his death each minute due,
If still he lived he scarcely knew.

But when the light of day arose,
To St. Ouan Count Richard goes,
Together calls the brotherhood —
In humid garb a brother stood!
Count Richard bids him forward pace
And meet the abbot face to face —
"Say, brother, what hast thou to rue?
What evil hast thou sought to do?
Next time take better heed, my friend,
How over planks by night you wend;
And make to us confession free
Of all that chanced last night to thee!"
With shame the monk was well nigh dead,
Above his ears his skin was red
To think he must his fault unfold;
Yet all at length he plainly told.
The Count averred he spake aright,
So came the simple truth to light;
And many a year in Normandy
This taunt was wont in vogue to be —
"My pious brother, 'ware of speed,
And how you cross a plank take heed!"

———

3. A Legend.

There stood a church well known to fame,
St. Michael of the Mount by name,
On Normandy's remotest edge
Upon a cliff's exalted ledge,
Surrounded by the surging tide
Save when, upon the landward side,
(What time the ebbing waves drew back),
Was opened out a beaten track.
The tide rolls inward twice a day
With forcible and rapid sway,
That all, who at the time of flow
Would cross, must at their peril go.
Oft pilgrims to the church repair
To gain in heaven a surer share.
Once, on a certain festival,
On pressed the pious pilgrims all
To celebrate the holy mass,
Just as the waters 'gan to pass.
They fled the narrow path along,
A hasty and tumultuous throng.
One woman, soon to prove at length
A mother, lost her little strength,
Impeded by the bitter smart
Than inly dwelt beneath her heart,
And, in the tumult overthrown,
Upon the shrinking sand lay prone.

To save himself each pilgrim strained,
While she, unheeded, there remained.
Across the others all had run
And now the rocky slope had won,
When horror! they the victim view,
Round whom the waters closer drew.
All other help was now too late,
The help of heaven they supplicate;
While she, who thought her death was near,
Nor saw a human friend appear,
To Jesus and the Virgin prayed,
And to the angels shrieked for aid.
No pilgrim heard her voice's sound,
But yet to heaven a way it found.
On high, the Virgin-mother sweet
Rose quickly from her golden seat,
And, all-compassionate, in haste
A veil around the woman placed,
Who, by its wonder-working might,
Was sheltered from the billows' spite!
For, 'mid the waves that round her flowed,
Was formed for her a dry abode!
The time of ebb was drawing near,
The pilgrims on the strand appear;
They long had deemed the woman lost,
But, as the tide the sand re-crossed,
She from amid the waves was seen
Emerging safe, with joyous mien,
And in her arms' embraces mild

She held a lovely new-born child.
Then gladly priest and lay unite
To glory in the wondrous sight,
Towards her point in glad amaze,
And Jesus and the Virgin praise.

---

4. Roland and Alda.

FROM AN OLD ROMANCE.

This poem, as the title intimates, seems to be very closely copied from some old Norman original. It is written in a kind of "asonante" verse, every line ending with a syllable containing the same vowel sound, until a short line occurs, when the vowel sound is changed. This peculiarity I have endeavoured to preserve.

Back to the town the Vianese* in haste
Withdrew; the gate was barred, the draw-bridge raised.
This when king Charles beheld, his blood with rage
Boiled fiercely, and right wrathfully he spake —
"Dash forward to th' assault, ye knightly race!

---

* In German, "die Vianer". This I guess to mean the inhabitants of Viana, in Navarre, at no great distance from Roncesvalles.

Who fails me now — whatever fief he claims,
Holds he in France strong fort or rich estate,
Fair castle, borough, tower, or marketplace,
All even with the ground shall soon be laid!"
Hearing such words as these, all forward came.
Some close beneath the walls pavises* bare,
And hammers and steel-headed hatchets swayed.
Straight to the walls the Vianese repaired,
And hurled adown huge beams and stony hail,
Till more than sixty of the youthful race
Of France's heroes fell, full sorely maimed.
"Imperial lord" — Sir Naims-im-Bart then spake,
If thou by force of arms this town wouldst gain
With all its lofty walls and ramparts fair,
Its thick and steadfast towers, unworn by age,
Which once with savage strength the heathen framed,
Methinks, 'twill never in thy life be ta'en!
Send therefore to the land of France in haste,
That carpenters be hitherward conveyed;
And when at last these walls shall meet their gaze,
Then bid them manifold machines prepare
That so the walls may fall!"

---

* The pavise, pavais, or pavache, was a very large shield, used by besiegers to defend themselves while they attacked a fort.

The Emperor hears him, and with anger fired,
"Montjoy!" with mighty voice he loudly cries,
"What makes you tremble so, my valiant knights?"
Hereat begins anew the stormy strife,
They heave, they hurl, they sling with furious might.
And lo! amongst them Alda, Venus-like,
Comes forward, proudly clad in robes of price,
With golden threads right skilfully bedight.
Red were her blooming cheeks, and blue her eyes.
She stepped upon the mighty rampart's height,
And when she viewed th' assault, the uproar wild,
Stooped down and seized a stone of wondrous size,
Which on a Gascon's helm she caused to light
So sternly, that the crest in twain it rived,
And scarcely he retained the breath of life.
This deed beheld brave Roland, keen of sight,
And thus with mighty voice the hero cries:
"By all the Saints I swear, upon this side
Will no one ever make the town his prize,
For I 'gainst womankind will never fight."
Not long delayed he, ere once more he cries:
"Who art thou, virgin fair, so Venus-like?
Receive my question with a gracious mind,
I ask thee but from ignorance, not slight."

"My name from thee I hide not" — she replies,
"By them that reared me was I Alda hight,
Daughter of Rayner, Genoa's prince and pride,
Sister of Oliver so keen of sight,
And niece of Gerhard, famed for high emprise.
Illustrious is my race, its empire wide.
Unwedded to this day have I survived,
And, by the saints and angels, so will bide.
For he I wed must please duke Gerhard's mind
And Oliver's, in whom all valour shines."
Then to himself made Roland answer light—
"Now by the saints, 'tis pity but thou find
Thyself soon nestling in these arms of mine!
For so I purpose, if the combat dire
To which Sir Oliver hath me defied
Shall leave me conqueror!"

Then spake again fair Alda, the discreet,
"Sir Knight, I nowise have from thee concealed
The knowledge thou didst pray me to reveal.
Then answer me in turn — if so thou please —
From whence art thou, and by what parents reared?
I marvel at thy large well-fastened shield,
Thy sword, that by thy side hangs bright and keen,

Thy lance, from which a pennon bravely streams,
And at thy dapple-gray and stately steed,
That swiftly as a wingèd arrow speeds.
'Mid those that stem our host thou tak'st the lead,
Before all others thou a hero seem'st.
By all my powers of guess, I well believe
That she thou lovest must be beauty's queen!"
Then Roland, laughing loud, made answer meet,
"Yea, lady, 'tis the truth that thou dost speak!
In all wide Christendom she hath no peer,
Nor — that I know — elsewhere!"

Yet Roland, hearing that she so replied,
Would not at once reveal his whole design,
But answered her in turn, dismissing guile.
"Dear lady, let at least this truth suffice,
By them that love me am I Roland hight."
Fair Alda heard him with a joyous mind;
"Art thou that Roland who — else rumour lies —
Wilt meet my brother soon in desperate strife?
Thou little knowest all his force and fire.
For if thou plighted art 'gainst him to strive,
I tell thee of a truth, it stirs mine ire;

For men will think thou seek'st me for thy
bride;
I hear such rumours are already rife.
Yea, by thy truth and service as a knight,
Had I not yesterday escaped thy gripe,
Thou hadst not been so merciful or kind
As e'er to set me free in any wise."
Roland her words remarked, and thus replied,
"I pray thee, of mine honour make not light."
The Emperor to the Count of Berri cries,
"Sir Lambert! tell me true, dismissing guile,
Who is the maid on yonder turret's height
Who oft to Roland speaks, and he replies?"
"Now by my loyalty," Sir Lambert cries,
"'Tis beauteous Alda, she whom all admire,
Of valiant Rayner, Genoa's prince, the child.
Soon to Roïn she goes — the Lombard's
bride."
"That will she never," cried the king, and
smiled,
"Roland himself hath set on her his mind;
And sooner should a hundred steel-clad knights
Be slain, than Alda prove the Lombard's bride."
So spake the king; but Roland straight retired
From Alda, who remained upon the height.
The king beheld him, and with slightest smile
Exclaimed — "Dear nephew, what dost thou
design
Towards yon maiden on the turret's height?

If thou, perchance, against her cherish ire,
I pray thee now in love, forgive her quite!"
Childe Roland heard, with shame his cheeks were fired
Beneath his uncle's gaze.

"Dear nephew mine," quoth Charles, the hero brave,
"For her dear sake, who with thee lately spake,
Hast thou upon one spot too long delayed.
For Oliver meanwhile dashed through the gate,
And with him knights a hundred, well arrayed,
Who by surprise thy followers have ta'en,
In twain have cleft some twenty of their pates,
And freed the prisoners which we lately made!
Of this was beauteous Alda well aware,
And did but jest with thee to keep thee safe!"
Childe Roland heard him, and for anger raved,
His countenance was flushed with furious rage.
But when the Emperor saw how Roland chafed,
He sought to turn aside his wrath again.
"Dear nephew, be not mad with rage," he spake;
"For her dear sake who with thee talked of late,

We'll turn us homeward to our tents again;
For love of her we'll bid the siege be raised."
Childe Roland answered — "Be it as thou say'st."
A trumpet blew — the mighty host in haste
Drew backward to their tents.

www.ingramcontent.com/pod-product-compliance
Lightning Source LLC
Chambersburg PA
CBHW052335110726
47901CB00005B/1236

* 9 7 8 3 7 4 4 7 9 7 8 9 4 *